Nyifie Brothers Publishing

SUICIDE FLATS

JOHNNY B. TRUANT

November, 1989

CHAPTER 1
STALE

Callum ambled into the kitchen, feeling like the dead. He noted the time (7:10am; for Pete's sake he'd already been awake for two hours), re-filled his mug, then added half and half. Small dark flakes appeared as the coffee lightened, circling like shipwreck survivors. It was residue from inside the carafe, he'd realized a few days ago. It never seemed to get washed anymore. So every day, he poured and was grossed out, poured and was grossed out. The alternative, for some reason, just didn't appeal.

Mildly disgusted, Callum carefully removed the flakes with a spoon. He told himself again to at least rub the carafe with a sponge so this wouldn't happen tomorrow. *Later, though*, he told himself. Right now he didn't have the energy. Apathy, yes — he had plenty of that — but not energy.

He returned the carafe to the Mr. Coffee, his resolution already forgotten.

Apathy intrigued Callum. It didn't change life; it just covered it with a shroud. Apathy made everything grey, every food flavorless, every smell diminished somehow. Even now, the wall clock's ticking was muted and flat, as if heard through earplugs. But there was more: Lately he'd begun to wonder if he was even in his own life at all — if the world that'd surrounded him these past 41 years was, in fact, *real*. It seemed more and more like he was observing himself from above — as if his soul already had one foot out the door. Thinking that way probably meant something (something psychological, something spiritual, something else), but again Callum found he didn't care. Distance was easier, once you learned to steer yourself by remote control.

A sound like bat's wings made him look to one side. Mary was at the table, turning a page of the newspaper. He thought: *Oh, right.* He'd spied her there when he'd entered. *How moderate. How exceedingly noticeable.*

"Morning," she said.

"Yes," he said. "It is."

She didn't look up. He leaned down to kiss her cheek, because her mouth was too far away.

"They're dancing on the Berlin Wall. It's crazy."

"Why does it matter where people dance?" Callum asked.

Mary looked up. For a second her eyes flashed concern, but then they too returned to apathy. She flattened the paper on the table so Callum could see. In the midst of newsprint were photos of people standing on something familiar — a structure atop which people definitely shouldn't be.

"Because it's *the Berlin Wall*, Callum."

"Oh. Weird."

"The Iron Curtain just fell, and you don't seem surprised."

"I *said* it was weird."

Mary took his hand where it hung at his side. "You okay?"

"Of course I'm okay."

"You sure?"

He nodded, then sat down because it was the best way to

make her stop asking if he was okay. A blue box of Rice Krispies stood in the round table's center.

"You're eating these?" Callum asked, taking the box.

"They're getting stale."

"They're Nathan's."

"Yeah, and they're getting stale. You don't have to eat them."

Mary's bowl, still with milk in the bottom, sat at her left hand. Callum took and refilled it, uncaring that it was used any more than he cared about washing the coffee carafe. Mary was right. The level in that particular box hadn't gone down in over a month. No sense letting it go to waste.

Cereal.

Then sugar.

Sugar.

Sugar.

Callum spooned from the little ceramic bowl until a small white island formed among the Krispies. It was how he used to eat them when he visited his grandparents as a kid, because Rice Krispies were bland without sweetener and because Grandma and Grandpa didn't care how much he rotted his teeth. He hadn't eaten this way for three decades, but here it was again. It was a regression. He should probably do something about it. Like talk to someone. But who cared; apathy was stronger.

"How is he?" Mary asked, her face back in the newspaper.

"The same."

"You been up long?"

"No," he said. It was sort of true. In any way that mattered, he never slept anymore. Bedtime was a transaction, not a physical function: just a horizontal place to think all the exact same things.

Callum added sugar to his coffee too, because what the hell.

He stirred for longer than necessary, staring, letting himself be hypnotized. On the mug's side were the words *Ministers do it Biblically.* Mary had given it to him as a joke to cheer him up, but the joke had gone sideways. Callum found himself unable to disuse the mug despite how out-of-character and inappropriate it was, simply because it was Mary who'd given it to him. He couldn't just stick it in the back of the cabinet and forget about it, now, could he? No; when a man had family, he held tight to every artifact of it — *everything*, right down to dime-store mugs.

Not everyone found the mug funny, though. He'd sipped from it on a video call with Father Cortés and gotten a lecture. Not that Callum cared. He'd realized quite suddenly that Cortés was and had always been a pious asshole who only pretended to be and do all the things he was so superior about. It made Callum wonder what others had been thinking about *him* all these years. *Righteous shithead, going on and on about God.* Feh. If there even was a God.

"I have to go in early today," Mary said without looking up from the newspaper. "They want me there for an audit."

"You're leaving?" Callum found himself angry. Maybe jealous. Both emotions mingled with shame. The house lately was the lowest note on a piano, the drone of a subsonic woofer — a tone so deep, it unsettled your skeleton. Neither of them wanted to be home for longer than it took to pretend they were reluctant to leave. Being at work was paradise compared to this. Grocery shopping was a carnival. He'd even renewed his drivers' license six months early last week, finding the DMV a breath of fresh air: everything vibrant, bright, and alive. It'd become a game: Whoever could leave home first without admitting they *wanted* to leave was the winner.

"It's just an hour early."

"Mary, I have work to do."

"So do it," she said.

"I'm overdue. I'm blocked. I need silence to concentrate. I ..." He almost added, *I was planning to leave early so I could try writing at a coffee shop,* but that was the wrong lie. He'd cursed himself with that thing about needing silence. His mind raced, trying to find something else to say. What was more silent than here, other than a tomb?

"Carrie will be here in an hour or so. If Nathan needs anything, she can handle it."

"Carrie makes noise, too."

"Well," Mary said, her monotone finally taking on an edge, "then I don't know what to tell you."

She didn't leave the table, but it was clear to Callum that she'd said all she planned to. Truth was, fair was fair and she'd beaten him to it; she'd announced believable plans first and was therefore allowed to leave while he — at least until the nurse showed up — would have to stay. Truth was, noise wasn't the problem and never had been. Callum used to write his sermons to the backbeat of chaos, able to work anywhere and any time back when he'd been young and had it all figured out. Now that nothing made sense, though, it was the pall that dogged him. The slow departure of their son's life was a physical presence, not just a concept. It was a foul wind that blew down every hallway. To stay here was to be suffocated by it, and yet at the same time as both yearned to escape, neither wanted to go.

The conflict was impossible. There was no way to have the love without the pain — and to Callum and Mary's shame, so often recently the pain felt stronger. They should be in his room every minute, Callum felt. Be there every second of every day, holding his hand. They *were* there, so often ... but they were also human. And it was oh-so-human, in moments of weakness, to feel the touch of pain's white-hot brand and desire nothing more than to run away.

"What are you auditing?" Callum asked. After his whining and her sharp tone, he felt the need for an olive branch.

"It's a public works thing."

She sounded pissed. Or more likely, she had the same chaotic stew inside that he had: a conflict so turbulent, it'd done alchemy and made emotions never seen before.

"Like road construction?"

She shook her head. "Something to do with the Rampart."

"The Rampart is public works?"

"I don't know, Callum. I just do what I'm told."

She stood, leaving the newspaper.

"You're going *now?*"

"Don't wait up tonight," she said. "I may be late."

CHAPTER 2
SERMON

Callum considered the idea that his wife might be having an affair, then dismissed it before the notion was fully formed. He'd known Mary most of their lives. Sex was not her pressure valve. Right now, an affair would feel like a job to her: one more project, complete with rules and deadlines, for her over-full brain to manage.

He watched her get into her car through the living room window, knowing there was no harm done but feeling bad for attempting to subvert her anyway. On Mary's way out the door, they'd traded a glance that'd lasted less than a quarter second. The glance said: *I'm furious; I'm frustrated; I'm tired; I'm worn as thin as a bus station rug … but somehow, even though my gut says otherwise, I'm able to believe it's not because of you.*

These days, words like that were worthy of a Valentine's Day card. Having enough sense not to blame each other was their new way of saying *I love you*.

He listened to Mary's departing engine until he could no longer hear it. Once it was gone, there was nothing to focus on. Nothing but the gloom.

He went upstairs, then peeked into Nathan's room. The boy was small and still, asleep again under the covers. Callum wondered if today would be a good day or a bad day. You could never tell, and it was unclear to him which was better. Bad days were, true to their name, *bad* ... but good days paradoxically had the potential (at least in Callum's opinion) to be worse. Good days raised hopes. Every good day Nathan had, Callum allowed himself against his better judgment to believe a corner had been turned. Every good spell was an Indian Summer, promising things were all right again ... but only for a while. Was it better to have Nathan infirm in bed like they'd mostly accepted, or was it better if the boy was up and around, acting normal as ever? Before this year, Callum would have chosen the second option — and, for the record, *still* would choose it for Nathan's sake. For his own sake, though, abject illness might actually be easier to take. With pessimism, at least the worst was already on the table. With pessimism a person never got his hopes up, and therefore couldn't be disappointed.

He needed to think about something else.

Leaving Nathan's room to wander like a watchman, Callum thought only about what was in front of him. Only what he saw. But then he remembered breakfast. And he thought: *The Rampart.*

Recalling Mary's audit, Callum began to get an idea for his sermon. As both a distraction and a practical thing, the idea was a breath of fresh air.

He really *was* blocked; that hadn't been a lie. Every Sunday he had to stand behind a lectern and espouse lessons he no longer believed, and for that reason his sermons had become increasingly hard to write. Every Sunday he had to face a church full of people who knew about Nathan, infusing every speech with context that was none of anyone else's business. It wasn't fair. Having to put on a brave face was bad enough in social situations, but atop that Callum had to do it as some sort of authority. *God is killing my son, but God's still pretty great and because of it I'm happy and not at all panicked and depressed;* that's what the congregation expected him to say — to make *them* feel better while he felt worse. He wasn't allowed to be angry. Not in public. It was beyond a burden, and in his weaker moments he hated them for it.

But the Rampart idea — seedling that it still was — was a good one. It was *so* good, in fact, that he'd have to be careful with it: a subject so incredibly obvious, it felt like a trap. Done right, Callum might be able to touch on notions that for once had nothing to do with happiness and well-being and the soft side of faith. In place of those mundane things, he'd be tapping religion's golden oldies: evil, the unexplainable, manifest malevolence, and the kind of faith that made cults.

He searched through a stack of *National Geographics* under his desk until he found the issue he remembered, now a few years old. Inside was a photo essay on Fortune's eccentricities: the forest with its twisted trees, the dead zone, the cultist lean-tos with their pagan symbols and carvings, the broken and burnt area. *Nat Geo* might even have been the first to give the whole area its gruesome but fitting name: *the Gore Point.*

Callum stopped when he saw pictures of the lake.

Eight years ago, a beautiful blue pool in the center of Wasatch-Cache National Forest had begun to turn inky and dark. Callum had never gone, but he'd seen *Geographic's* essay and plenty of news footage: picturesque Cecret Lake, now full of what looked like bile. Back in March, anyone in Fortune had been able to toggle between local and national news and see what looked like the same thing in different places: black-covered Alaskan shorelines from the Valdez spill, then black-covered lakeshores back home. Of the two, Cecret Lake looked far worse. You could tell that Exxon's oil was only on top of the water, whereas Cecret's filth went all the way down. Its water seemed to have been replaced. The stuff filling the lake now was darker and more viscous than oil: diseased and unreal somehow, like effluent from a smoker's tumor.

On the next page was a map of Fortune. The enormous stone Rampart — still standing as Berlin's wall fell — made an almost perfect circle with Wasatch-Cache and specifically Cecret Lake at the center. To Callum's bothered mind, the map looked less like a wheel with an axis and more like a sinister eye. The occupied parts of Fortune stood between the park and the Rampart all the way around, like an iris full of morons.

Callum had lived in Fortune before it was incorporated: basically his entire life, immigrating because his father wanted to get in on the Zen Element rush of the '50s. He'd been luggage, not someone who'd come to Fortune by choice. Callum, unlike those who'd moved here later, at least had an excuse for living in the most disturbing place in the world.

There were photos of Old Fortune in the magazine, too: a ghost town for years, then reoccupied when Zen times boomed again and cleared land got scarce. The oldest neighborhoods were near the mines. Callum still had a childlike fear of the Zen mines, which'd been converted from creepy old shafts to ... well, to *who-knew*-what in the years between. Only now was he realizing that he didn't have the second half of that equation. Everyone knew the mines had been upgraded during the 1970s after some incident in ... '63, '64? Who knew. He'd been barely older than a teenager then. And yet nobody, as far as Callum was aware, really knew what the mines were these days — or where Zen Element was found, now that the shafts were gone.

Did it even *come* from the mines?

Or did it come from something else?

Living in Fortune gave citizens a slow creep of oddness, gradually exposing them so it wasn't odd at all until you stepped back and examined the gestalt. The oddity was more sudden for outsiders, like the people from other parts who'd read the magazine Callum held in his hands and come away horrified. For *those* people, Fortune was an enigma, a wasteland, a haunted house, and a conspiracy all at once. Strange: Even though Callum had been here through all of it, he'd never really considered Fortune unusual.

But it was. It very much was.

Other towns didn't have a bad spot in their center, like a bruise on fruit.

Other towns didn't have vast dead zones where nothing grew — zones that emitted a quiet siren song for the troubled, who gathered there in cult-like covens or went in to end their lives. The place even had a name: *Suicide Flats*.

Other cities didn't produce a substance that, according to scientists, shouldn't be able to exist.

And others weren't the subject of rumor upon rumor:

The black lake isn't a twist of nature. It's a dark omen.

The Gore Point is full of ghosts, spirits, and other things that go bump in the night. That's why people kill themselves there. It's why the mines were closed; people say the last time one opened, it was full of Hellfire. It's why the trees have twisted into shapes like teardrops, and why far enough in, nothing grows. It's why people report strange animals roaming it that might not be animals — things with no rational source, no rhyme or reason.

Evil things.

Nightmare *things.*

Worst of all, the government knows all about it, and knows it's true. They've been covering it up.

Callum wasn't big on conspiracy theories, but Fortune's

theories sometimes sounded more plausible than the party line. Why else would the Rampart have been built? Officially, it was there to protect Zen Element production ... but that didn't make sense because the entire population was inside. The worst rumor of all (one Callum believed, even though he didn't want to) was that the Rampart existed not to keep others *out*, but to keep the Gore Point *in*. It wasn't there for Fortune's protection. It was there, many said, to protect the rest of the world from the dark and rotting heart of Fortune.

Callum turned the page. The story was over, though, and a new story began.

He closed the magazine and set it aside, thinking, trying to decide if he wanted to chase the sermon idea he'd had after all. It felt responsible, from a church perspective, to at least poke the idea ... but it also felt *ir*responsible and exploitative from a dozen other perspectives. It'd mean taking a sensationalist shot at an already sensational issue, rubbing salt in Fortune's wounds because Callum was tired of rubbing salt in his own.

There were people (some Satanist freaks who lived in the Flats, but also some with their heads on straight) who believed the Gore Point was a gate to Hell. It sort of made sense; it was a wound that never healed — a blight that, over the years, had only become more and more infected. Officially, scientists had no idea why. The soil was fertile but sterile, devoid even of bacterial life, but rainfall and sunlight were adequate. So why had microscopic life died? Why, when new bacteria was introduced, did *it* die, too? Ever since the lake went black, "authorities" like GEN had supposedly been investigating those questions, but the investigation was shrouded in secrecy. Nobody talked about it ... and after enough time, the people of Fortune had stopped asking.

So what *was* the Gore Point? Why *had* the lake turned? Why *had* the Rampart been built? *What*, for the literal love of Christ, had its designers been trying to contain?

Callum hadn't spoken about the Gore Point in his sermons. Few religious figures had, except those on the fringe. It was a matter of public courtesy — a favor they were all doing for the city to spare it the panic that, now that Callum really thought about it, had been festering beneath Fortune's polite veneer for as long as anyone could remember.

He shook his head. He couldn't in good conscience open that wound, could he? He stood, deciding that writing the sermon he'd had in mind was a mistake.

A sound broke the home's silence: the front door, creaking open. It meant the nurse had arrived to look after Nathan. And Callum thought: *Maybe it's a sign.* Carrie's arrival meant he could leave, and she'd come at the exact moment he'd been considering something rash. If he wanted to go where he'd never gone before — just to see, just to feel the issue out — now would be the perfect time.

No. Don't, a voice inside him said. *You can't. Talking about the Gore Point will only freak people out. It'll only get them riled up. It's cruel to ask whether Hell lives in the heart of Fortune, and whether evil is coming. Think of all the people who'll arrive content on Sunday morning, then spend Sunday afternoon terrified for their mortal souls.*

Yes, Callum thought. *All those people.* All those complacent, doe-eyed fools who stared at him every week from the safety of the pews, taking his family's woes as reasons to be grateful. Using *his* pain to make themselves feel better.

"Fuck them," he muttered.

For a second he stopped, shocked by his own words and the sudden vitriol behind them. He never swore. But then the moment dissolved, and he felt right again.

He barely paused. He grabbed his bag, called out to Carrie that he was leaving, and headed out for the Gore Point.

But even as he went, he had to wonder: Maybe the rumors were true after all. Maybe he, like the rest of Fortune, had fallen under the spell of some malevolent specter.

CHAPTER 3
THE GORE POINT

They'd put signs at the outskirts of Suicide Flats. It was the work of some public health group, Callum assumed: folks who wanted to get in one last word for the desperate, before they did what they were about to do.

Your life is a precious gift, read one sign. *Help is available.* Below that, a phone number. There was a small waterproof box clipped to the post it was nailed to, but when Callum lifted its lid, he found it empty. In a rough semicircle around the sign, maybe ten feet out, were scores of small white cards that'd seen much heat and weather. Callum walked over and picked one up. On its front was the name of a suicide-prevention group and the same phone number as the sign, presumably so the death-bound folks who hadn't brought pencil and paper could still take the group's information with them if they reconsidered.

At some point, someone seemed to have taken all the cards from the metal box and flung them away in irritation or anger. Callum spied writing on one of them, so he picked it up to investigate. The scrawled message read like a subversive fortune cookie: *WE ARE ALL THE DAMNED.*

He opened his fingers, letting the card flutter to the dead earth below. He didn't like holding it. The things people said about the apron of Suicide Flats were true, and the card carried a booster shot of the same: bad vibes like a contagion, in the air like the reek of a skunk. To Callum, it all felt very familiar. This place understood him. This place knew how life truly was — how bad just carrying on could be. There were no polite smiles around him now. No pious lost souls ready to believe whatever fairy tales they were told. There was nobody at Callum's side to tell him how sad they were for him, then offer an upbeat twist to erase his pain and make themselves (rather than Callum) feel better. *God has a plan,* they might say. *I'll pray for you.*

Callum didn't want to be prayed for. His own prayers went unanswered. He didn't want pity, or sympathy, or a hand to hold. Callum knew God just fine, and he knew God was not in this place. It was nice, for a change, to be left alone.

He'd brought a map of the area with him from home, but so far it'd been unnecessary. Entering the park was like beginning a high-octane game of Hotter or Colder. In one direction, he could feel the air thicken: not heat but *like* heat — the dry sauna kind that's so thick you can't breathe. He knew, from that dark compass, where the lake must be. He also knew how frightened just being here made him for no clear reason, and yet he still wanted to keep walking.

He knew he would not turn back. The terribleness of the Gore Point was at least honest. It didn't lie to him like the rest of life did.

The pain in his chest had been at critical for months now, so this new existential dread, this new breed of fear, was actually refreshing by comparison. The juju here felt black and white to Callum: a clear triumph of wrong over right. Unlike his constant thoughts of Nathan, this place begged no ambiguity. There was no *if* to the Gore Point. No approach-avoidance wherein *both* ways of feeling were somehow wrong like the way things were at home. It was the difference between fear of falling and actually falling. Once you fell, there was no more hesitation at the ledge. After you stepped off, you no longer feared the terrors of the future, because they were already here.

He looked around, seeing nobody. He'd half expected a patrol or checkpoint of some sort. Were there still rangers in the park? How about guards, if only to keep the suicides from piling up as a health hazard? Their decay must seep into the groundwater, right? Was that how this — whatever *this* was — would spread? Were those who drank from Fortune's reservoir literally drinking the dead?

"If the government is covering something up, they're not doing a very good job," Callum said aloud.

The second the words came out, he wished he'd kept them to himself. It felt strange to speak here, like shouting inside a cathedral. He wasn't even sure why he'd spoken at all. To have some sound, maybe, because otherwise there was none. Occasionally wind rustled the tree leaves in the greenbelt behind him (a brittle and dead sound, carrying the way sound carries when it's very cold), but he was only now realizing he'd heard nothing beyond it: no insects or lizards scuttling from his footsteps, no bird calls, no flowing water, no distant howl of coyotes. Their lack made a conspicuous sort of quiet: intentional somehow, as if an unknown party was listening and needed silence to hear.

"Right. Straight ahead," Callum said as he made his feet move. Again, he didn't think before speaking. It was his way of whistling in the dark. Any conversation was better than none, even if the conversant was himself.

The landscape was unrecognizable. He'd come here with

his father back when the land was still green and Cecret's waters were still blue, but now the gentle verdant hills were a scorched wasteland. The dead echo he'd felt before was still in the air, ringing from a sound that had never originally been made. He snugged his sweatshirt around him, unsure if he was hot or cold. His skin was sweating from intense heat, but the air was November-cold. Every time he unzipped, he thought he might freeze to death.

Surely there'd be someone at the lake. If the conspiracy rumors were true, surely he'd find federal agents over the next rise.

But there was nothing. Nothing except the tiny black pool in the pit of the mountain valley, its water as black as ink.

Oh yes, he thought as he set eyes on it. *There is definitely a sermon here.*

Or rather, there were *many* sermons here. There might, in fact, be nothing *other* than sermons here. His feet had stopped at the crest of the hill above the lake, and now it would take intense will to soldier on. Callum had never before felt such clear malevolence. It'd spooked him; that was the layman's way to say it. Why did people only *whisper* about the evil of this place, as if there might be any question? It was obvious. *Beyond* obvious. His skeleton wanted to escape his flesh, running back to the greenbelt without him. He was having trouble focusing on the vista ahead — trouble, in some odd way, believing that what he saw was actually *HERE*, was actually *NOW*. Like the commercials said: *Is it live, or is it Memorex?*

It didn't feel like Memorex, but it definitely didn't feel *live*.

You should leave.

The voice in his head, telling him to go, seemed to almost not be his own. It was the same dark voice that came to him in the pit of night, wishing it would all be over. It was the voice of unreason one feels at the edge of a high-rise balcony, wondering what it'd feel like to jump. *One little push with the balls of your feet is all it'd take to go over the railing,* that voice might say. *Like this.* And then you'd feel your calves flex a bit, showing you how.

That black urge wasn't really suicidal; that was the interesting part. It was merely curious. Callum had talked about that deadly impulse, that deadly feeling, with a friend once, while they were in the back of a taxi. The cabbie, who hadn't known his place or that he was speaking to a minister, had turned around and added his opinion: *Do you know what that voice is? It's the voice of the Devil.*

After they'd left the taxi, Callum had laughed at that. But he wasn't laughing now.

You should leave. You shouldn't be here. It's not because you're a man of God. It's the opposite. It's because maybe you're a fraud — because maybe all this time, you've only been pretending.

"Sir? Excuse me ... *Sir?*"

Callum almost jumped out of his skin. He didn't realize how deeply he'd been inside his own head until his attention was yanked back to the here-and-now. Before he could even consider where the new, out-loud voice was coming from, his brain detoured into something like anger. He felt deceived. He'd thought he was alone; he'd been quite sure the land was empty. Seconds earlier, he'd known he could wade right into the tar of the lake if he wanted to. Which, in some morbid way, he realized now that he'd been wanting to.

His eyes focused. He returned to real things. The anger departed instantly, and Callum found himself wondering why it'd ever been there.

A thin man in his 30s was approaching from what looked almost like an Army Jeep. He must have driven up while Callum was staring at the lake, thinking unreal thoughts. How had Callum missed it? How had he gotten this close without Callum hearing a thing?

"Can I help you, sir?" the man asked. He was wearing a uniform that looked mostly like a park ranger's, but not quite. Rangers here didn't normally wear a sidearm. This man did.

"No. No thank you."

"This is a restricted area, sir."

"I thought it was a park," Callum told him.

"Yes, sir. But you must have seen the signs on the way in."

"I'm not planning to kill myself."

"Not *those* signs, sir. I'm referring to the big ones at the entrance. Behind the orange-and-white lift gates."

"I didn't see any signs."

The ranger's face changed. He had the patient false politeness common to all police-type enforcers: that tendency to call even drooling crackheads trying to stab them "sir" or "ma'am." Callum's last words, it seemed, had pushed that politeness too far. This man didn't like being played for a fool.

"Did you *walk* into the park, sir?" he asked.

"No, I drove."

"On the road."

"Of course on the road!"

"And you parked nearby. You didn't pull off halfway and hike in?"

"I used the lot by the nature station. What's the problem?"

"If you drove all the way up to the nature station, there's no way you could have missed the signs ... *sir*. I'm afraid this area is off-limits. I'm afraid nobody's supposed to be here."

"Why?"

"There's some sort of biological contagion in the area."

"No," Callum said. "I meant, *Why are you afraid?*"

The ranger paused, confused. "Sir?"

Callum took a breath, then asked the question he'd actually meant to ask. "What kind of biological contagion? This area's been dead for years."

"Yes. That's why it's being investigated."

"So you *are* covering something up. Is *that* what you're saying?"

Callum heard his own voice, heard its tone, and wondered why he was arguing. He didn't feel like himself. He kept slipping to an internal place, losing track of what was happening around him. He wondered if he was having some sort of a breakdown. Things with Nathan had been beyond rough lately, and Callum, because he was apparently a *fucking voice of comfort* to the *fucking fuckwad constituents in this fuckhole of a town,* had to keep pushing his emotions down and slapping on a happy face so the idiot shithead sheep could sleep at night. It was pathetic. *They* were pathetic! Why should he lie to all of them and say that God was good? Maybe he should tell them the truth — tell them that in the end they'd find only loneliness and pain, and there was no Heavenly Father to wipe their taints for them and tell them they'd done well in life despite the everyday lying and hypocrisy and goat-fucking perversion of all of them. That God would forgive them for coveting each other's high-school daughters and masturbating furiously at each other's windows, for cheating on their taxes and stealing books from the library and gum from the Stop N' Go, for picking their noses at stoplights and wiping boogers under the seats of borrowed cars, for hovering too high over gas station toilets and accidentally shitting on the floor, then shrugging and leaving it there because a faceless immigrant would clean it up. Maybe *that's* why Callum was angry. Maybe *that's* why he was arguing with the ranger, parroting conspiracy theories he didn't even believe, challenging the man's authority, saying he didn't see the huge BIOHAZARD — DO NOT ENTER signs at the gate even though maybe he did, even though he'd been quite sure minutes ago that there *were* no signs, that nothing was amiss here, that THIS FUCKING JACKASS COCKSUCKER HAD NO AUTHORITY TO CHALLENGE HIM AND THAT IT'D BE WITHIN CALLUM'S GOD-GIVEN RIGHT TO STAB HIM IN THE BRAIN AND PISS IN HIS EYE SOCKETS AND—

"—all right? *Sir?*"

Callum blinked. "What?"

"I said, *Are you all right?*"

"I'm ..." He'd planned to say yes. But instead, Callum shook away the strange, alien feeling that'd subsumed him moments ago and said, "I ... I haven't been feeling well."

The voice inside said, *Push him down. Take his gun.*

But Callum just repeated himself: "I haven't felt very well at all lately."

There was a moment of tension inside Callum. It felt like his thoughts were ripping in half ... as if part of him was still in front of the ranger but another part of his mind — the furious, black part that'd been inside him all along, trying to behave while Proper Callum put on a brave face — broke free and moved away. For a split second, Callum felt like he was two people in two places: the good minister, and the dark id that was *so fucking sick* of all the smiling and lying and pretending to be okay — the part that wanted to misbehave, to do all the things a good minister would never do.

Then it was over and he was himself again, and he felt very, very tired.

His head swam. His legs buckled. The ranger grabbed his arm for support, but Callum waved him away. "I'm fine," he said.

"You sure?"

"I'm sure."

The ranger was about to say more but Callum was already walking back, seeking departure from this place like a man in the desert seeks water. All thoughts of delivering a sermon about the ill tidings afoot in Wasatch-Cache National Forest were draining from him, the opposite of wanted. What he *wanted* was his bed. He wanted a bath. He wanted to close himself in the damp dark for a while and pretend that none of the world existed.

"Careful on the way out, sir," the ranger called after him.

But Callum didn't hear. He was over the rise, his thoughts already gone.

CHAPTER 4
UNSEEN

Special Agent Richard Borgner — known as "Chappie" amongst his colleagues — watched the place where the man had disappeared until he could no longer hear footsteps. He considered going after him. He wanted to know how he'd gotten through the roadblock. They hadn't secured the park completely because it looked suspicious (that's how the freaks kept getting in to conduct their séances and kill themselves), but they'd blocked the roads well enough that there was no getting around. If the man he'd just spoken with had indeed parked by the nature center, he'd've either had to crash through one of the barricades or off-roaded through the underbrush to one side. Chappie's guess was the latter, but either was a detainable offense.

Instead of chasing, he returned to his Jeep and clicked the radio.

"Allie, you still up at the checkpoint?" he said into the mic.

"Yeah," said a rough female voice. "What'cha need, Chappie?"

"I just sent someone your way. Male, Caucasian, 40s, average build. Alone."

"Sent him from where?"

"Down at Cecret. Found him just standing by the lake. Staring at it."

Special Agent Alexandra Jiminez put on her professional voice. "He was *at the lake?*"

"At the lake," Chappie confirmed.

"Not just in the Flats?"

"He said he parked in Lot Four."

"Wait. He *drove* in? He wasn't a walker?"

"Looked like a normal civvie. Nice, neat haircut. Like a banker or accountant."

"Suicidal?"

"Strange," Chappie replied. "But not at all like the usual kids who come out here to do their thing. Utterly average-looking. I'm telling you, he seemed ready to put down a blanket and have a picnic."

Although that wasn't quite true, was it? The man had *looked* average, but he hadn't *acted* average at all. Chappie had been in Grenada in '83 and had wondered many times if he'd ever see home again, but it'd still unsettled him less than the conversation he'd just had. There was something to the man that bothered him, just like there was something to this *place* — something Chappie hadn't liked from the moment he arrived three weeks ago. He heard things at night around here. Thought he *saw* things at night. The brass knew something about the Gore Point that they weren't sharing, telling him only that if he *did* see something that wasn't a wolf or a bear, he should use the weapon they'd given him: the big half-sword, half-fork thing they called a "Rollard." If he needed more than the Rollard, he was supposed to call a local outfit called GEN that supposedly did research, but that everyone knew did far more. *GEN has better weapons if you end up needing them,* Chappie had been told ... but they hadn't said what kind of weapons, or why they might be needed.

"Keep an eye out for the guy as he exits," Chappie went on. "He seemed kind of sick. I think he'll just get in his car and go, but I want to make sure. I don't want him to end up wandering."

"I'll send someone to Four," Allie said.

Chappie nodded to himself. "Hey, Allie?"

"Yeah?"

"There are cameras at the barricades, right?"

"Sure. No one is stationed there, but yeah, cameras."

Chappie knew that. The balance in Wasatch-Cache was to cordon off the Gore Point without actually cordoning it off. They needed to keep people out without appearing to keep anyone out. Civilians were supposed to see the signs and self-govern, but the agency had placed hidden cameras to make sure they did.

"Is someone watching them? Watching the cameras?"

"Of course."

"You?"

"No, Miguel."

"Well, check on him, will you? I'd like to know why he let this guy by without radioing me. Make sure he's not napping on the job."

"Sure."

"And Allie?"

"Yeah, Chappie."

He paused. Then he said, "Never mind."

Chappie hung the radio mic back on its receiver. He'd wanted to say more, but it felt ridiculous to do so. They all had their theories about what was going on here — why GEN and others had them guarding a ring of forest that'd inexplicably died and a crystal-blue lake that'd one day turned black. They had theories, but nobody liked to say them aloud. They were too odd. Too silly. Too superstitious for agents of their caliber — the kinds of fears more at-home with children scared of monsters in their closets at night.

What he'd wanted to convey — what he couldn't find words to convey — was the odd energy coming from the man who'd just left. In the low morning sun, Chappie would have sworn he'd almost *seen* that energy: a thick, cylindrical bond of gossamer running between the man and Cecret Lake, as if the lake was reaching out to him. As if it'd found something inside the newcomer that it wanted … and that, by the end, it'd somehow taken.

But that was silly, wasn't it?

Chappie returned to his Jeep as the inky lake, unseen behind him, began to boil.

CHAPTER 5
OUT OF CONTROL

The new phone that GEN had installed in Eldon Porter's home office began to ring. There was a little light on top that flashed in warbling rhythm with the ringer. It looked like a tiny version of the cherry on police cruisers. Eldon supposed the light was meant to indicate which phone was ringing (seeing as the government types who used such phones probably had many of them lined up for their various operations' hotlines), but Eldon had just the one in addition to their home phone, which made an entirely different noise. Because there was no chance of confusion to begin with, the GEN phone's light came off as self-important. This phone clearly thought it was better than other phones. Its flashing was the eager-beaver equivalent of a Teacher's Pet, waving its hand in a sad attempt to grab attention.

Eldon picked it up. The hotline didn't ring often, and it made his heart flutter.

"This is Eldon Porter."

"Identify."

"Four one one dash three beta. Six alpha three four one one."

"Where is the sun on Tuesday?"

"Yesterday, my tires went flat."

There was a pause and the sound of shuffling papers as the operator verified the countersign. Then: "Hold please."

Eldon waited, more nervous now. He wasn't used to all this cloak and dagger. They'd gotten him as a grad student, offering more money than any private sector job ever would, then turned things into James Bond so slowly that at first Eldon hadn't even noticed. First, he'd needed a security clearance. Then, he'd needed an identification number. Then he'd started hearing from relatives who wanted to know why the government had called them to check up on him. Old professors were asked for references. The last time he went into downtown Fortune to pay a parking ticket, the clerk there had practically saluted him, saying that of course the ticket wouldn't be a problem.

Strange things were afoot, and now he had a scrambler phone on his desk. Five years ago he'd been fresh out of grad school, considering a job at K-Mart to help pay the bills while his physics degrees became more and more useless, but then suddenly they'd become so use*ful* that every guy in a suit and concealed shoulder holster had wanted his attention. He was earning twice what his father earned after climbing the ladder at IBM his entire life, and yet he couldn't tell anyone what he did for work. There was only so much tension a guy could take.

"Eldon, hi," said a harried-sounding voice on the other end of the phone.

"Brianna? Why are *you* calling me?" He did wonder, but he was relieved. Brianna was an average person, just like him. She'd just turned 28. Eldon, only 14 months older, could relate to Brianna far better than Colonel McNamera, who he'd half expected to have placed the relay call. "Aren't you supposed to be at the lab?"

"I *am* at the lab. I'm calling about your little pet."

"What about it?" It wasn't actually a pet, of course. Brianna meant the rift.

"It's acting up. You may want to come down here and see."

"'Acting up'? What's that mean?"

"Well, you've seen mostly safe, longish wavelengths coming from it up until now, right?"

"680, 700," Eldon said. The rift put out mostly red light, spanning into infrared. Until he activated it, the rift's emissions were less harmful than a toaster's. Its wavelengths cycled up and down in two distinct bands, the lower-energy ones dipping below radio waves to ULF, which was what surface support used to communicate with submarines. Standing in front of the rift all day for years wouldn't even give you a tan.

"Well, it's a nice fiery blue right now," Brianna said. "*Dark* blue, pulsing into indigo and violet. I'd wear lead if I went in there now. I didn't want to fire up the equipment without talking to you first, but I'm sure it's into UV, probably farther."

Eldon sat down, confused. Donning a lead vest was probably overkill, but from what Brianna said, the rift had certainly become more energetic. He'd want X-ray protection maybe, UV googles certainly. Usually when Eldon activated the thing, it still only turned green. They'd had the rift open for over a year now and not once had its wavelengths gone shorter than the visible spectrum.

"Have you tried opening a conduit? See what the other side has to say?"

"That's your territory, brother. I just work here."

"Do me a favor," Eldon said. "Get on the network from your station and connect to my computer. I want to know what's going on with Element production."

"Already checked. That's the other thing. It's not wafting Zen Element at all."

"Not at all?" Eldon had a hard time believing that. You could get bigger amounts of Zen Element from other sources (assuming the other plane didn't catch you doing it), but *officially* speaking, Element only came from rifts. Rifts were like a leaking faucet. Sometimes they leaked a lot of Zen Element and sometimes just a little, but entropy was entropy and that meant it *always* flowed. Every rift effluxed; that was inevitable given the extreme heat of the other plane compared to Earth's plane. The only way to stop the efflux would be to equalize or reverse the planes' temperatures, which obviously wasn't happening … or for the other plane to somehow go out of its way to suck atmosphere backward across the boundary.

Behind Eldon, the fax machine hummed to life.

"I've just sent you an energetics report," Brianna explained. "It looks to me like effluent is being redirected to another local source."

Eldon ripped the transmission from the roll, trying to read the report's small type through the fax machine's distortion. Brianna's assessment seemed to be right, though Eldon didn't understand how. There *were* no other rifts, as far as he knew — nearby *or* far away. Communication between the planes had thus far been stepwise and careful. The other plane's first explorers had arrived unexpectedly one day and scared the living shit out of some hikers (who were then paid handsomely to move away and never talk about it again), and thereafter it'd felt smartest to keep communication within government circles. Right now, their main point of contact — such that *that* meant anything — was Eldon Porter. It gave him job security, at least.

But the more Eldon stared at the report, the more it was starting to seem like there was, in fact, a second rift. It wasn't inside GEN's lab; it was somewhere out in the wild. He'd have to check the maps, but he'd gotten to know the GPS coordinates pretty well by now. Based on the data in his hands, the new rift was somewhere inside the Suicide Flats. That was where the first explorers had come across, but there'd been no incursions since Cecret Lake turned black.

"Okay, hang tight," Eldon said.

Nervous but unable to say why, Eldon hurriedly gathered his things and raced to the lab. The drive used to have a beautiful view, but now that view was of the Rampart. Its huge concrete mass had its own majesty, and Eldon usually found himself awed by it. Today, though, it struck him as foreboding.

Since the '60s — long before Eldon was involved and before the relevant agencies were more than infants — those who knew about the interplanar rifts had regarded them with a wary eye. Before the '60s, there'd been nothing but excitement ... but then the mine fires began and the Mine Zero incident occurred and that Russian man living in Fortune had apparently gone all the way back home in the strangest way possible. Official reports made in late '63 had changed the way the government saw the other plane, and that's when the Army had doubled its involvement and scientific work had fallen under Uncle Sam's umbrella. The Rampart's construction was the natural consequence.

Eldon, even knowing the real story, usually felt protected by the huge wall around the city. Today, on the other hand, he felt for the first time as if he might be on the wrong side of it. If something was happening at the Gore Point, they should all be *outside* the Rampart, not in.

Eldon cleared security, waved to Brianna to let her know he was taking over, then closed himself inside his partitioned-off lab and drew the blackout shades. He peeked at the rift and saw it as blue as Brianna had said. He didn't don protective gear because there was really no need to inspect it more closely — no reason to go into the rift chamber and risk exposure.

He opened the door of what looked like a black closet and entered it instead. He didn't like this next part, mostly because he didn't understand it.

Despite GEN's raised eyebrow regarding the intentions of the other plane, they'd nonetheless worked so far on a *just-trust-me* basis with it. There'd been no alternative. In one sense, the other plane was the only reason GEN knew how to open rifts, but in a much truer sense, nobody thus far *really* knew how to open rifts. They'd managed it despite themselves, almost as if some other force had taught them how.

Which it basically had.

One day, after studying the strange things that'd come over in that first exploratory group (grey-skinned, deformed and dismembered creatures with horns and sharp teeth), Eldon had suddenly known it all. Looking back, he could only conclude that the creatures had given him the information psychically. It was the only possibility. They'd taught him without teaching, and after that encounter Eldon had opened the first rift from the human side. Better modes of communication had followed, like the black box he was inside now. But as with everything, the box worked on a practical sort of faith. Eldon didn't know how he communicated with the other plane from inside the box. He only knew that somehow, he always did.

Eldon sat inside the chamber. It was a converted Faraday cage, originally used to test signal-generating equipment in an EM-free space. Post-conversion, the original structure was encased in plywood and sealed tight against light intrusion. It was barely big enough for the chair he sat in. Even though there was equipment running in the lab and the enclosure's walls were thin, he never heard a thing when he was in here. It was quiet enough to hear the churn of his organs, the rush of his own blood.

Eldon sat, holding a question firmly at the center of his attention. He waited. Then, just when he thought nobody over there could hear him, he started to get a picture inside his mind: a sense more like memory than new information, as if he was recalling something he'd known all along.

First, Eldon saw himself. This part *was* basically memory. He saw a years-ago Eldon Porter standing in front of a line-backer-sized red creature with huge, down-curling horns like a ram's, the two of them sharing mindspace in a way Eldon had only been able to process days later. A feeling came with it: one of success, of satisfaction, and comfort.

This is how it's supposed to work, Eldon thought. The idea was his own, but being imparted to him by someone on the other side.

He felt into the memory/vision, noticing how although no words were possible, emotion was. The others' concept of emotion was foreign to Eldon — different from human emotion. It was hard to explain, but it was all very familiar: the creatures and humans were different, but "good" and "bad" applied roughly the same to both. The creatures had sampled Eldon's feelings and intention, and Eldon had sampled theirs. It was vibes only, but so far vibes had been enough.

After a minute or so, the memory of himself was replaced by a new memory: a "memory" that might be happening right now or very recently. It wasn't truly recall of the past. This time, the vibes were very different. Whoever Eldon was "talking to" over there didn't seem to know how to conceptualize it.

Eldon saw a man in his mind's eye. He saw the black pool of Cecret Lake in front of him. The man seemed almost unimportant to the vision. What mattered more was what looked like a black serpent slithering from the man's chest and into the lake. To meet that serpent, an energetic presence was reaching out from the plane's thinnest spot, curious about it.

Desiring it.

The serpent felt terrible to Eldon. *What was it?* What could it be, other than doom? He wanted to pull his mind away from the vision, to refuse it. But there was a message here: something the other side wanted to understand but didn't. That dark presence — which had changed shape, becoming an eclipsing black cloud — was like a contagion, siphoned from the man and into the mind of the other plane.

Eldon imagined the man's energy synchronizing with the other plane's energy. Causing resonance. It was like pollution tailor-made for them: foul, but also addictive. Destructive, but somehow irresistible.

Terrible.

Eldon could feel it from where he sat: a horrible mood filled with pain and loss and anger. It was the worst day of anyone's life, siphoned from the man by the other plane's complementary vibes. And as Eldon felt it (as he watched the almost-a-memory of a man who wasn't himself), he understood: the black snake of emotion had entered the water, then crossed through a rift at the lake's bottom. It'd gone into *them.* It was human pain like the other side had never seen ... and part of their group mind, as it was driven to madness, wanted more.

What is it? Eldon wondered. But then, suddenly and unasked, he knew. *Grief.* It was *grief* he saw coming from the man standing beside the lake. It was grief he felt, as if it was his own.

We do not understand this, the other plane's hive mind said to Eldon. *We do not want it, but we cannot resist it.*

Eldon imagined sharks swimming in pools of blood with

all sense gone, driven to frenzy by the only instinct left: the need to feed.

Then he saw the black lake boil as the tiny interplanar fissure at its bottom cracked and opened wide. He watched, breathless, as one of the creatures from the other side swam to the surface, its idiot mind in overdrive and hungry for more.

Eldon's heart leapt into his throat. A fiend — one with an individuated mind, driven mad by the new, never-before-sensed serpent of horrible human emotion — had just crossed over and now was loose in Fortune.

You must prepare, the other plane's thought-stream told Eldon.

Eldon, afraid to hear the answer, asked why.

Because we want *it … but we cannot* control *it,* it told him.

CHAPTER 6

NIGHT TERRORS

G*et up.*

Callum's eyes opened. He wasn't sure if he was awake or still dreaming. The day had been terrible and strange, and when he'd fallen asleep, it had been like dying. That's how it'd struck him as he lay in bed next to Mary with the TV on: like he wasn't just getting tired, but was instead slipping away.

He'd fallen asleep every night of his life and not once had he had a near-death experience, so he knew this was different. It came with a sense of reluctance, then release. He'd heard that on their deathbeds, people often came to see the end as a relief: a wonderful feeling of no longer needing to juggle the balls of life and permission to finally stop trying. That's how he'd felt all day after he left the black lakeside: as if the constant pain in his chest over Nathan had simply gone away. As if he was suddenly, inexplicably, and irresponsibly just fine. There was no sadness. There was no grief. *What* dying son? Callum had, until bedtime, felt a million times better.

But wasn't the same said about intentional deaths —

about suicides? And didn't that sort of make sense? After all, where had Callum been today? Why, he'd been to Suicide Flats: the place where all worries ended, and for a short time everything was okay. Too late, it'd occurred to him to be frightened. Maybe the Flats had infected him while he was there, and what he felt now was just delayed fatalism. He'd slit no wrists and taken no booze with sleeping pills, and yet now it seemed suicide had come for him just the same.

Sleep came. He had dreams. He was awake to them, fully lucid. He wondered in those dreams if he'd been right about dying and this was the afterlife. Was he still on Earth, or had he woken in Heaven?

Or, like all parents who apparently didn't care about their dying children, had he woken in Hell?

He tossed. He turned. For hours, he wavered between awake and asleep, cognizant and dreaming. It became impossible to tell which was which. Was his bed the truth? Sometimes he thought yes, but then an impossible thing would happen and he'd know — or at least try to believe: *No. I'm only dreaming.*

Or dead.

And in Hell.

Burning for my sins. For my negligence. For my lack of caring.

Forever.

And ever.

And ever.

Now he stared up from his pillow, watching as the corner streetlight played through tree leaves to make a moving menagerie on the ceiling. Had he really just heard someone telling him to get up? Reality had been so fuzzy lately. This wasn't the first time life itself had felt unreal. This wasn't the first time in recent months that he'd wondered if he'd actually woken from a dream ... or was instead still in one.

Get up and go downstairs.

He sat up. Everyone had an internal voice, but Callum didn't usually hear his so clearly. He wondered if he was losing his mind.

Downstairs, it said. *And hurry.*

He rose, foggy either because he'd just woken or because he was still dreaming. His brain was thick with torpor: an old man trying to stand, wobbling and unsure. The voice, which should either worry or scare him, did neither. He accepted it the way a man in a dream accepts everything.

He looked at the hallway door, then went to the bathroom instead. That'd show it. Some dream voice wanted Callum to walk downstairs in the pit of night for no reason? Why, he was his own man. He'd go to the bathroom first.

He left the door to the bedroom ajar so he could do what needed doing without turning on an overhead light. He didn't want to ruin his night vision. He planned to go back to bed quickly, after he did whatever he was supposed to do on the first floor. There was no need to wake up more than necessary when odd voices came calling.

He wondered if Mary would hear. If he'd wake her.

Mary.

And his mind said, *Bloody Mary.*

It was a different voice this time — this time his own. Freed of sense by his middle-of-the-night confusion, Callum's brain returned to childhood, to sleepover parties, to games the kids played. To the spook stories they told. The one he'd never shaken was the legend of Bloody Mary. Supposedly if you stood in front of a mirror at night with all the lights off and said "Bloody Mary" three times, a horrible bleeding specter would appear behind you, ghost-lit from within. Even back then, even under pressure, even under the threat of ridicule by his peers, Callum had never once had the guts to try it. He'd spent his entire adult life — even knowing better — avoiding mirrors in the dark. He'd either reach for the light switch immediately when entering the dark bathroom, or, like now, simply avert his eyes.

It was silly. It was childish. But things felt safer that way.

He finished and washed his hands, keeping his eyes down. Then, on impulse, he looked up.

Behind him in the mirror was a woman dressed entirely in white and wearing a veil. It was impossible to see her face because the veil was covered in blood. The rest of her clothes were half pristine, half soaked with gore. All he could see above the neck was her mouth. It was rotted: the mouth of a corpse.

He startled. Almost screamed. But the woman wasn't there, and never had been.

Get ahold of yourself, he thought.

Yes. And go downstairs, said that other voice.

He plodded slowly to the ground floor, unafraid again because he knew this had to be a dream. Because in dreams, events happened and then ended without leaving a hangover. He was simply *here, now,* reaching the staircase's bottom. All of this was perfectly normal.

Now go outside.

But no. That was too far. Too ridiculous.

Then he went outside.

The backyard was half shadow, half speared by the yellow glow of a light on the alleyway utility pole. Everything was still. A neighbor's porch chimes and the distant kicking-on of an air conditioner comprised the entire soundscape. Standing inside the fenced boundary of his small suburban lot, Callum felt strangely conspicuous. It seemed as if a spotlight would soon come on and pin him where he stood — like a burglar in security lights, or a convict trying to escape.

Someone was out here, he decided. Someone was waiting.

"Hello?"

But his word aloud in the night felt as conspicuous as speaking inside the Gore Point.

In the shed.

Callum's eyes ticked toward his toolshed. It was a tiny thing from some big-box home improvement store, planted in the yard's corner a decade before they'd bought the house. The floor was rotting out, the paint on the sides peeling. It was only big enough to hang shovels and store his small walk-behind lawnmower. With all that filled the shed now, only one person could stand inside with the door closed. One person peeking through the doors, waiting for Callum to lift the open padlock from the latch.

Ridiculous. Nobody's in the shed. Why am I out here? I should go back to bed.

It was true. You couldn't go inside a shed and then replace the padlock on the outside. That's probably why the lock wasn't actually on the latch and was instead lying in the grass at the shed's threshold. He could see it from where he stood under the porchlight: a lump at the foot of the thing, even though Callum had mowed the grass just two days ago and replaced the lock when he was finished.

Obviously you didn't replace the lock. Obviously, you dropped it in the grass by mistake.

But he was quite sure he'd replaced it. He never closed the hasp because he'd long ago lost the key, but he hung it anyway to keep the door from blowing open. The hasp's bottom had corroded, forming a spike of rust. Standing in the dark now, Callum's thumb went to the side of his index finger, rubbing the scrape that spike had made less than 36 hours ago. He remembered how the rust had worried him, and how he'd called the doctor's office to ensure his tetanus shot was up to date.

Okay, then the lock blew off. You didn't notice because the wind was surgically precise: a tiny burst strong and agile enough to blow only on the lock and nothing else. It blew once, unseated the lock, then stopped entirely.

"I'm going back to bed," Callum told the backyard.

His hips twisted, but before his head followed, he saw movement. A shadow below the ill-fitting shed doors moved as if agitated. As if annoyed that Callum had come all the way into the backyard to play, but was now going back inside without so much as a game of Hopscotch.

Callum told himself he didn't see it. There was nothing in the shed. Nothing in the backyard. No dark creature had called him from his slumber because he, Callum, had something it wanted ... because it'd sampled something it'd never sampled before and was now addicted — and now it wanted more.

Crazy. You're crazy, Callum told himself. He must still be in bed sleeping. Still dreaming the tortured dreams of the damned.

He went inside and closed the door. With the porch light cut off, the kitchen seemed unnaturally dark and still. He didn't like being here. Didn't like being awake. Didn't like trying to convince himself that he *wasn't* awake, because the worst thing a nightmare could do was to hear your rationalizations and convince you that despite your reasons, what you were experiencing was real. And that's the way Callum was starting to feel: that despite all the strange and impossible things going on, none of this was dreams. He was really awake. Really in his quiet kitchen in the middle of the night. Really thirty feet away from a garden shed with its lock removed, its door slightly ajar, and something horrible inside. A voice really *had* spoken to him upstairs — not out loud, but somehow inside his head. It really had called him down here. To open his back door. To cross to the shed. To open it. And see.

No.

Callum went to the refrigerator, less eager for a snack than for the light inside. He didn't want to cross to the wall switch. Didn't want to turn on the overheads, admitting he needed their comfort. Opening the fridge would do. The fridge offered just enough light. Just enough to scare away the demons.

Inside the refrigerator, right at the front, was a restaurant-quality whipped-cream canister. Mary had joked that once she was done with the cream inside, they could use the leftover gas as whippits. A little bit of nitrous to get you high — to banish the world and banish the pain.

Its outer shell was made of aluminum. Shiny. Reflective. In its curved surface, Callum saw the shape of something standing behind him.

He turned, expecting Bloody Mary. Expecting to see that there was nothing there, and tonight was an endless string wherein his macabre imagination ran wild. Instead, in the wan light of the open refrigerator, Callum saw a small black creature standing upright. It was about the height of a prepubescent child. It stood with a hunch, its head forward of its shoulders. Its face was almost entirely mouth. Almost entirely gleaming white teeth, coated with phlegm. It seemed to be grinning — a sinister smile that stretched from where an ear should be to where another ear should be. It seemed to have no eyes. No hair. It'd left footprints of wet earth on the linoleum and splotches of goo between them, as if the horrid thing itself was dripping.

For a moment, Callum couldn't breathe. He was entirely paralyzed, inside and out. It occurred to him to rationalize. To tell himself that this *proved* he was having a nightmare, and none of this was real. Those thoughts occurred to him and were swept immediately aside. Once they were gone, he had only emptiness and terror. Life stopped right here. Right now.

He'd become a mute and thoughtless statue: a prisoner inside his own moveless shell.

More, the creature seemed to say, its mouth opening to hiss a single foul syllable. But after one beat, two beats, Callum realized he was only watching it breathe. When he'd heard "More," it'd been inside himself. The thing was speaking directly into him: a direct thought-violation, impossible to shut out.

More, it said again inside him.

Callum fell back against the open refrigerator. A jug of milk tottered, fell, and burst open on the floor. His paralysis snapped at the same time but his body betrayed him, able to run only into the refuge of the appliance behind him. The archway to the living room was on his left, but he'd have to come around the door — toward the creature — before he could reach it. He could rush for the hallway and stairs, but that way was behind the thing ... and, even if he successfully got past, he'd only trap himself further.

He'd need to go upstairs. To rouse Mary. Take Nathan in his arms and carry him out, hoping the boy wasn't too sick, too fragile, to be taken. But what then? They couldn't come back downstairs; they'd have to escape through a second-floor window. Even if they'd had a fire ladder (they didn't), how would he use it? He couldn't descend a wobbly rope ladder while holding Nathan, and chances were Nathan was far too weak to descend it himself.

His eyes darted left. He grabbed the largest knife from the butcher block and held it in front of him.

"Get out," Callum muttered to the demon in his kitchen.

It watched him. It watched as well as it could, without eyes.

"I said *get out!*" He found himself roused and reckless by the onslaught of adrenaline. Everything was suddenly a little less unreal and a lot less scary. Did it matter what the thing was? No. It was a *threat* and nothing more. Callum's body, having chosen *fight* over *flight*, was ready to kill it or die trying.

The thing stepped forward. Its mouth opened, showing two rings of teeth behind its already-overcrowded front row. Its breath was the stench of rotting meat.

"Come on," Callum said, parrying to meet it. "Come on and try me, you bastard!"

It moved like lightning. Before Callum could blink, the thing had sprung at his chest, knocking him to the floor. Then it was above him, pinning him, dripping what passed for saliva onto his face. Its hands were clawed, like the talons of a raptor. And it was *hot*, like a brand pulled from fire.

Callum waited to die. Waited for the monster to open its big mouth and begin taking bites. Instead, he felt a force of some kind streaming out of it, prying at his mind and heart like invisible fingers. All the while, he heard the thing's dark voice inside his head, using his own language and brain against him.

More. What you gave before, we want MORE!

Callum felt a rough hand inside his head, his thoughts rummaged and tossed about like burglars ransacking a house for hidden treasures. He tried to fight it, but he'd never waged mental war and didn't know which psychological muscles to flex. He tried to move, but the thought-rape had made him forget his body. He felt the thing's brand-hot skin burning his own. He could feel the dark, putrid heat of its breath on his skin as its toothy mouth opened and closed.

Callum went limp, unable to resist. He waited in surrender. Waited to have his soul removed, his body shredded.

But then the creature stopped.

Its head perked up, turned, and hesitated in the stillness as if hearing a sound.

Then it sprang from him, ran for the door, and was gone.

CHAPTER 7

LETDOWN

"Callum. *Callum?*"

He came around slowly. Mary was above him, lightly slapping his cheeks. He felt something cold behind him and realized it was the still-open refrigerator. Morning light streamed through the windows. There was a sour smell in the air, and his back was wet. It was the milk, he remembered. The milk bottle that'd broken when a demon knocked him into his Frigidaire.

"What happened? Are you okay?"

He wasn't sure. He blinked a few times, then made himself sit up. He wanted to scream, but in his torpor he wasn't sure why. It hadn't all come back yet. Or rather: It was coming back fine, but it all sounded so ridiculous. He'd dreamed while he sleepwalked, was all. Nothing to see here.

"Yeah. I think I'm okay."

"Why are you down here? Why ... ?" She didn't say the rest, maybe because this oddity could only handle one step at a time. "Did you faint? Are you ill?"

"I ..."

"Were you outside? The porch light was on and the door was open." He looked and saw it closed, assuming Mary had done that before spotting him. He wanted to protest. If the door was open, it wasn't his fault. He was quite sure he'd closed it before all those impossible, insane things had happened.

"Callum, what's ... What happened last night?"

Callum blinked a few more times. His shoulders were against the produce drawer, which wasn't as cool as it should be. He seemed to remember checking the time on his way down and finding it early. If that was right, the fridge had been open all night. Everything would be a loss by now.

He looked at his wife. Her eyes were filled with a mixture of worry and fear. The fear wasn't for him, though. This was fear for herself, fear for Nathan, fear for the sanity of the world. Mary had been stretched every bit as thin these last months as Callum, but she'd borne it better. This was what it'd taken to catch a glimpse of her last straw: finding her less-capable husband unconscious in a pool of souring milk, clearly on his way to a mental breakdown. Thinking this, Callum saw a third emotion in Mary's eyes that he'd missed before: *resentment.* If he lost his mind, he'd be off the hook. He'd be carted off to a psychiatric ward to recover and be cared for ... while Mary, the strong one, was left to bear the burden alone.

"I ..."

He could still see all of last night in his mind's eye, not at all convinced it was unreal. His heart sped up, preparing again for fighting or fleeing. He clearly remembered the creature that'd been standing where the knocked-over kitchen chair laid now. He recalled its heat, its smell, and terror nearly strong enough to void his bladder. He remembered it all, but it was daytime now. Had it actually happened? He was so sure it had, yet so sure it hadn't. Daylight had a way of making all fears foolish.

His eyes shot from place to place. He wasn't as calm as his voice was trying to be.

"What's wrong?" Mary asked, impatient now.

"Help me up," he said.

He allowed himself to be led to a chair, trying to buy himself some time to decide what he believed and wanted to say. Mary said the door to the backyard had been open, and from where he sat he could still see dirty footprints on the floor. They seemed to be claw-shaped, but only vaguely. Maybe they were his own. Wasn't it possible he'd tracked the dirt in himself? That would be so much better to believe.

"Are you lightheaded?" Mary asked.

"It's getting better."

"Did you pass out?"

Callum looked down at his sleep shirt, seeing it filthy with yard dirt but not ripped, which was how it'd seemed last night. There were dried spots all over (his clothes, the floor), but any liquid could have made them: milk, water, or demon saliva. He glanced at his wrists, which the thing had grabbed to pin him. The places he'd imagined it touching were red, but not blistered. He looked rubbed raw in those places, but the abrasions could have come from anything. And so he had to ask himself: What was more likely — that a creature with brand-hot skin had attacked him without leaving burns, or that he was going crazy?

Help me, God. I'm losing my mind.

"I'm going to call Doctor Burton," Mary said, making sure Callum was steady before crossing to the wall phone.

"No. Don't."

"Don't be stupid, Callum. Look at you!"

"I'm okay. I don't want to add to your burden."

But she was already at the phone. Already dialing. He could see in her gaze that she loved him more than anything ... but that at the same time, she hated him for all the new worry he'd laid atop her already overloaded shoulders.

He was *already* a burden. *Already* weak.

In the ways that mattered, he'd already let her down.

CHAPTER 8
MAYHEM

While Minister Callum MacReady was disappointing his wife, the town of Fortune was waking to a morning of mischief, destruction, and the occasional bolt of terror.

RAE JEFFRIES, who ran the local library board with an iron fist and grew geraniums in vast rows in her garden, walked into the dooryard between her back porch and garage with pink gloves in hand and every intention of beating the sun to the punch. Her alabaster skin burned easily, even in the cooler months. It was just after 7am, and still Rae wore her big floppy hat. The garden would be in shade until midmorning this time of year ... but when it came to the sun, you could never be too careful.

Today would be a good day in the garden. She'd been seeing a lot of earthworm activity recently, which was good. She'd also seen snails, which were good as long as they stuck to the compost pile and didn't discover the delicious plants fifty feet away. The snail situation merited watching. It seemed unlikely that they'd obediently stay where Rae wanted them. Snails weren't smart, but you never knew. She'd walled in the compost with rotting boards, but it's not like they couldn't climb right out.

She took her handheld spade and rake from the bin on the porch. A smile grew wide on her face. Her husband might be a son of a bitch, but he never bothered her out here. The garden was her sanctuary. She'd wondered sometimes about renting space in the community greenhouse on Fosworth Court, where she could garden UV-free all year, but she hadn't pulled the trigger. Paul could be a real son of a bitch about extra expenses. He could be a son of a bitch about a lot of things. On general principle, Rae tried to avoid him as much as possible.

She rounded the corner and gasped.

Her geraniums were completely decimated. Someone had stomped right through them. The destruction was so complete, in fact, that the whole thing seemed deliberate.

"Fucking fuckwad fuckfaces!" she said aloud. Rae was not one for eloquence and, as far as profanity was concerned, never consulted a thesaurus.

She knelt, furious at how thorough her interlopers had been. It had to be that group of teenagers who hung out at the Stop N' Go. They'd stomped on absolutely everything. In fact, every footprint seemed to be three footprints in one. Instead of oval shoe shapes, they'd made shapes that looked like three-tipped maple leaves, presumably by stomping thrice in the same pattern each time. Why? Just to be punks, she had to assume.

Except there was a problem with that. Three teenage shoe prints in a fan design would be much larger than what she saw. These prints were small — as if it wasn't teens, but toddlers. Or if it *was* teens, they'd been wearing strange shoes that made the shapes with only one step instead of three. Rae didn't know which it was, but she knew animals hadn't done it. Nothing this size could hop her ten-foot fence, but even dumb teens could operate a gate latch.

Her head turned, and she gasped again. The vandals hadn't opened the gate; they'd smashed right through it — maybe with a golf cart.

There were no tire tracks, but Rae didn't notice or consider that.

She also didn't notice all the blood. Not until later, after the rest of it happened.

NICHOLAS FLANAGAN — "MUDGE" to his friends — frowned through his window at the DIY deer feeder he'd made from an old industrial birdcage. It was still full of deer corn, as if none of the usual crew had visited overnight. That was strange. Normally, Mudge's yard was the buffet that deer couldn't stop talking about. They ate the corn; they ate his landscaping; they sometimes stood on their hind legs to pull peaches from his peach tree. Mudge's neighbors were not fans. For some reason the deer were not courteous enough to stick with devouring only Mudge's plants (which were freely on offer) and instead ate *their* plants, too. Lacy Grey, who lived next door, had planted tulips when she'd first moved in. Silly woman. Tulips never survived.

There'd been *some* activity at the feeder overnight, though. Mudge could see that from here. At the feeder's base, yesterday's fresher, more-brightly-colored corn overlaid last week's dull and weathered remnants. So the deer had come; they'd at least jostled the cage enough to rain kernels. They just hadn't *eaten* the corn they spilled. Why was that? Usually the feeder was half-empty by morning, and the ground was nearly pristine.

Still at the window, Mudge frowned more deeply. The feeder, he saw now, hadn't just been bumped. It was askew, as if it'd been rammed. What's more, several of the bars inside were bent. The small, furry corpse of something was behind the main pole, its blood on the bars. It almost looked like the animal — a squirrel, he thought — had been inside the feeder at first, then yanked out with extreme, body-destroying prejudice.

"You want some Fruity Pebbles, Nicholas?"

Mudge turned. His wife Lettie always ate kids' cereal on Saturday mornings. She also watched kids' TV shows on the weekends: not the truly shitty ones, but the kind adults could tolerate if they tried. She'd done it ever since the kids lived at home, then never lost the habit. It felt like clinging to Mudge, but who was he to judge?

"Something beat up the feeder pretty bad last night," he said. "I think there's a dead squirrel out there, like maybe it got caught in the feeder. Or maybe something pulled it out and tried to eat it. What'd do that?"

"I'm just asking because there's only one bowl of Pebbles left," Lettie said as if she hadn't heard him. "If you want it, I can have Crunchberries."

"No, you go on," Mudge said, waving a dismissive hand. "Come gander. Tell me what you think."

Lettie came to stand next to him at the window. He winced. She'd developed an old person smell recently — something he really needed to find a way to tell her without offending her because it skeeved him out. It'd been a long time since the kids left. It was *their* kids — Mudge and Lettie's grandkids — who competed for the cereal now.

"Well isn't that something," she said.

"Coyote?" He said it with a silent E: *ki-yote.*

"Do coyotes eat squirrels?"

"Dunno. Lookie how the the bars are bent. See?"

"I see."

"Well, could a coyote do that?"

"What're you thinkin', Nicholas? Bear?"

"Maybe. But that's a strong cage I used. Have to be a black bear 'round here, and black bears are little." It'd take a grizzly to bend bars like that. There was more, too: He didn't think a bear could catch a squirrel, if they even ate them.

"Hang tight, darling," he said. He crossed to the living room and pulled his shotgun from the gun cabinet. He loaded it with birdshot — not enough to kill a big bear, but plenty to make it run. "I'll be back in two shakes."

The day was beautiful, but still Mudge's heart rate doubled once he was outside. He wasn't sure why. Wasn't sure why his nerves were suddenly on high alert, his hands tight on the shotgun. He'd moved it into kill position at his hip without meaning to, whereas he'd normally hang it low. He could hear his neighbors out doing their business: Carol Brown three houses down singing while she watered her begonias and kids playing not far away. Strange that he was out here with his wits on fire, tense like a man about to be jumped.

His subconscious noticed the oddities before Mudge did. He'd spied the squirrel's body, which now seemed to be bitten in half. Its entrails were a half-dried pile of red spaghetti. The bars of the feeder's cage were bent far more than he'd seen from the window, two of them coated with blood. And there was a smell in the air. Coppery. Its reek was an assault to the senses, once he noticed it. It was the squirrel's blood, he decided. Only he knew from the start that it was way too strong for that to be all.

Past the feeder, out of sight from the back window, he found the bodies of three deer.

They'd been ripped open at the belly as if with knives, their insides scooped out like autumn pumpkins.

CHICKENS WERE SHREDDED. Foxes were blamed. Billy McNamera's smokehouse was smashed to bits and all the meat was stolen … but it was a rushed job by the vandals who'd done it; they'd dropped entire racks of ribs and bitten chunks from a few cured steaks right through the T-bone. Four different homes across town were broken into, but for reasons unknown the intruder had left without stealing anything, without bothering the people sleeping upstairs. Doors were raked with powerful claws. Windows were broken. Alarms were set off. Asha Vikar had one of those fancy night-vision cameras set up, but the tape was corrupted; microseconds after a scampering, human-shaped black thing entered the video's frame, the recording fuzzed out completely. She took it to a techy friend days later, who said that only a very strong magnet would do something like that … or another powerful source of energy.

Power fritzed overnight sporadically throughout the affected area. Barbara Johnston's sheets, which she'd left out to dry, were half-burnt by morning. Two fires caught in other homes, one minor and one that began at the drapes and decimated half a kitchen. Alan Chen discovered a pool of sticky red goo on his living room's hardwood floor beside a window that'd been smashed — by wind, a rock, or an intruder, he never knew which. The goo was the wrong color and wrong smell for blood (for *human* blood, anyway), so Alan simply wiped it up with a rag. Some of the stuff stained his palm, and three days later he realized a scar that'd been on that palm his entire adult life had healed.

The place the goo had sat on the hardwood made a spot better-polished than any polish could do — almost as if the wood there had reversed its age, and was brand new again.

AND BACK IN HIS LAB, under renewed interest by the GEN think-tank, Eldon Porter watched the tiny captive rift he'd made as its ionized aurora shifted color — sometimes its usual low-energy red, sometimes a short-wavelength dark blue or violet. He'd been unable to get more from the communication chamber and had been awake all night because of it. Lab techs kept bringing him coffee. Eldon downed it black, not tasting it, just trying to stay sharp enough to understand.

He'd thought a lot about the vision the other plane had given him yesterday before it'd cut off and stopped talking. Missives from the other side were strange things; they didn't come in obvious ways and didn't come all at once. Every time Eldon had spoken with the hive mind on the other side of the rift (the other side of *any* rift, including the one that'd opened yesterday under Cecret Lake), he'd found himself dwelling on it for days afterward. Bits of the message seemed to bury them-selves deep in his mind, resurfacing over time. It sort of made sense. If the chamber's "present moment" communication felt like recent memories, why couldn't other parts of the message feel like memories from farther back? Completely under-standing what they told him never felt like a logical act. It was more like remembering.

Eldon thought he understood what'd happened yesterday inside the Gore Point now, and he didn't like it one bit.

The other plane had only touched human consciousness recently. So-called "fiends" had been visiting the human plane since before humans existed (deep-bore rock samples proved that; ore believed to be the source of Zen Element turned out to actually be coated with fiend blood as its true source, going back hundreds of thousands of years), but Eldon was the first person the fiends actually shared minds with. Before that, their visits struck Eldon as covert explorations. Possibly raids. Regardless, prior rifts-crossings had avoided humans entirely, with the obvious exception of the Mine Zero incident — and even then, Eldon suspected the fiends had only shown themselves because humans had entered their turf. When the Mine Zero crew discovered the old prime rift deep beneath Fortune's surface in '62 (that rift was closed now, and Eldon thought it was for the same reason: caution or discretion), the miners had forced the fiends' hand. Eldon could only imagine the depth of the explorers' terror, finding what they'd found in Fortune's bosom.

It'd only been a few months since GEN's investigation of the strange, anti-entropic substance the feds called "Zen Element" had turned from theoretical to practical. Those in-the-know had suspected there were beings living on the nuclear-hot other side of interplanar rifts since the '50s and had confirmed it with the Mine Zero report, but it'd taken 26 more years before those beings tried to communicate. They'd sent a first soldier, and that soldier taught GEN all it now knew. Some called it a partnership, but Eldon knew better. He'd caught glimpses of what was over there ... and of course, he'd glimpsed their minds.

It's not precisely animosity *toward us that they feel*, Eldon had told his superiors, *but it may as well be.*

The beings that GEN called "fiends" — and the lab techs quietly called "demons" — didn't want to murder and maim, Eldon told his bosses. Still, they were a hive mind most of the time, and their ruling caste seemed by Eldon's estimation to live for centuries. They didn't want to kill humans, but they also didn't understand why killing was a big deal. If you're a hive mind whose parts live for hundred or even thousands of years, why would any single part matter? Individual beings were just chaff compared to the whole. To fiends, killing hundreds of meaningless individuals would be like getting a haircut.

Eldon could think of two palatable futures regarding rifts and the races. In one future, the beings on the other side might come to understand and respect humanity — which, incidentally, was what the wide-eyed among them already believed. In the other future, all rifts would close and the planes would thereafter keep to themselves, never interacting again.

The alternative to those brighter futures was what kept Eldon up at night: the idea that one day, armies of fiends would cross over for good, conquering our plane like conquistadors in the New World.

Eldon's job was to investigate, research, and act as a diplomat. He was supposed to help the fiends understand humanity and find common ground. But yesterday, something he'd been wondering and worrying about had finally happened. The fiends had been tapping into human intellect for months through Eldon ... but now they'd sampled emotion as well.

Yesterday, someone had approached a pre-rift inside the Gore Point while radiating a stronger emotional signal than the other plane had seen before. Suicidal teens entered the Gore Point all the time, but that was chicken-and-egg; they *became* suicidal due to the Point's energy rather than arriving with wrists half-slit. Yesterday's visitor, however, had offered bad vibes many times stronger ... and the fiends, sensing it, had eaten it up.

That dark emotional cloud had given fiends on other side of the Cecret Lake rift a snack. It'd only whetted their appetites, though; after the snack, they'd wanted more. The "wanting" was not subtle. It felt more like obsession to Eldon. Maybe even addiction.

After the visitor left, the pre-rift on the lake's bottom had opened. Eldon suspected now that all that bad juju had caused a fiend near the boundary to individuate, losing oversight from the hive mind. If that was true, it was truly an *individual* who'd opened the rift, not the whole of them. Steam had boiled through the lake's bile, and the night vision cameras had shown something emerge. GEN had protections in place for just such an event, but none had triggered. Either GEN had drawn all the wrong conclusions about what an incursion might look like ... or maybe GEN — and Eldon — had been deliberately misled.

Now, a fiend was out there in Fortune somewhere. It was holding itself in check as it roamed through unsuspecting neighborhoods, likely still clinging to the fiends' thus-far decision to stay unseen. But its willpower had to be fading, Eldon thought. Its sense of restraint — its so-far avoidance of humans — wouldn't last long.

Worse, energetics from Eldon's captive rift suggested that more might be coming. The individual's mind wasn't completely severed from the collective, and that meant the hive had tasted delicious despair as well. So far, only one fiend had been driven to frenzy, but Eldon felt increasingly sure that others would follow.

The chamber had said: *We cannot control it.*

If that was true, a plague had begun last night ... and Eldon — and possibly the fiends' hive mind itself — knew no way to stop it.

CHAPTER 9
FUGUE

Callum sipped his Orange Julius. Someone across the mall's atrium was playing Madonna. It wasn't official mall music; Callum could tell that much from the silence of a nearby speaker. People just did that kind of thing anymore: blasting their own music as if everyone wanted to hear it. It made him sick.

"Minister MacReady?"

Callum heard the voice. Sort of recognized it. But he had other things on his mind, and other things to do here. He was waiting. Waiting outside the food court at the mall. Something would happen soon, and when it did, it'd require all his attention.

"Callum," the voice said. Its tone had gone from Hello to no-bullshit, as if it knew he'd ignore a formal address but notice a personal one.

Callum looked up. Bob Burton was standing on his right, holding bags from JC Penny. His girls were at his side, both of their hair in third-grade pigtails. They looked like the dead twins from *The Shining*.

"Hi," Bob said after Callum met his eyes but before he said hello. That was a good move on Bob's part. Callum had no plans to say hello first. This was his place, and Bob was a distraction.

"Hi," Callum said, because Bob was waiting.

"You okay, buddy? Did Mary get ahold of you?"

"Mary is my wife."

Bob's brow furrowed. Then he said, "She called me."

"Really."

"Yeah."

"Why?"

"First time she called, it was for medical advice. She said she found you downstairs in the kitchen this morning. She said it was like you'd been sleepwalking, but I got the feeling it was more than that."

Callum grunted. This was none of Bob's fucking business.

"But then she called back. Said you ran off when she went to call me the first time. She's been looking for you ever since. She called because she was worried, Callum."

"Sorry. She's been a bitch lately."

Bob straightened, seemed to recalibrate, then bent to say something to his daughters. He handed a five dollar bill to one of them, took their bags in his own hands, and then the kids ran off.

"Going to buy tampons?" Callum asked after they were gone.

"To the arcade." Bob sat in one of the empty chairs at the small orange table, giving Callum a sideways look. "How long have you been here?"

"All my life," Callum said.

"Mary also asked if anything funny came up at your appointment last week."

"'Funny,'" Callum repeated. "Like *Seinfeld*."

"Funny like strange," Bob corrected. "Medically." He hesitated and then added, "... or psychologically."

"*Was* anything hilariously strange at my appointment?" Callum asked. *"Medically or psychologically?"*

"It's strange right now," Bob said.

"Really." Callum sipped his Orange Julius.

"What's going on with you?" Bob asked.

"I'm enjoying a refreshing mall beverage and listening to Madonna."

Bob resettled on the chair, then gave Callum a look that Callum supposed was intended to be serious. "Mary's worried. She thinks you're having some sort of a breakdown."

Callum looked at Bob's face. He laughed, then turned back to watching the atrium.

"I'm serious. *She's* serious. She said you were unconscious and covered in sour milk. Is that true?"

"Not anymore," Callum said. "I had gym clothes in the car."

Bob waited for Callum to elaborate. When Callum didn't, he went on. "Are you going to go back home? Or at least call Mary and let her know you're okay?"

Callum turned his head. Ever since leaving the kitchen, he'd been seeing the world through a black shroud. It was because he was still in a nightmare. A nightmare that never ended. And that was just fine, because it meant he'd probably been in it for days, weeks, months, or a year. That was the only logical conclusion: He *wasn't* living a slowly dying Hell and having to act cheerful about it for the benefit of his congregation. That was absurd. Too absurd for reality. No; the only sensible answer was that none of this was — or ever had been — real.

The now-familiar dark voice inside him said, *Watch the fountain.*

Callum looked. The fountain was an aquatic ballet set to

flashing lights. He watched the water jump across the mall's open center in graceful arcs while kids who shouldn't be in the fountain but were anyway tried to dodge them. The beauty of everything happening right now, Callum thought as he took it all in, was that nothing mattered. If this was a dream, he could say and do whatever he wanted. Who cared what transgressions he made, if none of them were real? Dreams came with a magic eraser that righted all wrongs when they ended. Everything would go back to normal if he ever woke up.

"Callum! I'm talking to you!"

Callum looked again at his doctor, watching Bob's curiosity turn to frustrated concern. Callum found that he didn't care — not about Bob's worries, not about Mary's worries ... not about anything, really. He felt his psyche reach out to something invisible, something unseen — something he understood more than he'd understood anyone lately. There was order to the world, once you accepted that everything was chaos. The paradox didn't bother Callum at all, nor did how differently he felt today than yesterday or last night. It was like a line had been crossed inside him. Some hidden knowledge had finally snapped into place, and ever since, everything had made sense. This was what life had become. This was, apparently, who he was always supposed to be.

Callum the kind.

Callum the inspirational.

What hot load of bullshit that was, and had always been.

"I think you should come with me," Bob said.

"Why?"

"Because I'm your doctor."

"Not today, you're not."

"What?" Bob stood, his mouth cocking into a sarcastic half-laugh: the kind of expression a person makes when nothing is funny at all. "Am I going to have to drag you out of here?"

Callum kept his eyes on the fountain. Something very important was about to happen there. In fact, something very important was *already* happening there. Callum could see it. An adult was staggering through the water arcs along with the children, heedless even when they sprayed him in the face. He was wearing a suit, but it was ill-fitting: oversized in the back, apparently, because it hung in blousy folds at the front. As if it was split, and was about to fall forward. His shirt looked the same. His slacks were drooping, belt seemingly undone, only the bulk of his hips keeping them from falling down. His head hung forward, the way it would if he were sleepwalking. Or if his neck was broken.

Bob's hand settled on Callum's shoulder. Callum spun where he sat, glaring into the doctor's eyes.

"Take your fucking hand back or I'll bite it off," he hissed.

Bob stepped back, his hand still hovering. His eyes were wide.

Then, at that exact moment, everyone inside the atrium started to scream.

CHAPTER 10

LEGIONS

Eldon looked down at the hand-sized energy detector Denny Brennan had given him. Its workings made no sense. Brennan was a tinkerer who'd always been able to build things, but looking at the device in his hands now, Eldon could only conclude that the rumors were true: GEN had given their people something new and unknown to play with. That was the only explanation for the inexplicable thing he'd been given, tinkerer or not.

Denny's gadget looked like a walkie-talkie that'd been opened up, stuffed with nonsensical electronic equipment, then re-sealed in inexpert fashion. Disconnected wires hung from the back for no apparent reason. A gel-like pouch of plastic was visible at one of the open seams, filled to bursting with clear goo. The front plate of a handheld football video game was attached to the thing's innards with colored leads, secured with nothing fancier than a rubber band. The LEDs on the game's display, instead of representing a football and players, now meant something else. That "something else" had made a lot more sense to Denny than to Eldon — probably because Denny had knowledge that Eldon, even with his own high clearance, wasn't allowed to know.

It resonates with in-vivo Zen Element, Denny had told him, intercepting Eldon to give him the device before Eldon could leave the lab. Eldon had been too scatterbrained at the time to ask the most obvious question: *What made you find me to give this to me, and how did you have any idea I'd need it?* Eldon had reported his findings and fears up the food chain, but none of those he'd called on the hotline had sounded concerned. He could only conclude that Denny, who had ambitions far above his pay grade, had overheard and felt he knew better than the brass.

Resonates?

Yes, Denny had told him. *Zen Element is easy to home in on. All you need is to look for energy that works the opposite of how energy works in our universe. You understand about entropy?*

Eldon understood. Entropy said that all things moved from order to disorder, and that energy never self-organized in the way Zen Element's energy seemed to. What Denny said implied that all his device needed to do was to look for energetic signatures that were impossible, then point the user toward them like a compass.

But Eldon had lost Denny after that. Even the lowliest GEN intern understood the science of interplanar rifts better than he did, even though he'd built a rift and was the only person the hive mind would talk to. In the end, Eldon had taken the device and run as he'd been planning to run, now with apparent direction. The difference between heeding Denny's "Zen detector" and knowing anything about how it worked was the difference between watching a television and knowing how to build one. He didn't need to understand it, as long as he could work it.

Sort of.

Now, sitting alone in his car outside the Fortune mall, he pressed buttons with no idea what they did or meant. Denny had said the device was pre-prototype — less than a proof of concept. To zero in on a source of Zen Element (an escaped fiend on the Earth plane, for instance, its blood full of the stuff), Eldon was either supposed to run for a touchdown or try for a field goal. He couldn't remember which.

A knock on the driver-side window nearly made him shit his pants.

He looked over, then used the crank to roll down the window. The 18-year-old soldier that Denny had persuaded to go with him stood on the curb outside. Eldon felt sorry for the kid. His job at GEN was to act as a glorified night watchman. Now that he'd followed what must feel like Eldon's wild hair to the mall of all places, his mood was equal parts intimidated and obedient.

"Are we going inside, sir? Do you think it's inside?" The soldier's hand was on his sidearm. That was a good sign; it meant that on the drive over, as he'd followed Eldon through traffic, he'd come to believe Eldon's claim: The string of destructive incidents overnight in Fortune wasn't due to teenagers, but instead the work of an escaped *something* they should both be afraid of.

Eldon looked at Brennan's football-game monstrosity. Its lights were flashing like crazy, but Eldon couldn't remember how to read it.

"I don't know."

"Do you really think this is happening?"

"I don't know."

"Because I was thinking, sir. I was thinking about one of the briefings we were given. About containment for the GEN facility."

"And?" Eldon didn't look up. He was still trying to make

sense of the Zen detector, certain that time was already far too short, and chaos was right around the corner.

"They don't tell us much, sir ..."

Eldon looked up when the soldier hesitated. He saw him swallow, clearly afraid. The kid might not actually be eighteen, but Eldon would give a testicle if he was more than twenty. He hadn't seen combat or hostile territory. He'd probably joined ROTC in high school to pay for college and expected easy sailing. What he hadn't expected was combat ... and what *nobody* expected was the coming of Hell on Earth.

"They don't tell us much, but someone said something about our weapons. About how they should be upgraded, because bullets might not be enough if ... if something ..."

"Here," Eldon said, reaching into the passenger seat.

He handed the boy the grocery bag Denny had given him, inside of which was an experimental GEN weapon called a Paulson pistol. Truth was, bullets probably worked fine on fiends if you hit them in the right spot and used enough of them, but the kid would be safer with the Paulson than non-military Eldon would be. Everyone from top to bottom said that Rollards were the best overall weapon against fiends because of the physical damage they could do — one reason Eldon had brought his lab's Rollard, too. The real hitch with bullets was that they were small. It was hard to know where to wound a fiend enough to stop it using only a bullet, seeing as their organs (if they had any) worked differently than humans'.

The kid looked at the thing. "Sir?"

"It fires some sort of an energetic round. Better than bullets, I guess."

"How do I work it?"

"It's got a trigger. I assume you point and pull." After that was anyone's guess. Denny hadn't elaborated; he'd just handed it over seeing as Eldon planned to go fiend-hunting without backup. Apparently the weapon was theoretical and experimental. His only real comment on it had been, *This will probably work.*

Eldon stepped out of the car. He'd pointed the football-game device at the mall a bit ago and it'd lit up and made noise. Going inside was as good a bet as any.

From here, the mall looked calm and normal. Nobody was yelling or running out covered in blood and bile. In the past, fiends had always tried very hard to stay out of sight when they were on the Earth side. Eldon hoped things would stay that way as the rogue demon sought the dark vibes it wanted so badly, but who knew? What he'd seen and heard from the other plane's hive mind suggested that this was all unforeseen and unexplored territory. Eventually, if there was no other way to get the fix it wanted, the escaped fiend might well break cover.

The soldier tucked the Paulson pistol into his waistband, opposite the M9 in his holster. He looked at Eldon and said, "What about you, sir?"

Eldon pulled his long white lab coat from the back seat. He put his left arm through the sleeve, then pulled the Rollard from the back-seat footwell and looped its strap over his right shoulder before pulling the lab coat the rest of the way on. He'd look funny entering the mall like some mad scientist with a lumpy coat, but he'd look a whole lot funnier if he carried the half-broadsword, half-devil's-trident Rollard openly in his hand.

Eldon nodded at the soldier. The soldier glanced at the Rollard and nodded back.

"What's your name?" Eldon asked.

"Weatherby."

"Your first name."

"Donnie."

"You up for this, Donnie?" Eldon asked. He felt sorry for the kid. *Donnie?* The name only made him seem younger, more carefree, and more ill-fitting for what might be coming.

Donnie gave a grim half-smile with no joy in it at all. "Depends what 'this' is," he said. "But I'll do my best, sir."

Eldon considered saying more. He thought about telling the soldier more of what he knew and what he thought might be true, and he thought about saying something about himself to reassure him — namely, that Eldon wasn't entirely a nerdy scientist. He'd worked dual career possibilities for far longer than was sensible, certain until just a few years ago that he still might end up a fireman. He'd done most of the training; he could lug a hundred pounds of five-inch hose up a stairwell and carry a full-grown man over his shoulder. There were times when Eldon actually wished he'd gone that way — that he could be a fighter instead of a thinker: a killer of riftborne threats rather than a studier of them. Today, he supposed, was his chance. He'd just have to think of it that way — and, hopefully, convince Donnie that he was more competent than he'd so-far felt.

In the end, though, Eldon settled on another nod — this time with what he hoped was a devil-may-care smile.

"There's just one of them, though?" said the kid. "You think there's just one ... *demon?*"

Eldon allowed the word. "Fiend" was a euphemism anyway. They all knew what the other place was, and what its inhabitants should be called.

"Just one." He *hoped* it'd stop at one, before this particular E.T. had a chance to phone his frenzy back home.

"I just can't help thinking about my grandfather with his Bible, sir," Donnie said, looking at his feet. "In Mark 5:9, when

Jesus performs an exorcism ... well, the demon inside *that* man says it's not just *one*. It's *many*."

Eldon nodded. He wasn't religious himself, but his parents sure had been. *"'I am legion,'"* Eldon quoted. "That's what it says."

"Yes sir."

Eldon was watching the young soldier's eyes when he heard the first scream come from the mall. Then the second. Then the third. It was now or never.

"Well, there's only one fiend this time, but there's two of us," Eldon said, slapping Donnie on the back and turning toward the entrance. "This time, *we're* the legions."

CHAPTER 11

SHARP-DRESSED MAN

ob was somewhere near Callum, repeating his name until it lost all meaning, but Callum had no idea where. Normal directions and distances had become meaningless. It was more of that dream logic — that casual dismissal of the most obvious unrealities — even though a buried, bound-and-gagged part of Callum knew without question that he'd never been dreaming.

This was real. Horribly, terribly real.

The man in the fountain continued his grim march, blood now visible as it wicked through the fabric of his white dress shirt from an unseen wound. His eyes, looking up from that broken-neck downturn of his head, were on Callum. He was coming not to hurt him, but to meet him. They had business, the man and the minister. The fact that Callum knew it so clearly terrified that hidden part of himself: the normal, everyday man he'd been until yesterday. Until he'd stood by the black lake, and felt all his cares leave him ... and become *this*.

"CALLUM!"

This time Bob grabbed Callum by the wrist, not to get his attention so much as to drag him away. Because something was wrong. Something was very, very wrong. Only now was Callum noticing how the shallow pool of water at the on-comer's feet had turned crimson. Only now was he seeing the way the children ahead of the man were confused while those behind him were running for their mothers. Something about his back side was worse than his front. And all the while, the red water beneath him swirled, expanding like a gathering storm cloud.

"Jesus, Callum. *Come on!*"

Amidst the screaming of children. The screaming of adults. The chaos in front of them, as people ran from a man who was only walking forward. Only sloughing dead flesh into the fountain. Only coming to pieces, and yet still on the move. Amidst all of it, what did Bob want from Callum? Was he afraid, or was he still punting for Mary and her helicoptering, for her obnoxious nagging, for all things mundane and dull?

Finally something was happening, Callum thought. *Finally*, there was more to his life than piety and pain. And Bob, with all his droll inanity, wanted to pull him away from it? It was beyond offensive.

Callum looked at his doctor, finding only disdain. He wanted to rip through his chest. Break the bones of his ribcage. He wanted to see if he could take the man's heart in his hands — what the throb of his life ending might feel like.

"What if Hell has come to Fortune … *Bob?*" Callum growled. "Where *are* your girls, anyway? Are you sure they're at the arcade? While you stand here pulling my cock, what if they're already burning?"

Bob took two steps back. He glared doe-like for a few more seconds, wide-eyed and dumb, then dropped his shopping bags and ran.

Callum climbed over the food court railing, moving into the mall's main concourse. He still held his Orange Julius. His feet moved forward of their own accord, closing the distance between himself and the bloody businessman.

The man's head slouched a hard notch forward, breaking eye contact. It hung too low now, practically upside-down on his chest. As if something had finally split, a new glut of blood splashed into the water behind him. His staggering slowed — not precisely zombie-like; more the gait of someone trying to lug too heavy a load. But what load was there? The man carried nothing.

His suit coat slipped forward as his shoulders rounded under the weight of his sagging head. Only no; that was wrong: It wasn't the coat that slipped from his body. More like his *body itself* was slipping away from something else.

Something behind it. Or inside it.

Something that had ripped the man open from behind and was now wearing his body like a costume.

And Callum understood.

He blinked. Behind his eyelids, he saw a desolate place that was at once unknown and intimately familiar. It was a red and parched place made of rocks and bluffs with a scorched sky — a place where, Callum somehow knew, his skin would blacken in the heat, curling up like paper in an oven. He'd never been there, and yet he'd been away too long. The dream feeling deepened: Callum dragged forward by his own body, now out of his control.

I should be afraid.

But he wasn't afraid.

His mind went to the life he'd had yesterday. To the morning prior, when — after checking his son's vitals and finding him unchanged — he'd gone to the kitchen to parody sanity with his wife. She'd asked how Nathan was. Callum had said "the same." But he *hadn't* been the same an hour earlier, had he? At 4:30am, by his only child's bedside, Callum had found himself wondering if this was the end. There was resignation in that moment, and depths of sorrow far deeper than any ink-filled lake. He'd cried, quietly, running a hand over the boy's hair and thinking of the most pointless reminiscences: hair born blond and baby-fine, darkening with age. Hair on the day of its first haircut. Hair that would soon be underground or in ashes, returning to the earth from whence it came. He'd gone to the guest bedroom after that, shut the door, and curled up on the double bed Nathan had slept on until they'd stumbled across a cheap, roomier queen. He hadn't wanted to move ever again. What was the point?

His hand. Nathan's hair. Here in the mall, he couldn't stop replaying it.

Yes, said a voice inside him. *Give us more.*

He opened his eyes, only realizing when he did that they'd been closed for minutes. He'd been in that parched red place all alone while his body marched forward. The mall now felt strange and alien, as if it was here, not there, in which he was a visitor. A wisp of what looked like black smoke was drifting from his own chest to that of the coming man. It elongated, pulsed, became a horizontal drip like a wash of too much watercolor paint.

Something from Callum was going into the man. Something taken, something stolen. Something Callum thought he'd wanted gone, and the other was happy to take.

The man's suitcoat fell the rest of the way forward, as if his shoulders had finally reached the point of being unable to hold it. His shoulders came with the coat. His torso and head came after that.

The corpse splashed into the water chest-first, spattering the fountain's edges with thin red speckles. Once the dead man was face-down, Callum saw that he'd been ripped open from the back as if by a razor-sharp autopsy blade. The thing that had been inside it, however, was still standing: the horribly, intimately familiar thing that'd been using the businessman's body as a disguise.

It stepped out of the corpse's shell. It continued walking toward Callum.

Part of Callum alarmed. It tried to pull him from this strange fugue and make him run. But the other part — the co-opted, spellbound part — was far stronger. He watched his plodding feet approach the small black monster with its enormous mouth, its rows and rows and rows of sharklike teeth. He watched himself as if from the outside, wondering if this was where the life of Minister Callum MacReady ended.

More.

And a voice inside Callum said, *There is no more. You have all I've got. All I am. All I've ever been.* He saw the image of himself smoothing Nathan's hair over and over again, knowing that the creature in front of him was somehow reveling in the pained memory, replaying it inside Callum's mind without Callum's permission — over and over, like an obsession. The wisp of smoke between them surged each time he felt his private pain, moving from Callum's chest to the demon's chest. It was feeding on his pain. His grief. His sorrow. It was drinking every last dark emotion from Callum's soul: trying to get it all like slurping the dregs from a cup's bottom with a straw.

More.

Its head turned, making their smoky connection warble and break apart. Paint-drip fingers of the same smoke shot from it, extending toward onlookers who'd frozen, unable to look away. It was searching. Probing the other people around the fountain, wondering if they had pain as rich as Callum's to sample.

MORE.

And then something else happened — something that Callum was sure only he could see. A bolt of that same black energy, like grey paint dripping upward at lighting speed, shot from the creature's head and shattered the atrium's glass skylight.

It's calling others, Callum thought. *It's seen what's in these people, and rung a dinner bell for more like it to follow.*

And come.

And feast.

The creature, free of its discarded skin suit, came toward him with its claws out. Its mouth opened. Last night, it had been overwhelmed in finding him — maybe confused, maybe drunk on what nourished it. Now, it wasn't confused at all. It knew what it wanted. It'd raised a call.

Now, it would feed.

And yet Callum still came toward it willingly, that desolate other place still hiding behind his eyelids, appearing every time he blinked. With his heart sucked dry, he was coming back to himself — back to his everyday sense. With it came horror. The Catholics — especially the old school — still sometimes talked about possession. Callum used to laugh at the idea. But no. It was real.

It'd had him. It *still* had his body, as it walked toward its doom. And Callum — mostly himself again, trapped inside — could do nothing to stop it.

More.

Its mouth opened wider. Its teeth were too bile-coated to gleam, filling the whole of what should be its face.

He could smell its breath.

He could feel the heat coming from inside it, scalding like air from a blast furnace.

WARRIOR

Something struck Callum broadside, throwing him to the hard stone floor just outside the walk-in fountain. He hit very hard, barely avoiding a concussing blow to the head. His right shoulder took the brunt of it, torquing with a white-hot bold of pain. But there was good news: The pain brought him the rest of the way around. He re-gained control of his body and could suddenly flee like everyone else ... if he was still unwounded enough to run.

And if someone wasn't on top of him.

"Stay down," said a gruff voice.

The man on top of Callum stood up, using Callum for leverage and slamming his wingbones against the floor in the process. Callum, free of the fugue that'd so recently had him, looked up to see his tackler as a standing god above him: a man broad across the middle and built like a fireman, but wearing a lab coat (complete with pocket protector) of all things. Sunlight from the broken skylight made his white garb shine.

The man's intense eyes locked on Callum's, reminding him to stay where he was. There was menace in them, but menace born of deadly efficiency. *I don't have time right now to deal with your bullshit,* those eyes said, *so if I have to hurt you to keep you safe, I will.*

The man swept his coat back and swung what he'd concealed beneath it into the open. It was a huge and heavy-looking weapon with two ends, one of which had a side like a three-tined fork and a side like a broadaxe. The handle end bore a spear-sharp point. After unfastening the strap that'd been hiding it under his coat, the man wielded the thing with two hands, like a scythe.

Callum crab-scrambled backward. He struck a clutch of chairs against the railing he'd so recently climbed over, now at the depth of terror. Nothing made sense. No part of this happened in a sane world. Not the oil-black thing with its claws and teeth and throat that hissed like a leaking pressure vessel. Not the broad-shouldered man in a lab coat, holding his weapon like a reaper's blade. There was another person in the mix, too, Callum saw now: a kid in Army uniform who'd come with the man. Instead of holding a recognizable weapon, he had what looked like a child's toy: too small to be a gun, or at least a respectable one. It was the size of a Derringer, at home more in a flapper's garter than a soldier's hands. It also looked entirely unfinished. The thing was all loose wires and tubes, with a comic blue bubble structure on its small barrel.

The big man held a hand up to the kid, ordering him to stand down.

"Don't shoot it!" he said. "For the love of God, don't shoot it unless you have to."

Callum looked to the soldier, wondering at the man's order. If there was one thing Callum would do with the monster in the fountain, it'd be to shoot it. He wouldn't automatically shoot criminals, even those who broke into his house and pointed guns of their own ... but he'd shoot this as knee-jerk as he'd step on a roach.

Something beeped. The white-coated man dropped his gaze carefully, finding its source in one of his big pockets. Callum spied the thing: It looked like a walkie talkie smashed together with a video game. Whatever the man saw on its display must have alarmed him, because he looked back to the soldier as if expecting to find him on fire.

"Think of something else, Donnie," he said. "You hear me? *Think of something else!*"

The soldier, apparently named Donnie, had frozen completely. His dumb little pop gun was still pointed at the monster, but his face had turned into a wax sculpture of horror. His eyes were somewhere else, somewhere far away.

"Donnie? *Donnie, listen to me!*"

He stepped between the creature and the soldier. Now Donnie's weapon was pointed at the scientist's back while the scientist moved his weapon to one hand, the other held up in a universal gesture of pacification.

He said to the monster, "I'm *Eldon*. Do you understand? *I'm Eldon Porter.*"

Callum wanted to blink. To believe again in dreams and nightmares. The man — *Eldon*, apparently — was treating the thing like a guest at his cocktail party. *We've met before, haven't we? My name is Eldon, remember? You're the monster that lived in my closet as a kid, right? That's right; ha ha ha. Drop those claws and let's grab a drink together.*

A puff of black gas had begun to drift from the soldier's chest, wafting its way past Eldon like cigarette smoke in a draft. It was the same gas Callum had seen moving from himself to the creature: terrible emotions, aerosolized and invisible to all who'd never had it sucked from their hearts before.

The smoke reached the creature. It seemed to gain strength, to stand up taller. It moved into a sunbeam and Callum could see the gore that covered it: the lifeblood of the man it'd opened like luggage so it could wear him like a costume. Behind Eldon, the kid called Donnie began to scream.

"Move away, Donnie," Eldon said over his shoulder. "Get out of the fountain."

But Donnie was too far gone. His eyes rolled back as all sense left them, his mouth drawn down at both ends like a sad clown's frown. He looked to Callum like a Nazi in the climactic scene of *Raiders*, his entire face about to melt. The sounds he began making were barely human. The smoke trail throbbed like a heartbeat, the creature growing stronger as the soldier grew weaker.

"DONNIE GET THE FUCK OUT OF HERE, YOU FUCKING HEAR ME?"

Callum saw a flash of light. Nearby, a trash can exploded like a bomb. The kid had fired his weapon: a toy's appearance with the heft of a rocket launcher.

The smoke line darkened and doubled. The creature roared. Keeping his eyes on the monster, Eldon reared back with one hand and shoved Donnie hard enough to trip him over the fountain's edge. *"I said stand down! You want to start a war?"*

War? Callum, despite his fear and confusion, sat taller. *What war?* The man in the lab coat was still acting like he wanted to make peace instead of using his blade. Why had they come with weapons, if not to use them?

The black creature lowered itself to all fours and bound forward like an alien dog. Eldon struck it with the dull length of his weapon's handle, making it tumble. It rolled over twice in the fountain's shallow pool, its back striking its former man-suit as it went.

Donnie raised his gun, if that's what it was. His hands were shaking; his second shot went as wide as the first. This time the ball of light it fired went farther: all the way across the atrium, blowing a car-sized hole in the second-floor Spencer's Gifts. Through it, Callum could see sky.

The creature grabbed the soldier by the leg. It ripped it away like warm taffy. Blood spurted from the stump, turning the water around him an even darker shade of red. All the fight went from Donnie after that. Instantly he turned pale, his face slack. The weapon stayed in his hand, but the hand went as stupid as the rest of him. He screamed, then went into shock. After that he lay still with arms out and chest up: a man accepting his own vivisection.

At that, Eldon seemed to give up on the idea of peace. Funny thing about about peace: It wasn't something only one side could agree to, and so far the monster wasn't playing.

The black creature dropped Donnie's severed leg. It stood on two feet again, opening its mouth to reveal all those teeth. Only ... something was different. Something was *wrong*. Then Callum saw: When the thing had come at him last night, it'd been as tall as an elementary-schooler. When it came out of the dead man, it'd seemed a bit larger: up to Callum's shoulders, maybe. But now it stood taller than Eldon ... and Eldon was a big man.

It was feeding. And as it fed, it was *growing*.

"Okay," Eldon said to it, holding his weapon like he meant to use it. "All right. Let's see what happens."

The thing bellowed through the atrium. Its voice had grown with its enlarged chest: a frightful roar from an even more frightful nightmare. Its clawed limbs went wide. Then it stilled, facing off, and Callum saw what looked like a tiny hand made of that same black smoke coming from it, reaching toward its adversary.

He looked to Eldon, expecting to see the same connection he'd seen before — as the creature, somehow, siphoned essence from Eldon in the way it'd siphoned something from him and the soldier, now lost and whimpering behind him. But Eldon's face was steely. As if he understood. As if he'd expected it to try whatever it was trying, and knew how to gird himself against it.

The creature roared again. The black hand broke apart like morning fog and its stance shifted forward, its eyeless face on Eldon. It was through trying to suck him dry, and preparing instead for battle.

They circled. Standing off. Waiting to parry like swordsmen.

"Come on," Eldon muttered, seemingly to himself.

The creature struck first. Now standing at least six-six, its wingspan had grown formidable. It shifted toward Eldon as it raked a clawed hand through the air. Eldon reacted almost too late, leaning away from its long reach microseconds before its claws opened his throat. Its first finger alone made contact, opening a shallow gash on his chin. Eldon wiped at it, annoyed.

He re-gripped his weapon. New calculations streamed through his eyes, his whole body adjusting to the thing's bigger size. Callum had no idea what was happening, but it couldn't be clearer that Eldon did. Somehow, in some way, he'd entered the mall knowing exactly what he'd find.

And knowing, hopefully, how to kill it.

While Eldon and the tall black thing circled, Donnie had regained some wits. As Callum watched, he fumbled with his tiny weapon. His shaking, white-tipped fingers were having trouble holding it ... but bit by bit, he managed.

Come on, kid, Callum thought. *Find a clean shot. You can do it.*

Eldon and the creature circled. In the mall-gone-silent, the splash of their fountain footsteps was unnaturally loud.

Eldon feinted forward. The monster took the bait, pulling away and making what it was meant to be a counterstrike. Eldon, who hadn't actually swung his blade, stood ready. When the creature swiped, so did Eldon. The axe end of his double-sided weapon — long and curved, like a medieval executioner's axe — embedded itself in the creature's side.

It roared. Black liquid, like ink, gushed from the wound. It dropped into the red water but did not mix with it: a viscous blight that refused to dissolve, reminding Callum of a hole to nowhere.

The creature swung again. Again Eldon was ready, this time spinning the other way to impale it with the fork side of his weapon. He moved like a warrior, not the geek his lab coat implied. Callum could see broad shoulders working, the man's breath coming in smooth and focused rhythm. And Callum thought, *Who IS this guy? Where did he come from, and how can he be so ready for something so unreal?*

But his confident thoughts came too soon. The monster seemed unhurt by the second blow; it seemed to have allowed it to open its own opportunity. The area Eldon struck was armored, and the fork of his weapon rebounded with bone-jarring force.

As Eldon recovered, the creature struck. Eldon's blow had moved him too close for the thing to rake him with claws, but it could — and did — knock him down. It hit him with a swift back-swipe of its elbow. Eldon flew off his feet, then landed hard in the water.

He contorted in pain. An involuntary grunt came from him. The creature didn't hesitate; it followed Eldon down and moved to pin him, to rip open his throat. But Eldon, by accident or intention, had a surprise for the creature when it did:

He'd managed to land with the pointed handle end of his weapon pointed skyward.

The creature's momentum threw it onto the spear. The point ran through its side like mounting a severed head on a pike. The new wound bled and the creature howled, but the run-through was still too near the surface, too far away from the monster's core to do more than piss it off. It pressed itself upright with its opposite arm. Eldon's weapon, still embedded in the creature, came with it.

It screeched with victory. It raised its claws above a now-defenseless,-flat-on-his-back Eldon. Eldon's defensive instincts made him raise his arms and tuck his legs, curling nearly fetal with forearms crossed on his chest. But there would be no defense against the blow that came next. Not with only flesh and bone between them, there wouldn't.

Callum cringed, but the death blow didn't come. Instead, a bright flash bloomed from where the soldier was lying, where he'd been honing all the focus he had left on the small, powerful weapon in his unsteady hands. His aim was dead-on. This time, the blast that'd blown through the second-floor Spencer's blew through the monster's torso instead.

Except that it didn't. The round struck the creature true as true, but no hole appeared in its middle. It did not bleed. Instead, the ball of light diffused across the black thing's skin, then died to nothing. As if instead of being hurt by the round, it'd absorbed it.

And grown stronger.

From his position cowering amongst mall chairs, Callum watched as the big creature grew even bigger. Its body swelled and throbbed like a werewolf's transformation, distending in seconds. Its round head became more like a muzzle. The muzzle twisted, widening, breaking open with an audible crack. More teeth grew, even outside of the reversing cavity of its mouth. Its claws extended, then multiplied. It had eyes now, Callum could see — or at least parodies of eyes. They were red holes rimmed with undulating silver: pools of blood floating in shimmering mercury. It was growing horns, too: horns like the Devil.

It roared again — not with pain this time, but with power. The roar, like everything else about it, had become so much bigger.

It turned on its would-be murderer. With the casual rake of one claw, it turned Donnie into thick, meaty ribbons.

It grew.

And *grew*.

The monster was still growing when Eldon leapt for its leg, then climbed it like a tree. One shuffle up was all it took to reach the spot where his weapon remained embedded, dangling from the thing's now-enormous side. Eldon jumped to reach it, catching the head's two sides with one hand each. For a moment he hung like a man on a zipline, then his weight pulled the weapon free. Mid-air, as he fell, his hands climbed its handle. He flipped the thing around on landing and swung without hesitation.

The creature was over ten feet tall when Eldon severed its leg. Instead of stopping, Eldon continued his swing, whipping himself around for a second pass as the leg fell away. By the time he finished his second circle and brought the axe-head back to center, gravity had brought the demon's belly within reach. He opened it deftly, spilling its otherworldly intestines.

The monster fell the rest of the way. Eldon stepped back, then brought his weapon overhead like a lumberjack splitting a log. This time he severed its head. And then, blessedly, its corpse shuddered and went still.

For a moment there was nothing. Nothing at all, save the idiot splash of the fountain's arcing water. It hadn't gotten the memo that in such an insensible world, fountains no longer mattered.

There were no other people remaining: just Callum, Eldon, two dead men, and a storybook monster that might, for all they knew, come back to life any second. Everyone else, at some point in all the terror and melee, had run away. They were alone now, and far too quiet for comfort.

Red water dripped from the blade in the big man's hand. Callum could only see his profile. He was still watching the beast's body. Looking on, Callum felt irrationally that now that he'd killed the beast, he'd come for Callum.

And then, thanks to God, it'll all be over, Callum thought.

The man — Eldon, his name was, still in his now-shredded lab coat — turned only his head.

"Is ... Is it over?" Callum asked.

A sound began: a rustling, shuffling, multitudinous rattle from everywhere outside at once, counterpointed by screams and unearthly roars. Eldon tipped his head to listen. As he did, Callum saw dark shapes flash through the broken atrium skylight, screeching and full of unknown menace.

"Not even close," he said.

CHAPTER 13
ONE BEIGE SHOE

They ran.

There was never any question; Callum simply assumed he should stick with Eldon now that normal bets were off. When an enormous black monster showed up inside a dead man, you followed the guy who arrived out of the blue to kill it — *especially* after the place it happened wound up deserted. It was hard to believe that not twenty minutes ago, the mall had been as lively as a Tiffany concert. He still had spilled Orange Julius on his shirt, for Pete's sake.

Where did Bob go? he found himself wondering. Eldon's flight took them past the arcade, and Callum couldn't resist looking inside. The games didn't know the world had changed; they were beeping and booping just the same as always. It was so strange, to see such ordinariness beside such disorder.

The effect was hollow. Liminal. The echoes, when the air went silent, had their own echoes.

They stopped at the double set of glass exit doors that spanned the full length of a terminal wall. The doors were covered in filth and smeared fingerprints, as if mall-goers had shoved through them heedless of whatever they may have been carrying. A few were frosted in a web of incomplete shatter, as if they'd been banged into with extreme prejudice. Drink cups, shopping bags, and even a shoe or two littered the in-between. Propping one of the doors open was an old woman's corpse. By Callum's best guess, she'd been stomped to death.

Eldon went to the woman's body, knelt, put two fingers to her exposed neck, then stood without comment. So she was dead. So what? So many other people were dying today.

Callum looked outside. Indistinct shapes shot past, bathed in November shadow. A thin, grey-skinned thing walking upright crept between cars in the up-front handicap zones before slinking out of sight. It moved like a raptor, and from what Callum could see, half its head was missing, its jaw hanging low like backyard swing. There were crashing, smashing sounds in the distance and even from here, Callum could see three distinct columns of smoke on the horizon. Four cars were stalled in a pair of two-car collisions. Between the doors and the parking lot, two people lay dead in the street. One woman seemed to have been hit by a car, her hips sideways and one arm bent the wrong way. The other had been hit by something else — something that'd slashed them from belly to throat, then ripped out enough intestine to use as a jumprope.

Eldon pulled the device Callum had spied earlier from his pocket, consulted diodes and displays that seemed meaningless, then returned it and looked outside. Finally he turned to meet Callum's eyes, unsurprised to see he'd tagged along. His own eyes were blue and softer than Callum expected. There was blood spatter on his face and neck, plus something on one cheek that looked like dark green moss: a smear that almost reached his mouth.

"It had you, didn't it?" he asked.

"What?"

"That fiend. That ... creature. *It had you.*"

"I don't understand," Callum said. But he did. And Eldon *knew* he did, and knew that yes, it'd *had* Callum plenty before the battle came and Callum had snapped out of it. The horror of it was too new, though — too inexplicable to give voice.

Something in the distance exploded. There was a scream. Nothing in their view changed; whatever just happened was out of sight.

"What's your name?"

"Callum. Pastor Callum MacReady."

"Pastor," he said thoughtfully, then let it go. "I'm Eldon Porter. Are you okay, Father? Are you hurt?"

"I'm not Catholic," Callum said, as if that was important right now. "Just 'Callum' will do."

"Okay," Eldon said, humoring his irrelevance. "Are you okay ... *Callum?*"

It was a good question. Callum had to inspect himself to know. "I think so."

"So you can run."

"I ... *Wait.* You want to *go outside?*"

Eldon nodded. It was a subtle movement: down only, no corresponding up. "No choice. That fiend came here because *you* were here. How do you think I found it?"

Callum didn't know how to answer that. The electronic device in Eldon's pocket must be some sort of a detector, but it made more sense that Eldon would have followed the monster here (the *fiend,* was the word he'd used) rather than Callum. Why would anyone want to find Callum? And how would they, unless they asked Mary?

"It came for *me?*"

"Were you inside the Gore Point yesterday, Callum? You were, weren't you?"

Callum didn't answer right away. He felt like he might somehow be in trouble. The ranger hadn't wanted him at Cecret Lake — said he wasn't supposed to pass the huge DO NOT ENTER signs he'd definitely seen even though he hadn't remembered it until later. Looking back, Callum had expected to be followed out of the park just to make sure he left like he'd been told to, but there'd been no following. He'd gone out the way he'd come, but as far as he could tell nobody'd seen him at all.

"Yes, but only because my wife works for a firm that was doing an audit on the Rampart, and—"

"It came here because you were here," Eldon repeated. "It was looking for you, and I think part of you was looking for it."

"What's that mean?"

Eldon stared outside again as if he hadn't heard.

"They're distracted," he said. Callum assumed he meant the other horrors that seemed to have invaded Fortune in the past half hour. "There's a lot of noise out there now. My guess is that for a while, they'll be more drawn to the one I killed than to you."

"What the hell are you talking about?" Then, something more important made the question he'd just asked unimportant by comparison. "What makes you think they won't follow me anymore?"

"Oh, they still will. They *absolutely* will. But not as strongly because the bond is broken — and probably not at all right now."

"Why?"

"Because this is the frenzy, and everything's new."

Callum found himself irritated with Eldon's half-answers — the infuriating way he hoarded what he knew and refused to share it. From the ignorant, terrified, confusing place Callum stood, it seemed he was doing it just to be a jerk.

"Oh? Did your little video game tell you that?" He eyed Eldon's pocket, where the device's wires were visible. "How the hell do *you* know that 'the bond is broken'? How do *you* know it doesn't *'have'* me anymore?"

Eldon pulled a Leatherman multi-tool from his pants pocket, opened the sharpest blade, and put it in Callum's hand. "Kill yourself," he said.

Callum looked at the knife, dumbfounded. After a few seconds Eldon took it back and put it away. *"That's* how I know," he said.

Outside, a woman came running around the building's side, her eyes wide with panic. Her scalp was half-absent, blood running down her face in rivulets like an inverted crown. She made it as far as the concrete apron by the bike racks before a dark, winged thing swooped from above and lifted her off like a falcon takes a mouse. One beige shoe fell, tipped sideways, and was still. Eldon stared at it, wondering why he wasn't more terrified. Maybe it was because he'd reached his limit long ago. He'd gone past it. He now was a man on empty — *past* empty, into the place where surreality lived.

Eldon spoke into the quiet, calm like they hadn't just seen a nightmare pluck a woman from the street.

"My lab is all the way across town. We can't stay here, but it's too far to go there. They're massing." He tapped his pocket with the device in it. "I've never seen energetics like are happening now. Staying outside too long is a mistake. You're going to have to trust me on that. We should find a place, then bunker down until the energy changes. *If* it changes."

"Are you going to tell me what's going on?"

"Hell is going on. You understand Hell, right? *Pastor?"*

Callum considered asking more, but he nodded instead.

Yes. He understood Hell just fine. He'd never believed it truly existed — not really — but some things, the soul simply recognized as true.

"We could go to my house," he said.

"Where do you live?"

"Concord Place. Walking distance."

"Do you have a basement?"

"It's an old house. We have a root cellar."

"Earth? Or concrete and cinder blocks?"

"Cinder blocks. It's not *that* old."

"Earth floors would be better, but a root cellar's still better than a basement." Callum wanted to ask why, but that was his brain again, trying to use intellect to make sense of the senseless. "We can't walk to your place though. I think you know why."

Callum looked at the beige shoe. He knew why.

"We'll have to run to my car. See it there in the red zone? I wasn't too worried about getting a ticket."

Callum looked. It was maybe a hundred feet from the doors, but the woman the flying thing had taken had only been about twenty.

"What happens if we don't make it?"

"Come on. You know the answer to that."

Eldon put a hand on the door in front of him, then pulled the big metal weapon away from his body again as if he planned to use it. Its blade was slick with the monster's blood.

"Wait," Callum said.

Eldon paused.

"You have to give me something. Some kind of weapon. Let me go back and get the gun that soldier had. I think it's still in the fountain."

"It's right here," Eldon said, patting his coat's opposite

pocket. Had Callum blacked out? He didn't at all remember Eldon picking it up.

"Give it to me."

He shook his head. "You saw what happened when Donnie shot it at the one back there."

"Oh," Callum said. He'd forgotten that. Shooting the beast was what'd made it triple in size and grow stronger. How had the makers missed that when they'd designed the thing?

"It fires Zen Element rounds. There's Zen in their blood. It must have ... *absorbed* the blast somehow." He shrugged, mostly to himself. "It might be a class issue. I *thought* there'd be classes."

"What are 'classes'?" Callum said.

"It's complicated. There's a lot that nobody understands, and there's a lot that a *few* people understand but haven't bothered to share. Personally, I was pro-disclosure. I was overruled."

Callum wanted to ask again what Eldon meant, but he was sure he'd get the same answer: *It's complicated. It's need-to-know. So just put your head down, kid, and do what I say.*

"I don't think we have a choice of what comes next. I don't like it either, but I think it's run or die." Eldon looked over seriously. "I won't lie to you, Callum. It might be run *and* die, but at least if we run we have half a chance." He took a breath, still watching the apron outside the mall with its mayhem and single beige shoe. "Maybe it's okay. Turns out I'm better with a Rollard than I thought." He indicated the sword-like weapon. "I'll do my best to cover you."

"No," Callum said.

"*'No'?*"

"I don't want to run. I'm not running. I'm not going outside if ..." He trailed off. He didn't want to say what he'd meant to, because it felt a bit too close to the bone: ... *if armageddon has come.*

"Okay," said Eldon. He pushed the glass door, preparing to exit alone.

Callum grabbed him by the back of the coat. It was a sneaky way to press the issue. Callum realized he'd rather face Hell with someone who knew what was happening than be alone.

Eldon stopped with the interior door still partway open. He looked back, but his expression said his patience had run out.

"You'll cover me?" Callum asked.

Eldon nodded.

"Okay. Then let's go."

CHAPTER 14

LET'S DO THIS

Callum didn't realize how hard his heart was beating until the first time they dove for cover. After, while they crouched behind a pair of garbage cans waiting to be spotted, he noticed it: the deep and hollow thrum of a tympani. To Callum's ears, his heartbeat was as loud as signal drums. They'd hear it beyond the Rampart: Fortune's not-unexpected demise, calling out its death rattle.

Rampart. That made him think of Mary, who'd done work there again today. But even more it made him think of Nathan.

Callum looked at Eldon. Everything out here was too bright. He decided it was because his eyes were open as wide as they could go with terror, letting in all the world's light. There was a coppery taste in his mouth, like sucking on a penny. His breath was a cagey thing; Callum held onto it, but felt like the smallest lapse of attention would cause it to run away. And that *heartbeat.* That enormous, seismic heartbeat. Soon Eldon would shout at him for it — or kill him to still it so the thing they'd ducked to avoid wouldn't find them.

Callum peeked between the garbage cans. He could still see

it, out among the cars. He didn't *want* to see it, but he couldn't bring himself to look away.

After exiting the mall, they'd entered the front indent of the mall's footprint. Landscapers had made a courtyard-like place there that might have been quaint if not for all the dead people and body parts. They'd been walking low, hurrying without running, when they'd spied something in the lot beyond the corner that reminded Callum of a minotaur. It was brick red, seven feet tall, and had a pair of horns on its head as thick as his thighs. Its head wasn't exactly bull- or boar-like, though — more like a very large human skull that'd been mostly (but not entirely) stripped of flesh.

"Berserker," Eldon whispered. Apparently that was the name of the thing, though Callum had no idea why it had a name at all — why this was something anyone in the world knew, and wasn't shocked by. "At least I think."

"You've seen this before?"

"Sort of." Eldon tapped his head. "Like a dream."

"What's—?" Callum started to say, but Eldon put an urgent finger to his lips to stop him. He shook his head slowly, then moved the finger to point to one side. Callum shifted so he could see what Eldon was indicating, still using the gap between the cans. His heart-pounding problem almost resolved itself when he did. He thought it might seize and then stop, ending Callum MacReady's part in all of this.

There was something else out there, even closer to them than the minotaur. It looked like a human-sized scorpion, right down to the barbed tail. Its head was almost human, though, with big flaps of black something-or-other on the sides. Seeing it terrified Callum beyond any terror he'd had before ... but it did at least explain a sound he'd been hearing: Its pointed legs were tap-tapping across the hoods and roofs of cars in the parking lot, buckling them with its weight. To Callum, it sounded like the scuttling of an oversized roach — plus the occasional crush and shatter.

Callum opened his mouth, but Eldon again put his finger to his lips. It shot there lightning-fast this time, pressing hard enough to turn his flesh white.

Eldon shook his head, then cupped his hands behind both of his ears. Callum understood: The flaps on the scorpion-thing's head were for hearing. If they spoke aloud now, it'd find them for sure.

Callum was too scared to wonder anymore how Eldon knew any of this. He didn't bother to nod back.

Eldon gestured: *Follow me the other way around.*

They sneaked beneath a low stone bench and a set of courtyard chairs. Beyond them was the mall's sign: a stone thing that sat on the concrete. Eldon watched the minotaur and scorpion for a minute while holding up a hand, then waved urgently and crouch-ran for a pair of cars that'd crashed just beyond the red-curb loading zone.

They made it to Eldon's car, though they had to enter it in view of the things they'd been running from. Both creatures looked away, and while they did, the humans opened the doors and piled in. Every step of the process was beyond unnerving. Would it see them first, or hear the opening of doors?

"We should be okay in here. I don't think it can hear *that* well," Eldon said. "But if it's okay with you, I'll wait to start the engine until they're gone."

"It's okay with me," Callum managed to say. He'd made himself into a ball in the passenger-side footwell. He'd seldom been more uncomfortable, but he sure wasn't planning to move just to feel better.

Eldon reached for the inside door controls, then used a small joystick to adjust the side mirror until he could see the creatures. He stared for a while. Then he started moving the mirror again, this time to scope the lot.

"Jesus," he whispered. "I count eleven of them, and that's just what I can see from here. It's okay, though. Most of them are small. Small enough to run over. We were lucky getting to the car. Sorry about that. I'd've parked closer, but I didn't think this situation would FUBAR so quickly. The fiend that bound itself to you must have really liked you. I don't know you, Callum, but I do know your pain must *really* be something for them to find you so delicious."

"What?" said Callum.

Eldon didn't hear him. He was still fiddling with the mirror. "You'd better tell me where we're headed. I don't want to be figuring it out on the way."

Callum told him. Then they waited again, Eldon still watching the big fiends in the mirror.

"You holding up?" Eldon asked.

"I guess," said Callum.

"Good. Because I'm not. You want to know something?"

"Sure?"

"I'm scared enough to shit peach pits. I don't mind telling you."

Callum wished he hadn't shared. Fear humanized Eldon, but Callum had been fine thinking of him as an unshakable savior.

"Are you military?" Callum asked.

He shook his head. "The guy with me was. I'm just a scientist."

That explained the lab coat, at least. "You knew how to fight it, though," Callum protested. "You didn't seem scared at all."

"Adrenaline and good luck. I st—"

Eldon stopped suddenly, ducking all the way down with

alarm. Something flew over them: a dark shadow that came and went in a blink. He rose again slowly, like a turtle peeking from its shell.

"I study them for a subsidiary of GEN," he finished. "You know GEN?"

Callum nodded.

"Science is all just guesswork. Even when we tell the world we've learned something, the truth is it never stops being a guess. My bosses think they know a lot more than I do, but don't let them fool you. *Everyone's* in the dark right now."

"What are they guessing *about*, though?" No, that was the wrong question. The right question was too big, too obvious. In all this absurdity, it somehow hadn't occurred to him to ask. "What the hell is going on here, Eldon?"

Eldon peeked up, peeked out. Then he locked eyes with Callum. "Tell you what. If we make it to your house, I'll tell you everything I know — including the stuff I'm not supposed to tell anyone. I don't think my security clearance means much anymore anyway. Nobody's putting *this* cat back in the bag. We got a deal?"

"Okay," said Callum.

"The berserker and that bug thing are out of sight." Eldon swiveled the mirror a bit more, then sat up. "There are some little ones over by GAP entrance, but I don't think they're fast." He stepped on the brake and inserted the car key. "You ready?"

Callum nodded reluctantly.

"Okay," Eldon said, starting the engine. "Let's do this."

CHAPTER 15
BY THE POWER OF GREYSKULL

Carrie Aiden Grey paced the MacReady house, jumping at every sound from the outside. She'd entered a state she'd seen in patients but never before experienced herself: a sort of fugue, but a cognizant one. Cognizance seemed like it should be a blessing (better to keep your mind than go mindless, right?), but it was more of a curse in practice. If she were to freak out, lose her marbles, and feel a sudden need to solve crossword puzzles while the world burned ... well, that kind of dumbness would, she'd decided, feel a whole lot better. The insane didn't know they were insane; they just lived in a different reality than everyone else. Considered that way, insanity sounded pretty good right about now.

She couldn't stop thinking, even though her thinking went nowhere. She couldn't stop obsessing, though there was nothing worth obsessing about. Panic was supposed to have a half-life; anyone in panic was, with time, supposed to get used to it. Panic eventually became garden variety fear. Sometimes, it devolved all the way down into worry. That wasn't happening for Carrie, though. But at least the panic — which refused to devolve — wasn't crippling her. It wasn't making her traipse upstairs to take a shower in her clothes, or shutting her down, making her curl into a ball under the table.

So far, Carrie had remained sensible, logical, and ambulatory. She had wits enough to do all sorts of things (running away, improvising weapons ... or at the very least, nailing furniture over the windows) but was too panicky to do any of them. It was the most unproductive, least helpful sort of feeling. She had all the awareness but could take none of the actions. She'd stripped fear to its worst pieces: All of the bad emotions, but none of the defense mechanisms to wipe her into blissful oblivion.

She'd drawn the blinds and turned off most of the lights. She kept hearing terrible things from the lawn: guttural roars, screams of pain, shrieks whose sources she couldn't imagine. Cars had crashed in the neighborhood from the sound of things — into each other, into objects, maybe even into a few of the houses. She'd peeked out just once and seen nothing but twisted metal, fire, and people who ran away for a few good minutes before something found and ate them.

She'd gone upstairs, to Nathan's room. Even knowing Mary had taken Nathan on his little field trip, she went. She'd already made his bed twice. Refilled his bedside water glass. Nathan liked salty snacks when he was able to eat, so she'd made sure — again, twice — that his stocks were full. She'd considered vacuuming even though she was a nursing student and not a maid ... until she remembered that vacuums made a lot of noise, and decided to sweep with a broom instead.

She wasn't even supposed to be here. She could be home right now, being this pointless about her own chores instead of the MacReadys.'

Bill us for the whole day, Mary had said when she and Nathan left. *Insurance covers it anyway.*

Then she'd smiled. At first, Carrie had thought Mary was having a stroke because it'd been so long since she'd seen Mary smile. But no, there was no stroke. For once, Mary was actually in a good mood.

Nathan had woken spry and nearly unaffected: the best day Carrie had seen. When Carrie then called Mary's office to tell her about it (there was no need, but Mary'd had so much bad news lately that Carrie wanted to give her some of the good), Mary had come right home to be with him. It was nice to see her enthusiasm, especially after all the worry Carrie had seen in her that morning: not for Nathan for a change, but for her husband instead.

What's wrong with Callum? Carrie had asked, but Mary had only shaken her head. Carrie got the feeling he'd left that morning under weird conditions and now Mary didn't know where he was. Was Callum having an affair? Secretly, Carrie hoped so. Gossip was her biggest vice, and infidelity from the local minister was gossip's biggest whopper.

After Mary left this morning, Carrie had started snooping. She went through Callum's drawers looking for love letters from someone else. She went through his shirts, looking for proverbial lipstick on the collar. But she'd found nothing to support her gossip. The only thing amiss turned out to be the garbage, which had a whole lot of fresh-looking food in it. For some reason, the MacReadys had thrown out all the perishables in their refrigerator. Maybe that's something couples did, when one of them was cheating.

What did Carrie know? Or care?

When Nathan woke, he yelled down the stairs for her. That had shocked Carrie. She usually had to strain to hear Nathan at all when he spoke, and here he was bellowing. So Carrie had gone up. She'd taken his unusually robust breakfast order and given him his meds, but Nathan hadn't seemed this morning like a kid who needed any meds at all.

When he said he wanted to go to the park for the day, that's when Carrie had called his mother, who'd come back home. Yesterday, Mary told Carrie, her job had put her at the Rampart — the huge wall that surrounded Fortune. It wasn't *just* a wall, though. There was something inside it that gave off energy that anyone standing beside it could feel. With her firm auditing the agency that maintained it, she'd been allowed to do something that Carrie for one hadn't even known was a thing: Mary and her co-workers had gone *inside* the Rampart.

There's an inside? Carrie had asked. *I thought it was just a wall.*

Mary, finally given her chance to be enigmatic, had smiled and said nothing.

But yes, there apparently was an inside to the Rampart, just like there was an inside to a big hydroelectric dam. It wasn't just a structure, Mary had implied without saying. It was instead more like a system. More like a machine.

Maybe, if Nathan felt so good today, he'd like to go with her to see it.

And so Mary and Nathan had gone. They'd left together. Carrie was given the all-clear to split early and go home while still collecting a full day's private nursing pay, but instead she'd decided to do a bit more searching for evidence of Callum's infidelity. The gossip, if she could find some, was too amazing to ignore.

She'd gotten tired. Laid down to watch some TV, because the MacReadys had cable and Carrie didn't. She'd fallen asleep, more exhausted from last night's revelry with friends than she'd realized. When the propane tank across the street exploded for reasons unknown some time later, she'd at-first thought it was fireworks.

She'd roused groggily, still half-dreaming of fireworks. Fireworks would be very pretty right now. Never mind that the shockwave had flattened the cilia in her ear so completely, she could barely hear. That part of things didn't register. Just like the fact that when she approached the front window to see, the fireball that'd leapt quickly to the neighboring house didn't register, either. Within minutes, both homes were ablaze ... and yet it wasn't until the headless grey thing walked right in front of the window that Carrie thought to reconsider her fireworks theory. It wasn't until *then* that she thought to be scared.

Seeing it, she'd forgotten how to breathe. She remembered in a gasp so profound, she became lightheaded as some sort of hyperoxic rebound. The grey thing turned as if it'd heard her. It would have been staring if it'd had eyes. Or a head.

Carrie screamed. That's when it heard her for sure, and leapt at her through the glass of the window.

Looking back, Carrie recalled that its lack of a head didn't stop it from having a mouth, which was nestled flat in the space between its paper-skinned shoulders. The thing hissed at her, then began emitting a low, whistling sub-breath that sounded to Carrie like the wheeze of someone with pneumonia.

She'd screamed again and run for the first place she saw, which happened to be the kitchen. She ended up backed halfway into the broom closet somehow (the still-open door was the reason, later, that she decided to occupy herself with catatonic housework) and found herself cornered. The creature followed, moving fast. It had long, straight claws that reminded her of a movie she'd seen at a birthday party five years earlier, when she'd been seventeen: the one about the burned guy with knives on one hand who came for you in your dreams.

The headless thing swiped its claws at her. Carrie, finding herself cornered without a weapon, had done the thing every young woman knew to do when she was attacked: she'd kicked it hard in the crotch. Milliseconds after launching the kick, she'd realized it was futile; this was some sort of demonic monster, not a man with testicles. Still, for some reason her attack had the desired affect. Did monsters have nuts? Thinking back later, Carrie Grey would answer yes.

She'd pushed the creature aside. It fell away like a drunken bar patron, knocking all of Mary's pans from where they hung inside the kitchen island. Carrie didn't hesitate after that. Displaying defensive sense she didn't know she had, she immediately reached for a heavy cast iron pan that'd landed beside the creature's Freddy Krueger hand. It was still too nut-sore to cut her, though, and she was able to grab it with ease.

She hit it on its non-head. Then hit it again. And again. And again.

A pall had descended after that, and Carrie had only come back to reality after the monster on the kitchen floor was completely unrecognizable. Her arm and shoulder muscles ached. She was covered with what looked like spattered black phlegm — which, by the way, had also formed a large pool on the floor. She'd looked at the clock, wondering if it would tell her how long she'd been beating the thing. Didn't matter, ultimately. There wasn't nearly enough structural integrity left in the thing for it to still be living.

She was breathing so hard by the time it was over, she'd thought she might pass out. She dropped the heavy pan with a clang. She simply couldn't hold it anymore; her forearms were completely fried. Even after dropping it, she found herself unable to open or close her hands. She could only stare at them, wondering if she'd hold both in half-claws — the palms-up, fingers-up cupping shape you make when a guy wants you to tickle his jimmies — for the rest of her life.

As she calmed, her eyes went to the cast iron pan. She had a dilemma. You weren't supposed to wash cast iron pans. Now the dead thing's blood would forever be part of its seasoning.

She'd left the kitchen. Closed the door. Opened the door and grabbed a broom from the closet. Closed the door one more time. After that, the kitchen had ceased to exist. Carrie had been pacing the house ever since, not vacant-minded like she'd earned the right to be. No, Carrie had remained perfectly clear on everything. She *knew* how fucked she was, and how fucked the neighborhood looked through the window, and possibly how fucked the entire world was by now. It wasn't a good feeling. But maybe it was okay, seeing as she'd need her wits to survive.

To survive what, Carrie? said a voice inside her. The voice was goading, clearly wearing a shit-eating grin. *What exactly is happening here, with you playing She-Ra in the middle?*

She didn't want to think about that. It (like the black and brown lump that definitely *wasn't* in the kitchen that didn't exist for Carrie anymore) was a bit too scary to consider.

Now, with all her wits and scared out of her mind, Carrie could only wait for something to happen.

Suddenly there was a crash. A big one. It was right outside — or maybe close enough to be *inside*. It sounded like someone had just annihilated the garage door, ramming all the way in.

Carrie un-nullified the kitchen's existence. When terrible things happened, she'd proven she knew the best way to handle it ... and what she needed to be She-Ra again was in the kitchen.

She came out with her familiar cast iron pan. Her hands still didn't want to hold it: a harder feat now, given how coated it was in monster blood. Her forearms kept threatening to cramp. She fought the pain, gripping harder. Then, instead of backing away from the door that led to the attached garage (the place where someone had caused a fuss; someone was coming to get her), Carrie moved closer. That's what She-Ra would do. She-Ra was master of all things. Master of the Universe. Not He-Man. He-Man was a pussy; She-Ra was the real mover and shaker. When He-Man asked She-Ra for a handjob, she made him lick her toes first. That was Carrie's take on the situation, anyway.

She stood to one side of the door, waiting. She wound up like Jose Canseco, holding the pan high.

The door opened. A big man entered, holding a metal weapon as big as He-Man's sword. And so, by the power of Greyskull, Carrie did her faithful one-two: she spun in front to kick him hard in the balls, then swung the pan to take off his head.

The kick landed, the man buckled, and because of it Carrie swung too high with the pan to hit him. She hit the doorjamb instead. Her overtaxed forearms, filled to bursting with paralyzing lactic acid, shuddered at the impact and immediately surrendered. Surrendered like Skeletor, who was also a pussy.

The heavy skillet hit the tile entryway with a sound like the world ending, spraying shards. Carrie, knowing that adrenaline was her friend, then chose a random, undifferentiated attack now that she'd lost her bludgeon. She shrieked and threw herself at the man, climbing his crumpled form like a ladder. Her thinking was that if she couldn't wound him, she'd overwhelm and confuse him to death instead.

The man toppled backward. He collided with something tall and soft that Carrie half-recognized but was too frenzied to allow into her consciousness. The weapon he'd been holding (it looked like a stainless steel battle axe) clattered to the floor.

Carrie reached for it; the man tossed her off and pushed her. She skidded three feet empty-handed, then rolled up and attacked again.

"CARRIE!"

She stopped. Nobody was supposed to know her name in this situation. Besides, it was the wrong name. If she couldn't be She-Ra, she'd consider Red Sonja. Anything but this "Carrie" bullshit.

Her head cleared by millimeters. A small person knocked at a door inside her brain, reminding her quietly to settle the fuck down for a second and maybe pay attention to who and where she was. And, of course, who it was was standing in front of her.

When reality returned, all the strength went from her legs. She almost collapsed, shocked at the relief she felt in seeing a familiar face. She couldn't help herself; she rushed around (and almost stepped on) the man she'd hobbled so that she could hug the man who'd entered the house behind him.

Her words came out in a rushed jumble, no spaces between them.

"OhmygodCallumIcantbelieveitsyou!"

She hugged Callum hard enough to squeeze his organs into his head and feet. Then Callum gently separated them, and that's when Carrie realized how incapacitatingly terrified she was. She'd been pushing her fear down, but now it'd broken loose. Looking at the beaten-up, blood-spattered form of her employer, she saw that he might be even more scared than she felt — and definitely worse for wear.

"Is that *blood* on you?" she asked.

Callum looked at his clothing, surprised. "I guess it is," he said. "What's on *you?*"

Like Callum, Carrie hadn't realized her appearance. She tipped her head down and saw a blouse that seemed to have gone through a tar shower. She looked like she'd stood behind a car trying to spin itself out of a snowbank made of black ink.

"Also blood," she said. "It's—"

The man at their feet groaned and began to stand. Carrie had forgotten he was there. He hadn't been cleared by her lizard brain, though, so her first instinct was to hit him again — this time, possibly a convenient knee to the face. Before she could do more than shift her weight, though, logic reasserted itself. Callum wouldn't show up with someone she should knee in the face. Society wasn't what it'd been this morning, but manners were still manners.

The big man straightened with difficulty. Even standing he remained in a half squat, feet wide like a bowlegged cowboy. They waited for a moment in awkward silence broken only by the distant, chaotic sounds of the neighborhood. The man was rugged, square-jawed, and for some reason wearing a lab coat that'd been shredded and covered in both kinds of blood: red *and* black, like some sort of consensus-maker. Carrie found the lab coat he most confusing thing about what'd just happened. Had she just smashed the nuts of Mr. Wizard?

"Eldon, this is my son's nurse, Carrie," Callum said to him, still eyeing Carrie as if she might not be done swinging. "Carrie, this is Eldon. Eldon ..."

"Porter," the man croaked, wincing. It's nice to meet you."

CHAPTER 16

ZOMBIE PROTOCOL

Callum closed the door behind him. When he'd realized the garage door opener was in his car instead of Eldon's (and after he'd remembered how bad an idea parking in the driveway would be right now), he'd told Eldon to go ahead and do some remodeling. It was actually kind of cool to have an excuse to do something like you see in movies. He'd lived a mild-mannered life as a minister. He'd never had an opportunity to do anything crazy, like crash through a garage door.

The crash hadn't gone as smoothly as the movies had him believe. Instead of breaking apart, the big aluminum panels had simply bent out of the way. If Eldon had been going slower, the car might have bounced right off. The Toyota had made it, though, and was now wedged three-quarters of the way in. It was scratched and dented to all hell. The windshield had starred and webbed. The garage door had bent around the chassis and made Callum's door impossible to open, so he'd exited via the side window like those hillbillies in *The Dukes of Hazard*.

Watching Eldon and Carrie nod awkwardly at one another, Callum remembered the biggest reason he'd come back home. Yes, it was closer than Eldon's lab, and no, they probably wouldn't have been able to get much farther given all the car wrecks and fires and half-eaten corpses they'd passed on the way — not to mention the nightmares out there doing the eating.

Those things were true, but he'd come most of all for his family.

"Mary?" he called, moving into the house. "Mary, where are you?"

He stepped over a broken chair, then a whole raft of shattered dishes. He saw their source; his mother-in-law's china cabinet had fallen forward, slamming into the side of the dining room table so that everything previously inside was now on the floor. What had happened here? The table from the kitchen was on its side, stood flat against what seemed to be a broken window — and not just *broken*, but broken-*through* as if some asshole had driven another Toyota through it. That's why the china cabinet was where it was, he saw now: its fallen-forward weight was keeping the kitchen table in place so nothing else could push through the window.

Flecks of dried black liquid spattered the hardwood. The kitchen door was closed, and that was weird because he'd forgotten it even *had* a door. Mary had wanted to remodel and open up the downstairs floor plan but they'd never been able to scrape together the money. Keeping the door permanently open was the compromise — Mary's way of keeping her floor plan at least a little open if it couldn't be open all the way.

Callum looked at the door now. Someone inside the kitchen must have spilled a pot of used motor oil, because he could see a pool of it leaking under the sweep.

"Mary!"

"She's … She's gone, Callum," said Carrie. "I wanted to call you, but I didn't know where—"

"*'Gone'?*"

Carrie snapped-to immediately. "No! Not like that. She's … All of this—" Carrie's eyes ticked toward the broken window, then the kitchen door. "—all of this happened after she left. I'm alone. I've *been* alone. And I … I …"

Callum held up his hands for her to settle. He wasn't thinking straight himself. Why would Mary be home now anyway? She was at work.

Except that wasn't what Carrie had said. She'd said *left*.

"She came home?" Callum asked.

Carrie nodded. "Then she left. She took Nathan. They were going to see the Rampart."

Callum felt his insides turn to ice. Something had just been stolen from him before he'd even thought to reassure himself that it was safe and sound.

"Nathan's gone too?"

Another nod, this one with a sniffle. Carrie looked like she'd been through a war, and the shock of it was only now hitting her. He wanted to know what'd happened, under-standing somewhere beneath his family-concern that none of what he saw felt right. But first *this*. Before anything else, *this* needed to be settled.

"He was having a good day," Carrie explained. "He wanted to go to the park. I called Mary at work. Thought she'd want to know. She said she was going inside the Rampart today, and thought Nathan might like to see it … so she came home and got him. I'm sorry."

Sorry. Why was she apologizing? They were all so scattered, so far beyond the norm — so completely out of order.

"*Inside* the Rampart? Do you mean on the other side of it?"

"She means *inside*," said a bass voice. It was Eldon;

Callum's fight-or-flight mind kept forgetting that whoever he hadn't been speaking to was in the room. "It's not just a wall."

"What is it, then?"

"A repellant," he replied.

They spent the next ten minutes securing the house. Everyone knew what to do, so it went quickly. They'd all seen zombie movies. The rules were mostly the same: barricade the doors, board-over the windows. Callum kept his tools in the basement rather than the garage, so nobody was afraid to get and use them. Callum also had a fortunate store of two-by-fours in the basement: the single purchase they'd made between deciding optimistically to remodel the kitchen and realizing they couldn't afford to when their loan was declined.

When Callum ran down for the final load of boards, his eyes caught the door to the old root cellar. Their home was a split-level: four half-floors instead of two full ones. The root cellar was another half-story down to one side, directly under the living and dining rooms.

Earth floors would be better, but a root cellar's still better than a basement, Eldon had said back at the mall. It was, beyond proximity, the deciding factor for Eldon in coming here. Callum hadn't had a chance to ask why.

He went to the door now, opened it, and pulled the chain light. He'd told Eldon that the floors were concrete, but in truth Callum had poured that concrete himself ... over the exact kind of packed-dirt floor Eldon wanted. He and his brothers had spent a day dumping wheelbarrows full of mixed slurry through the Kansas-style outside door, but because the work was so hard, they'd done it thinly and inexpertly. Without a sealed floor, bugs kept getting in. Now Callum wondered if he could get at the dirt floor if it made a difference.

Probably yes, assuming he could find the sledgehammer he thought he still had — and, of course, assuming it wasn't in the shed. He couldn't imagine why dirt floors would matter to anyone right now ... but then again, he still couldn't imagine *most* of the things he'd seen today.

After the windows and doors in the main room were boarded, Eldon pointed to the kitchen.

"Before I open that door," he said to Carrie, "maybe you should tell us what happened here."

So Carrie did. She told them how a creature had broken through the window and how she'd managed to kill it. So Eldon opened the kitchen door slowly, carefully, and then almost laughed. Seeing how badly she'd beaten the thing, the caution he'd used suddenly seemed silly.

They boarded the kitchen windows and the back door — the door through which the creature had entered last night back when Callum thought it might be a dream. He felt guilt at the thought. If he'd told someone right away that a monster had come into his house and nearly eaten his face in front of his open refrigerator, maybe none of this would have ...

But who was he kidding? Nobody would have believed him.

With the house secure — and sounds outside muted enough that it was possible to believe everything was normal — Callum resumed high-octane fretting about his wife and son. He'd gone into a panic right after hearing that they were gone, but Eldon had refused to let him dwell until their urgencies were handled.

Face it, Callum, he'd said. *Whatever's going on and wherever they are, there's nothing we can do about it right now. What we can do is keep us safe. Who's going to come to their rescue later if something kills you while you're worrying instead of doing what needs to be done?*

Callum had let himself be persuaded, and was glad for it once the board-up was underway. It was more comfortable to bury himself in work than to worry about his family. Callum knew that as well as anyone. Ever since Nathan got sick, he'd found facing what needed facing hard, and escape into something else easy. Wasn't that why he kept going to work at the church when things got bad and he couldn't take it anymore? Wasn't that, in fact, why he'd run off to Suicide Flats yesterday morning?

Yes, that was why. That's why you left, Callum: because you're a coward. Because even though your family needed you, you could only think of yourself. Mary was gone. Carrie would take care of Nathan, but you were the only parent around; it was up to you to bear the burden. He only had you, and what did you do? You went into the mouth of this community's deepest wound, planning to exploit it as … as what? As some sort of twisted, infantile revenge against your parishioners for daring to pity you?

He felt beyond guilty — beyond the extremities of remorse. He couldn't shake a feeling (and not a groundless one) that all of what was happening in Fortune was his fault. *He'd* gone to the black lake. *He'd* felt its pull — its siren song of beautiful annihilation. *Callum* was the one who'd entered a walking fugue, forgetting himself and where he'd gone. It was *Callum* to whom the creature had first shown itself, coming to him in the pit of the night as if hungry — as if drawn by forces stronger than itself. It was *Callum* who'd found himself mindless and mentally polluted the next morning — *Callum* to whom the thing had come again in the mall's atrium, this time wearing the skin of a dead man.

That fiend that bound itself to you must have really liked you, Eldon had said when they were hiding in the car in the mall parking lot. *I don't know you, but I know your pain must something for them to find it so delicious.*

What did that mean? Was he really the source of this? Was he being punished, and punishing the rest of Fortune (and maybe the world) because of it? Was it because he was a terrible person? A coward, a betrayer, a hypocrite? Was Callum this plague's Patient Zero? *Move over, Eve … there's a new source of original sin in town, and this one did a shitload more than pick an apple.*

But now, with the house quiet and as safe as they could make it — as they heard the chaos outside only as distant news from a foreign land they need not concern themselves with, because it was someone else's problem — the weight of it all settled on Callum like a yoke made of lead. Guilt was his religion's currency, but this wasn't the deal he'd made back in seminary. He was supposed to dole out the guilt, not be saddled with it.

"Your family is okay," Eldon said.

Callum looked over. Lost in his own thoughts, he hadn't seen Eldon sitting there. He'd taken off his lab coat. Without it, he looked almost too clean. Callum could change his own clothes to get rid of the gore (they were right upstairs after all), but he'd so-far found himself reluctant. If Callum was the problem, he should keep wearing his scarlet letter rather than change to hide it.

Self pity, huh? said that hectoring voice inside him. *Way to turn penance into self-importance.*

"You don't know they're okay," said Callum.

"No, but it's a safe guess. Carrie said they left a good half hour before all of this started. That's plenty of time to get to the south checkpoint, which is where the offices are. Unless they stopped and had lunch first, they'll've had a lot easier time than we've had. The people at the Rampart know how safe it is. If you want to take care of your family, your job is to stay alive. That means worrying about yourself, not them."

That'll be easy, said the voice. *You've certainly had enough practice at thinking about yourself when others need you.*

Carrie sat opposite both men, on the easy chair across the coffee table from the couch. She looked almost settled: a lot more serene than Callum felt. The house still had electricity despite all disaster-expectations predicting it wouldn't by now, so she'd microwaved a mug of water and made herself some tea. She'd had to step over the corpse of a monster to do it, but that was old hat by now. Only Callum was the weak one. Of their trio, it seemed that only Callum was handling this poorly.

"Maybe it's time," Carrie said to Eldon, "that you tell us what you know."

CHAPTER 17
HELL'S ORIGINS

"Beneath our world," Eldon began, "there is another. We try to keep definitions of that world as neutral as we can. We call it 'another plane' or 'a different dimension.' We call the creatures that live there — and that have sometimes come over to our side, though never like this — 'fiends.' I'm a scientist, and I work with scientists. When I'm not working with scientists, I work with the government. Scientists and government like things they can quantify, which means they deal in fact. The government types want even more. They want *control*: facts not for their own sake, but as a means to an end.

"That's the culture I've lived and breathed for years now. But even in that fact-based culture, nobody's made of stone. Sometimes the most stolid fact-seekers I know still use the terms they grew up with — the ones that feel right even if they're not factual at all. Even they sometimes slip and use the most unsanctioned, unscientific word for what they feel 'the other plane' really is."

"'Hell,'" said Callum.

Eldon nodded. *"Hell. Demons.* I feel ridiculous saying it aloud, and even then I want to explain myself. I want to say, 'Hell is just a name.' 'Hell is a blanket term for a concept, and it doesn't need to be anything else.' Remove the superstitions, and what we usually call 'Hell' is nothing more than a set of conditions. It describes a specific set of physical characteristics that, even though we've never seen them before, we can at least *understand* ... just like the atomic weight of hydrogen is a characteristic we understand.

"The fiend plane is very hot, for instance — around 300 degrees celsius on average, which is hotter than a broiler. Its atmosphere is thick with sulfur. Its landscape, such that we've caught glimpses of it, is barren and red. The beings that live there are black, red, or grey-skinned, and what they bleed usually looks like bile. They have claws. A lot of them have horns — often huge upturned ones like the world's largest bull. Their bodies are broken and distorted forms of things we can describe: not 'unusual creatures with wholly new physiologies' so much as 'human-like things with their brains showing' or 'skinless dogs, but made of teeth and razors.'

"That part has always struck me as strange. Fiends have a way of conforming perfectly to what we, as a culture, have stored in our collective mythology as horrors. They are, in other words, *exactly what already scares us."*

Eldon took a breath.

"Now, I'm a scientist. I try very hard to never confuse correlation with causation. Just because two things coincide doesn't mean that one is the cause of the other. So when I see creatures that look like what we call 'demons' and come from a place that looks like what we call 'Hell,' I can think of a few reasons that would be. It might be coincidence, but that's a lot of coincidence. Alternatively, both could stem from the same cause outside of themselves (an unknown third factor that caused our myths *and* the fiends' morphologies without them causing each other), but in this case a third factor feels like splitting hairs.

"That leaves two possibilities: that X caused Y or Y caused X. The theory my colleagues favor says that the fiends are where our myths came from: We learned to fear them through experience because humankind has seen them before. It even makes sense. Excavated core samples suggest that our planes have been intertwined for a very long time: hundreds of thousands of years. If that's true — if humans have encountered fiends from time to time, especially back when the world was a more superstitious place — it would explain why our religions portray demons as looking and behaving just like fiends. They were our real-life boogeymen way back when, so they became legends as our societies evolved.

"It's a sensible theory, and it fits within what science can explain. If you use that framing, what we've always called 'demons' aren't that different from any other species. Fiends aren't immortal; you saw yourselves that they can be killed. They don't come for sinners more than anyone else. They don't flinch back from crosses. They don't burn in sunlight or if you splash them with holy water. They're just creatures that are different from us who live somewhere we only recently discovered. That's it. *That's all.* So that's the prevailing theory: Fiends resemble 'demons from Hell' because they're the *cause* of the legends we call 'demons' and 'Hell,' going all the way back to the dawn of civilization."

Eldon paused. For a few seconds he seemed to war with something, but then his body language changed so that Callum, watching, knew the topic was about to shift. He wanted to interject — to stop Eldon and make him finish. Something was missing from the rundown: a final possibility that Eldon believed more than the theory he'd just given, but for reasons unknown was choosing not to tell them.

That leaves two possibilities: that X caused Y or Y caused X. That's what Eldon said, but he'd only given them one side of the coin — that of fiends causing human legends. Why?

But Carrie spoke before Callum could, so he let it go.

"So *that's* what the government's been covering up," she said. "All the cultists and wackos out in the Flats talking about Satan were right all along. They *have* seen things. They *weren't* just crazy."

"More or less," Eldon said. "But it wasn't the other plane or creatures from it that interested people at first. Nobody — not even the government — knew there even *was* another plane until the last two-three decades. This didn't begin with Hell, or with demons. It began with Zen Element."

Callum sat back, suddenly understanding. Zen Element did so many astonishing things. Now, with all the pieces falling into place, it wasn't surprising to learn it'd come from somewhere else.

"Zen couldn't be covered up," Eldon told them. "Not at first. It was discovered publicly, so everyone knew about it. It was first found in the '50s, just like everyone believes. If GEN had existed back then or if the government had gotten to it first, they might have hidden knowledge of Zen Element or changed the story. But they didn't, so they couldn't.

"The first Zen-containing ore was analyzed at a public-sector firm called Weltin Labs. The person who discovered it, named Gerta Hedwing, had a brother who worked for Weltin. When she showed the 'special rock' she'd found in the park to her brother one night — how it glowed in the dark, and how she could keep her tea warm by putting her mug on top of it because it made its own heat — he was worried at first that it might be radioactive. At the time, decay of unstable isotopes was just about the only thing anyone could think of to explain self-generation of heat. So he took it away, told Gerta to wash her hands, her clothes, her furniture, and anything else the rock might have touched, and took it to the lab to run a bunch of tests. He found that it wasn't emitting radiation other than heat, some infrared, a tiny bit of UV, and sometimes the visible spectrum in between — but nothing high-energy, nothing harmful at all. It was just ... *heat*. Plain old heat that was seemingly being generated by the ore (or, as we know now, from Zen Element absorbed *into* the ore) in a way he couldn't explain. It seemed impossible. Even today it seems like it should be impossible."

"What is — making heat?" Carrie asked.

"Making energy from nothing," Eldon clarified. "Energy that's not coming from matter, or from an external source, or converted from mechanical energy or chemical energy or any other form of energy we know. Zen Element just sort of lights up all on its own. It's the only known substance that does."

"And that's impossible?"

"Obviously it's possible," said Eldon. "In movies, scientists say that things right in front of them are impossible because it's a dramatic thing to say, but that's not how science actually works. If you observe a genuine phenomenon, that phenomenon becomes your stake in the ground. You can't deny the phenomenon. You can't just say 'that's impossible' and move on. Put another way, nothing ever violates scientific law. If something real seems to be 'breaking the laws of physics,' physics has to change to accommodate it. Science isn't rigid. It can't be. It's constantly evolving and changing as it incorporates new observations, even if those observations upset theories we've believed for centuries.."

"So Zen Element comes from ... *from them?* From the other side?"

"Yes to both. If you've read anything about the Zen rush, you know that it was a lot like 1849 in California when prospectors started discovering gold. Energy from nothing has been a holy grail since we started to understand energy in the first place. Big thinkers got stars in their eyes, imagining a world where electricity would cost nothing and cars could run for free with no pollution. Small thinkers only needed to know that big thinkers saw value in it for them to see value in it, too, so entire amateur cottage industries sprang up around Zen Element almost overnight. People started digging for it. Panning for it. Zen was only found here, though, and that meant the United States had a monopoly. Other countries — Russia in particular — saw it as an imbalance of power, and therefore a threat. There's a whole energy race that ran alongside the arms race in the early years of the Cold War that not a lot of people know about.

"It was so, *so* localized. Zen Element wasn't just US-only. It wasn't even just *Utah*-only. The people I work with think of the area it's found as concentric circles. Cecret Lake is the bullseye. The dead area around it is the next ring out: something we think of as a 'zone of inhibition' but that's commonly called 'Suicide Flats.' We measure Suicide Flats a little differently than the public, so for us it extends into the forest a good fifty meters beyond the dead zone. GEN has an instrument that detects minuscule air pressure differentials — tiny compression and expansion pulses too subtle to be noticed consciously by humans, but that people tend to feel *sub*consciously as a vague sense of disquiet. People feel uneasy but can't say why, which is why it can push pre-suicidal people over the edge. Outside of that is the largest ring around Cecret Lake, where a sort of psionic energy I won't bore you with is elevated above normal background. The whole area — from that outer circle in — is how we define the Gore Point."

"Jesus," said Carrie. "That phrase takes on a whole new meaning once you know what it really is."

"It's kind of a sick joke," Eldon explained. "A 'gore point' is a feature along the exit ramp of a highway. One of GEN's techs supposedly heard it for the first time and remarked that if you're going to give something a name that sinister, it should be something better than a boring strip of concrete. 'Like the portal to Hell,' someone quipped, and the name stuck. It's been 'Gore Point' ever since."

He laughed, but the laugh was humorless. There were still screams, growling sounds, and screeches coming from outside. They hadn't stopped; they'd all just gotten used to them.

"You can technically still find Zen Element outside the dead area that every satellite can see and every newsmagazine has published photos of, but mostly people only look there. Before the Department of Energy — under a few disguises — closed the area a few years ago, anyone looking to make their fortune in Zen Element had to crowd into an area of only about five square miles. That's why it was regulated so quickly, and one of the reasons the original rush went bust."

"'*One* of the reasons'?" Callum asked. "Were there others?"

Eldon paused. His eyes rolled up, thinking. Then he stood, peeked through a gap in one of the boarded living room windows, and said, "I'm not supposed to talk about any of this stuff," he said. "If I tell you now, do you promise not to tell anyone else that demons are real?"

Callum blurted inappropriate laughter. Carrie stared at him, but Eldon gave a wry smile, pleased in their dire situation that his equally inappropriate joke was at least appreciated by someone — even if that someone's laugh was more a release of pent-up pressure than actual mirth. And certainly not joy.

"A lot of mines were dug in the hills during the first boom, because at first they thought Zen Element came from the rock itself. We know now that it's actually in their blood. Over time, fiends have come here and been injured, or come here and died, or come here and bled on purpose ... who knows how it happened. We know that for a long time, all that Zen just lying around was in a quiescent state: it was here, layers deep in the rock strata as the landscape changed over time. It's taken hundreds of thousands of years to build up all of the Zen Element in the Gore Point's land, but only after Gerta Hedwing's rock did anyone start looking for it. Cecret didn't turn black until '81, and it was just a handful of years before that that the vegetation died and Suicide Flats formed. I've spent a lot of time wondering why that was. I've asked around. Conducted a few of my own experiments, some with official permission and some without. If it's not the presence of Zen Element that's killed everything off, it must be something else. My only guess — and I have no evidence for this at all; it's just a gut feeling — is that it's the same pressure micro-differentials that we use to define the border of Suicide Flats that killed all the plants, the worms ... even the bacteria in that area. If it unsettles people in ways they don't understand, maybe it somehow disrupts critical life processes in ways we don't understand either. Who knows. It doesn't affect people who go there — not guards, not scientists, not rangers — so if that's what it is, it's selective. Almost ... intelligent."

"Wait ... the energy at the Suicide Flats is *'intelligent'*?"

Eldon waved it off, but Callum again saw the strange look in the man's eyes — the same look he'd had when he'd chosen not to tell them the other reason demons and their associated legends might be similar.

"It doesn't matter. Something changed, is all we know. The vegetation died, the zone of inhibition formed, and ever since we've seen more and more incursions. The entire area is 'thin.' It's a place where it's easy for them to punch through from their world to ours. When they do, it opens what looks like a flaming eye that hangs in the air. We call them 'rifts.' Rifts only open inside the Gore Point, even though at places like the lab, we're able to—" He stopped. Hard. "Never mind. The point is that although they've hidden from us when they do, fiends have been coming into our world quite a bit in the past few years. We can't stop them, but GEN has instruments that are able to tell when new rifts open. What's more, they can tell from soil samples where rifts have opened in the past, if they were big enough that their hallmarks are still there. That's how we know that not long after Old Fortune was built — the old gold-rush part of the city, where the original homes weren't much more than bivouacs — a very large rift opened inside one of the mines they'd dug. The energetics in that mine were ... let's say 'highly favorable' for such an event, and the mining company dug right into it. Not long after that, Old Fortune burned to the ground. Rather than rebuilding, it's like everyone got the Flats vibes into them and simply lost interest. The mines began to burn on their own, without fuel to keep them aflame. After that, all of them were closed. The rift, seemingly, closed when that happened."

"So that's the other reason Fortune went bust?" Carrie asked.

"Exactly. And for a while, things were quiet. But years later, in 1962, someone decided to reopen one of the mines — one that'd been renamed 'Mine Zero.' Right before all the mines were closed the first time, a group of miners disappeared inside Mine Zero. They left behind some very curious records, though, that made the military types very, *very* curious. So they decided to pop its top in '62, send in a new group of explorers, and try to ascertain the fate of the group that'd been lost. But they had a surprise in store for them. Mine Zero had been closed for years, starved of oxygen ... but when they opened it back up, they found it was still burning."

Callum's eyes went to the door to his basement, which was in turn the way to the root cellar another half-level down. All this talk of mines had him thinking of the thing Eldon said earlier about his cellar: that any root cellar was good, but that a dirt-floored one would be better. Did this story have anything to do with it? Was dirt good because stone was bad? The whole state was made of bedrock, so maybe Eldon felt that a dirt-floored cellar would, at least, have no connection to the domain of shafts and mines. But who knew?

"The group they sent in found a very, *very* large rift in a chamber at its bottom. Colloquially, those in the know call it 'Hell's Cathedral.' Something very strange happened in that place — something I've asked about, but I'm told is far above my security clearance. I only really know that it made the top people involved change their way of thinking about rifts and the Gore Point. They stopped thinking of Zen energy as passive and started to think of it as directed somehow. *Guided.* As if they, on the other side, can control it."

Callum felt a shiver. He'd certainly felt *controlled* over the past 24 hours or so, until fighting for his life at the mall snapped him out of it.

"Rifts only open inside the Gore Point," Eldon said, still standing near the window. "Whatever disrupts plant and bacterial life in the zone of inhibition — that doesn't seem to be able to affect anything outside the Gore Point, either."

He paused.

"The energy behind it, though—" *The energy he implies has a life of its own,* Callum thought. *The energy that isn't static, but instead intelligent.* "—behaves a lot like a quantum probability wave. You don't have to know what that means. Just know that it's able to affect things a whole lot further away. Including here. Including all of Fortune. And, if not for the Rampart, probably far beyond that. Beyond the country. Into space; who knows? Its probability grows lower the farther you go from the source, but it never really ends."

"If not for the Rampart," Callum repeated. It was very important to keep the Rampart in mind. By all accounts, it's where Mary and Nathan were.

"If not for the Rampart," Eldon repeated. "The Rampart does what walls can't do. It stops the wave. It keeps the energy inside Fortune. And that matters because they have to follow it, see. It's a link to home for them. An invisible lifeline, giving beings that don't belong in our world a way to survive here, for at least a while."

Eldon moved away from the window. He sat on the coffee table and faced Callum, as if this academic discussion was about to get personal.

"If that's where your family is," Eldon told Callum, "the good news is they're safe. The psionic wave — what we conveniently call 'Hell energy' — stops at the side of the wall facing Fortune."

"Is there bad news?" Callum asked.

"I don't know. But here's what I do know: I've never seen fiend activity like this. I've never even *read* about anything like this. In all the research we have — direct and extrapolated — nobody's seen activity even one-tenth this bad. For want of a better term, they're *hungry* now in a way they've never been. Not for bodies, but for energy they've never sampled before. There's a lot of that new energy inside Fortune for them, but there are a lot of them in the collective hive mind who are only sampling it now, through their species bond ... and all the others, waking up to it on the other side, are getting hungry too. There's a lot to make them hungry inside Fortune, but there's so much more outside the city. Right now, the Rampart is the only thing keeping them from it. The only thing standing in their way."

"But it's strong. It can keep them in."

Eldon said, "At this point, I honestly don't know."

Panic descended like a hammer. "Then I have to go there! I have to get them!"

"Callum." Eldon spoke gently, like a doctor breaking bad news to a patient. "You of all people are the *last* person who should go outside right now — to the Rampart or anywhere else. You need to stay put. Ideally in the root cellar, surrounded by a floor and walls made of non-psionic clay."

"What? Why?"

"Like I said, the first fiend didn't find you on accident. *I* didn't find you on accident."

Carrie's brow furrowed, having missed so much and far from understanding.

"There are two hundred thousand people in Fortune whose psyches are like spark lights to them. They're drawn to every one of those lights the way suicides are drawn to the Flats. But that's *nothing* compared to the way they're drawn to you."

"Why me?"

"Because they were virgins before you went into the Gore Point yesterday," Eldon said. "Because they'll never, ever forget you ... *because you were their first.*"

CHAPTER 18
GRAPHITE

Brianna Jacoby, age 28 and a vocal detractor of that step aerobics bullshit everyone was into recently, nearly high-kicked Denny Brennan in the face when he burst through her improvised lab-door barricade. Ironic: She'd probably have taken his head off if she'd done step aerobics after all. Turned out her squat-hardened legs didn't stretch that high.

She kicked beakers off the shelf next to him instead. Two flew through the air. One broke on the floor and Brianna managed to catch the other. Denny, alarmed too late and standing dumbly, watched her pluck it from the air as if this was some weird magic trick.

"Denny!"

Post-kick, she couldn't help but notice how different Denny looked today. He was usually dressed somewhat more formally than lab work required, invoking an old-man fashion older than his years. Denny was one of those men in his mid thirties who looked fifty because he wore sweater vests. Today, though, instead of looking like a pudgy Mr. Rogers, he was covered in what looked like blood-infused motor oil. It was an interesting change of pace.

She expected Denny to react to her trying to knock his teeth out: a startled, adrenaline response to ... well, truth was Brie had no idea what she'd thought she was responding to. It had been a strange, disorienting day. This morning alone, she'd finished her quarterly D.O.E. report, washed all of the glassware she and Eldon had been neglecting, and used the detached blade from the guillotine paper cutter to dismember a slobbering insect-faced thing that'd tried to tunnel into the lab through the hole in the drywall someone had made three weekends ago but nobody was owning up to. On a day like today, a girl sometimes got carried away and didn't know *who* she was kicking in the face.

But Denny didn't react. His eyes were wide. His hair, instead of its usual popcorn fluff, was instead a matted oily mess. Brie was reminded of her niece Lily, who watched that gross kids' show on Nickelodeon where the gag was getting slime poured on your head if you happened to say "I don't know." Denny looked like he'd been a guest star. Or possibly that he'd just gotten done playing *Double Dare,* which Lily also watched, having shoved himself through a comically large nostril and come out covered in snot.

Denny watched Brianna set the beaker she'd caught on the bench with great interest. He then stared at nothing in particular. His eyes were wide. Very wide.

"Graphite. Graphite is the key."

"What?"

Instead of answering, Denny stumbled his way past her. She stepped back to avoid being smeared with whatever covered him. It was unnaturally warm and smelled like bad meat.

"I need graphite." He began rummaging through the reagents on one of the lab's shelves.

"Where did you come from?" Brie asked.

"Seattle."

"I mean just now. Denny? *Denny*. Do you hear me? I asked how you got here."

He'd left the door ajar. Brie rushed to close it, glancing into the hallway before she did to make sure nothing had broken in (again) through the lobby. There seemed to be no rhyme or reason to what was happening outside. At first she'd looked to Eldon's rift for clues, seeing as she was now trapped with it and had little else to do. Maybe there'd be a correlation between the rift's emissions and the fiend activity? Unfortunately, there was no way to test her hypotheses. She couldn't see through the window to monitor the fiends outside after she'd pushed the monstrosity of their heavy filing cabinet against it (thank you, squat-strengthened legs), and the energetic reports they usually used had become so noisy that she could no longer tell where the rift energy was going because lately it'd been going *everywhere*. She and Eldon had spent years with those reports, working on the order of millivolts. The rift at the bottom of Cecret Lake, however, had begun at kilovolts and graduated recently to megavolts — and even that ignored the background scatter. Tracking that much energy using their old, ultra-sensitive tools was like using a stethoscope to listen to a nuclear explosion. You couldn't track nuance with that much power flying around.

As she closed the door, she realized she'd forgotten to lock it. That's how Denny had come in: He'd simply turned the knob. It meant that Brie, despite all her fortifications, had neglected the most obvious entry point and just gotten lucky. The fiends that'd entered the building were either as locustlike and mindless as the colonel said they were (and therefore didn't understand doors), or lacked the use of thumbs. Brie had piled a ton of stuff in front of the door to block it, but in her frenzy she'd forgotten it opened outward, not in.

She considered the now-locked door, wondering how the hell she'd barricade it from the outside. She decided the lock would have to be enough. The last fiend had come in through the drywall, after all. Its corpse was now in two piles on opposite ends of the room: homage to Brie's horror-movie worries that if she left its parts touching, it might recombine and come back to life. That seemed unlikely, but better safe than sorry.

After her first break-in, she'd pushed an upturned table against the drywall hole to seal it. She did the same with the door now, opting to at least block the space off if she couldn't jam the door. She was getting so much furniture-moving in today. All that non-step-aerobics weightlifting was simultaneously paying off and also not at all necessary this afternoon. After dealing with the demon apocalypse, she might go ahead and take the rest of the week off. Eat some ice cream, get fat, what the hell.

"Denny!" she tried again.

He turned.

"I'm glad you're here." She really was; facing this horror-show shit was terrifying on her own. Just having someone else to talk to — catatonic or not — was a huge relief. "But it's a meat-grinder out there. What the hell possessed you to come here instead of staying where you were?" There was more to it, too: Denny's lab at GEN was, if anyplace was, far more equipped to deal with a massive fiend invasion. GEN had made weapons. GEN also had energetic analysis tools, Zen sniffers, and had tons of inside knowledge they'd hoarded and refused to share with anyone else. Coming to Eldon and Brie's lab was a step backwards, like going from McDonald's to Burger King.

"I had to find Eldon," Denny said.

"Eldon's not here."

"I have to find him. I gave him a Paulson."

"Who's Paulson?"

"A weapon."

"What weapon? *Who's Paulson?*"

"A weapon. Paulson is the weapon we gave him. It's a pistol."

Brie didn't see why it mattered. If Eldon had a weapon beyond that big Rollard thing he'd taken, he was head and shoulders above everyone else. She, personally, would worry least about the person with a weapon ... if this was even worry she saw in Denny, rather than generalized mania.

"Where were you, Denny? Did you really drive all the way over from GEN?"

"Inside."

"Inside GEN?"

"Inside something else. I got out. Where's your graphite?"

Brie was confused by that. *Inside something else?* But Denny's freneticism was more urgent, so she let it go. He was being none-too-careful about going through their chemicals and reagents, knocking half of them to the floor. Fortunately, nothing he'd dropped so far was glass.

"Don't you have graphite in your lab?" With "graphite," Brie was thinking of #2 pencils. Why was Denny after pencil lead? While the world went to shit, he must want to take a standardized test.

"I needed to find Eldon."

"You said that."

"I need graphite."

"Yes, but—"

"Charcoal!" Denny turned, animated and still entirely manic, and reached for an activated charcoal filter at the top of one of the open fume hoods. He yanked it free and began banging it on the bench, trying to crack it open.

"Denny."

Nothing.

"DENNY."

Nothing.

So Brie embraced the cliche. She grabbed him by the shoulders, turned him around, and slapped him across the face. It was about time someone did that to a hysterical man instead of a hysterical woman.

Denny blinked. He looked almost offended. Brie recoiled instantly, repulsed by the feel of the stuff he was covered with. Now the bad-meat smell felt like it was inside her, infecting her now that she'd been fool enough to touch it.

"What the hell is this stuff all over you?"

Denny seemed sane now. The slap had worked. "Guts," he said.

"Whose guts?"

"Fiend guts. I was swallowed."

"'*Swallowed*'?"

"It's a long story. Luckily it was a big snake thing. Didn't have teeth." Denny wiped at himself; it seemed that as he returned to his senses, he was suddenly and disgustingly aware of the bile he was wearing.

"Jesus. So it just spit you out?"

"No. It was digesting me."

Brie recoiled again. So *that's* why her skin was tingling. If fiend physiology was anything at all like theirs and the black stuff had come from a digestive tract, it might contain acid. Did Earth acids work at 300 degrees C? She'd have to look it up when she was bored and horrified some day.

"How did you get out?"

"Science." He'd been fiddling with the charcoal air filter

and finally got it open. He poured its powdery gray contents onto the lab bench and said. "I had a theory. Ending up inside something forced me to test it." He picked some of the charcoal up between his fingers, then sifted it back to the pile like a chef adding salt. "Lead *blocks* Zen energy just like it blocks radiation, but carbon *absorbs* both. Apparently it can only hold so much, though. Too much Zen, agitated together with high-surface-area carbon like powered graphite—" Again he ran his fingers through the pile. "—or charcoal ... Well, I got this idea that it'd basically make a bomb. I was carrying a tub of graphite when the fiend swallowed me, so I opened the tub, cut the thing's insides with my car keys, and let its blood and the graphite mingle. Zen Element plus carbon. *Bomb.*"

"But you're alive. How are you alive if you escaped using a bomb?"

"It's not a normal bomb. Carbon is usually a stability enhancer, not a destabilizing element. That's why they use it in reactor control rods — to catch all the fissioning particles so they don't hit more isotope and start to chain beyond capacity. But this is Zen Element we're talking about. It works the other way. It's anti-entropic by nature, so I started to wonder what'd happen if you tried to stop it from organizing. I don't know how it worked, but it did. I figured that since I was already being digested, there was no real downside to giving it a shot."

Brianna blinked at that, strangely impressed. Everyone knew Denny was a genius, but his casual grasp of the most insanely backward principles involved in rift science was otherworldly. It certainly wasn't as easy for her.

After killing the fiend that had broken in, she'd played with its corpse a little. Why not? She was a scientist. Turned out its constitution was a bit different than they'd seen in the Zen blood they'd seen spilled before. Some of the higher-ups had been theorizing for a while that the fiends might come in several distinct "classes," all of which were radically different at the chemical level. It would, those higher-ups feared, make fiends very hard to fight if they ever crossed over *en masse*. You'd need differently energetic weapons for every class, and that'd be a problem unless they decided for some reason to only attack one class at a time — something, curiously, that the few samples Brie had tested so far seemed to indicate was actually happening now. The only thing that killed all classes was brute force, but the brute force applied by conventional guns was questionable because you had to know just where to shoot them. That's why Rollards were invented: the most efficient hand-to-hand weapon anyone could think of, because medieval combat was apparently the only reliable way to take down all of them ... assuming they were kind enough to come at the wielder one fiend at a time.

What Danny had done with his improvised fiend bomb wasn't wholly unfamiliar, but he'd deployed it in an entirely unexpected context, in the spur of what was surely a more-than-panicked moment. It was impressive.

"Wait," Brie said. *"Paulson.* Did Jack Paulson end up making the prototype he mentioned on the call last month? Did he name it after himself?" That was just like Paulson. He sometimes tried to grab Brianne's ass when they were all together, and he was exactly the kind of self-aggrandizing cock who'd spent his career looking for something to hang his name on.

"Yes. 'The Paulson pistol.' It fires concentrated Zen Element rounds."

"Shit. And you gave one to Eldon?"

"So you understand?"

"Yeah, I understand. I ran some tests on *that* one." She pointed at half of the dead fiend. If seeing it surprised Denny, he gave no sign. "Shooting it with Zen would have been like giving it a power-up. It wouldn't get weaker. It'd get stronger."

"And maybe *bigger*, too," said Denny. "GEN has evidence that relativistic matter/energy conversion works differently with Zen Element. They may be able to use Zen energy to produce new matter, like the opposite of fission."

That sounded beyond impossible, but so many previously impossible things had become possible since Zen Element was discovered. Brie had learned to roll with it.

"I tried to reach Eldon before he used the Paulson, but I called here and then his home but couldn't get him."

Brie didn't comment. She might have been busy dismembering an intruder when the phone rang.

"I figured I'd run over with some graphite in case you didn't have any, and maybe figure out where Eldon had gone while I was here. I had an idea for a weapon I figured would work better against the class of fiends in Fortune now assuming they're all a single class, which luckily we seem to have been right about and they *do* seem to be. The weapon I had in mind wasn't supposed to be a bomb, though. Smaller quantities of Element and a carbon powder of some kind, contained in a non-reactive shell, might resonate with the Zen in their blood over distance. You wouldn't have to shoot them at all — just sort of rattle the thing at them. That was the idea, anyway."

"But the streets ... I mean, there must be hundreds of—"

"I didn't know all of this would happen when I left GEN," Denny interrupted. "I gave Eldon a detector along with the Paulson: a prototype I fabricated yesterday when the energy started to redirect to Cecret Lake and I started to worry that something might open a rift and try to climb out. But I assumed *one* fiend might cross over, not a city's worth."

"Eldon said someone was at the lake yesterday. Some civilian. He got a vision of it when he used the chamber." Brianne nodded toward Eldon's office and the closet-like enclosure there that Eldon used to to communicate with the fiend hive mind on the other side. "Whoever it was, their aura was the most energetically terrible thing the fiends had ever sensed from our side. I guess it drove them crazy."

"I hate that word," Denny said. "'*Aura.*' What, are we supposed to burn incense and wave crystals at them?"

"Hey. We managed to talk them out of calling it a 'chakra.'" Although secretly among her scientific peers, Brianna believed in chakras. The human nervous system worked through electrochemical current, and the spine was, in that context, a huge live wire. Current created magnetism, and magnetism radiated outward beyond its source. Like it or not, humans *were* surrounded by fields of energy. "Chakra" was as good a name for them as any.

"Eldon told me about the guy by the lake, too. He must have been feeling a hell of a lot worse than even the usual suicides from what I can tell. Turns out they really liked his vibe on the other side." Denny scoffed. "Demons feeding on depression, despair, and hopelessness. They're not exactly bucking the cliche, are they? It's like when cops actually go to donut shops.

"Anyway, I thought I'd be safe to cross town. Energetics suggested that the one that *did* eventually come through the Cecret rift was somewhat individuated and separated — at least for a while — from the hive mind. I knew that might change, others might catch a whiff of what the escaped one was experiencing, and that might set them off and cause others to cross the rift as well. I just thought it'd take more time. A *lot* more time. And I certainly didn't expect *this*."

Brianne hadn't either, and the unknown of it was killing her. She'd never wanted a news broadcast more in her life.

Normally she hated the news: curated bad stuff, served up to alarm people more than inform them. Now, though, any news she could get would feel like a lifeline: a way to have some idea (*any* idea) what was happening in Fortune at large. Eldon said he thought his Patient Zero was somewhere near the mall, so had anything happened at the mall? How widespread was it? Was the Rampart holding? And come to think of it, were their *theories* holding? They'd had that theory about classes of fiends and it'd paid off; as far as Brie could tell, only one "class" was thus far crossing over. But what if they were wrong about other things, like the Rampart's ability to repel fiends and keep them inside the circle? What if they were wrong about the Gore Point being the only thin place on the planet? What if instead of rifts only opening inside it, they were opening everywhere?

She frowned, gazing again into Eldon's office.

"Denny?"

"Yeah?"

"Does GEN know how to close rifts?"

Denny opened his mouth, then hesitated.

"Come on. You aren't really going to 'security clearance' me right now, are you?"

Denny sighed. "We have theories. Nothing tested."

"Why not tested?"

"Because there are a lot of paranoid people above us. The colonel is actually the nicest, most polite, and least paranoid of them."

That was a disarming thought. The colonel was worse than Paulson, and held a hell of a lot more power.

"The thinking's always been that they know if we open a rift. They'd pretty much have to, seeing as *we* can figure out when *they* open rifts. That's how we knew when it happened at the bottom of Cecret Lake."

"And?"

"In order to test *closing* rifts, we'd have to have to *open* new ones first ... which the brass doesn't want to do, because they'll know we're doing it and maybe start to wonder if it's defensive research, which it absolutely would be. It's all head games with the military. So if we can't open new rifts, the only rift we'd be able to test closing is the one in there."

Denny pointed into Eldon's corner. The walls were shimmering blue and purple as they reflected the rift's aurora. It'd been those colors for a while: much more energetic than the longer-wavelength reds and oranges the rift usually emitted. It scared Brie. She'd never before seen the thing so radiant. It felt like it might give her cancer if she went in there now. As if it might just ... *blow.*

"Obviously we don't want to close the only rift we have. So like most of our work at GEN, we have lots of ideas but no way to try them out. Great plan, right? If anyone had tested the Paulson gun, I'd've known not to give it to Eldon. Not for this class of fiends, anyway."

"'*This class,*'" Brie repeated. "So you agree that there's only one class of fiends out there now?"

"Pretty sure of it, actually. We have ways of knowing."

Brie tried not to resent that. Her lab and GEN were on the same side, and yet the higher-ups kept people like her, who were doing important work, in the dark because they were paranoid and greedy. Because of it — because of something that could easily have been avoided if GEN had been more forthcoming — Eldon Porter might be dead now.

"How do you think you close rifts?"

"Glue, if you can believe it. Obviously not normal glue. There's a resin GEN developed that's able to affix matter that doesn't coexist with the thing you want it glued to."

"I think I'm going to need that explained, Denny. I'm only a Ph.D."

Denny sighed, not exasperated with Brianne but exhausted by all the red tape and cat-and-mouse that working with the Department of Energy required. "It has to do with quantum superposition. I don't understand it myself. They way it was explained to me was: Imagine you break a vase and half of it falls into another universe. Now pretend you want it glued back together while keeping the two halves where they are, in separate parallel universes."

"Bullshit."

Denny raised both hands in surrender.

"Do you have any?"

"Yeah. Of course." Denny reached into his pocket. "Let me check my First Aid kid. If it's not there, it must be in my wallet next to the condom that's been there since 1978."

"Well, then do you at least know what's *in* the resin? What's it made of?"

"Stable monotomic hydrogen."

"Monotomic hydrogen is inherently *un*stable. It wants to form H2. Unless it's ... you know ... inside a star."

"Apparently it's stable at room temperature when it's in quantum superposition. Don't ask. We're at the limit of so many things I don't even understand a tiny little bit."

"Then we have to go back to GEN," Brie said. "I don't know how we'll get there, but—"

"We're not going to GEN," Denny said.

Brianne persisted. "I think it'll be okay. I've been peeking out. It's usually mayhem, but sometimes I'll go two, three minutes between seeing a single fiend. My car's right by the building. If we—"

"We're not going to GEN," Denny repeated, "because GEN doesn't exist anymore. The thing that ate me was just one of an entire horde that descended on us all at once. They didn't just kill everyone. By the time I escaped that thing's gut, they'd torn the whole building to the ground."

Brie sat heavily on the lab couch — the deep, soft, but ultimately shitty one that Eldon wouldn't let her get rid of. What Denny was saying meant that although his "graphite rattler" idea might let them fight fiends without having to skewer every one of them with a blade, there'd be no way to stop more of them from crossing over to replace the dead ones. It was like trying to dry a bathtub after the handle breaks, once you can no longer turn off the water.

The room went silent. Only the pain and screaming from outside filled the otherwise empty soundspace.

Denny sat at a stool beside the bench with his pile of activated carbon. He seemed to be realizing the same thing as Brianne. Without a way to close the rifts, they were beyond fucked.

Fortune was beyond fucked.

And unless the Rampart would hold an eternity of fiends (something Brie doubted, if the numbers got big enough), *Earth*, as a whole, was fucked too.

Brie looked to the auroral shimmering in Eldon's sub-lab. It was blue and green now — the color of Caribbean water. Eventually Denny saw her gaze, turned his head, and joined her in watching. From where they sat, the spectral reflections of the captive rift were beautiful. It was sunset on the ocean, as the last of the light tossed the water's ballet onto everything around it.

But then, suddenly, the light show stopped. The rift, she could see from here, was gone.

It'd closed ... entirely on its own.

CHAPTER 19

CURE FOR PAIN

It was true. The demons *did* seem to like Callum.

They ended up bunkering-in through noon and well into the afternoon. With every passing hour, Callum grew more and more anxious. No matter what Eldon said about the Rampart being the safest place (seeing as it supposedly repelled demons … but c'mon; he'd also brought a weapon that made them more powerful instead of dead), Callum had no way to be sure. He had to take his family's safety on faith.

Problem was, *faith* was something he had in short supply these days.

Eldon had sent Callum to the root cellar like a problem child while he and Carrie got chummy upstairs. Eldon claimed the cellar was best for Callum because his presence was like ringing a dinner bell, but that was yet another thing he had to trust. There was, in fact, a *lot* of "trusting Eldon" going on right now, and the situation wasn't exactly working out in Callum's favor. With Carrie in the mix, and with Carrie on Eldon's side, Callum found himself outnumbered in his own home. Carrie trusted Eldon because Eldon was broad-shouldered, handsome, strong, and not much older than her. That's the way Callum saw it, anyway. Callum, by contrast, was smaller, older, weaker ... and an active liability, if you believed what Eldon was saying. Maybe they'd tie him up next. Or just kill him; why not?

Apparently Callum was irresistible to demons because he'd introduced Hell to pain. That struck Callum as absurd. And even if it wasn't outright absurd, it was unfair. Christianity and popular culture both had strong opinions on Hell and its contents, and both would agree that if pain and Hell had an arrangement, it was that the latter had birthed the former. Think about it. God is good; Satan is bad. God is love; Satan is hate. Heaven is joy ... and Hell is pain.

But it's not Hell. Not as you know it.

That was true, too. Yes, Hell had risen — but no, it wasn't the same Hell everyone had been promised. The whole world had turned out to be a lie. Callum had been kind and pious his entire life. He hadn't even allowed himself a wild time in college. He'd obeyed the law, paid his taxes, and helped old people cross busy streets. He'd donated to charities, worked in soup kitchens, and avoided coveting his neighbor's wife. And *this* was how God had repaid him? With a son who was terminally ill — for whom there was apparently no hope at all?

The whole situation was really fucked up. Callum thought those words (*fucked up. Fuck. Fuckity fuckity fuck*) with vitriolic relish, having tried them out with his actual mouth while he'd been ... *possessed?* Was that what he'd been this morning: *possessed?* Yes, when he'd been possessed, he'd said the terrible words he'd spent his life avoiding. Even *condemning* on occasion, as it suited the Lord.

But what had the Lord done for Callum recently? He'd given his son inoperable cancer, unleashed demons on him (specifically *him)*, murdered half his town, put his family in unknown jeopardy, then conspired with the man and woman now occupying his house to throw Callum in the root cellar so they could have sex on Eldon and Mary's bed. Probably.

So honestly, kind of fuck what the Lord wanted right now.

According to Eldon, Callum wasn't just a victim of this particular demon apocalypse. He was, conveniently enough, its cause. According to Eldon, Callum had gone to Suicide Flats yesterday (definitely *not* to commit suicide. He'd thought about that and wondered if maybe he'd wanted to kill himself without realizing it, just to alleviate the pain — a little death here and there, no big deal — but had decided *NO, DEFI-NITELY NOT,* even though thinking about offing himself now sounded pretty good actually) and awoken something inside the tiny black lake at its middle. There was a weak spot at the lake's bottom just like there'd been a weak spot deep in the mines in Eldon's story, and when Callum arrived at its shore, that weak spot had broken open. A demon near the boundary between worlds had sensed all the terrible, fucked up, God-isn't-so-good-after-all emotions inside Callum and wanted to ... what? ... *eat* them? Eldon described it like sharks reacting to blood in the water. It was barely the demon's fault. Callum, like a temptress — like Eve, who'd started the whole "sin" business — had driven it crazy.

Shame on you for being in pain, Callum. It was very inconsiderate of you to have such sadness and guilt and unending torment in your life. Of course *the demon came through a rift to follow you and take what you had by force. It wasn't the demon's fault. You tempted it. Maybe you just wanted attention, Callum. From where everyone else is standing, you were asking for it.*

Even now — even after the world had filled with minions of the underworld — Callum *still* wasn't off the hook. He remained the temptress. To save everyone else, he was supposed to take his seductive, tempting self out of circulation.

He should hide himself away, so the demons might learn to be civilized and behave or something. That's what it sounded like, anyway. That's the particular breed of mumbo-jumbo that Eldon had been spewing, but to Callum, that's all it sounded like: *mumbo jumbo.* What: Earthen floors and walls were supposed to keep his pain safe in here so it wouldn't frenzy the demons? Because although *everyone* out there had ill emotions and pain, Callum's was the *best* pain? What a load of crap. This was only happening because Eldon wanted to get Carrie alone.

Careful, said a voice inside.

Yes, yes. He got it. Ha ha; very funny. Callum was acting unlike his usual self again. Maybe he was possessed again. Or maybe this *was* his usual self and had been all along. Maybe "good and righteous Callum" was the lie. Maybe *that* was the possession (possession by the *real* great deceiver: not Satan but God) rather than who he truly was.

Maybe the real Callum was bad. Maybe he was evil. Who could say?

Upstairs, Eldon had claimed to be strategizing ways to fight what was happening. He'd talked about trying to get to his lab — to a rift they'd opened there. To Callum, as he hid dutifully in the basement and his mood grew darker, it sounded like maybe Eldon, not Callum, was to blame for the demons. *Who'd* been deliberately speaking with them? *Who* had a bona-fide rift — a portal to the place where the demons lived — in the place he worked every day?

If you've talked to the demons, you must have known this was coming. You must know how to stop them. You must, surely, have made plans.

But when Callum had said those things to Eldon, Eldon had given him an answer that wasn't an answer: *It doesn't really work like that.*

Yeah, well, maybe Callum was tired of taking orders from

someone whose authority seemed to be running out. Eldon had a weapon and he'd killed one demon. *One.* So what? Did that really mean he knew everything?

Maybe the demons *weren't* after Callum because of his pain. Maybe not then … maybe not ever. Maybe *Eldon's* plan was the foolish one. Maybe Callum, whose only goal was to find and save his family, had the better plan. And what's more, maybe Callum was through letting his pain be a liability atop a liability. Maybe, for once, he'd come up with his own cure for pain.

His fists tightened. He was tired of sitting around. He'd been sitting around for his entire life. He'd obeyed the rules and done what others told him to for his entire life, too. Over the past handful of hours, he'd told Eldon several times that he was worried, that he wanted to go after Mary and Nathan. *If they're at the Rampart, they're safe,* Eldon would say in return, spoken slowly like Callum was an idiot. *But if you go after them, the fiends will follow you … and that's the best way to make sure they're UNsafe.*

Yeah, well, Callum was unconvinced. For one, Mary and Nathan might not be at the Rampart at all, in which case they'd be hiding somewhere and very much in danger. He'd have to find them if that was the case, but he had a few ideas. They could be at Mary's office, or any of a few friends' houses. And if he *couldn't* find them? Well, that would be okay, too. He'd at least have tried. More than likely, he'd die in the effort.

Which, again, would be okay too.

Callum went to the stairs. Climbed the half-level from the root cellar to the normal basement. He came around the corner, listened at the stairwell, and determined from the volume of Eldon and Carrie's chatting (getting pretty friendly over there, weren't they?) that they must be on the far side of the living room. So Callum climbed another half-flight to the main level, navigating the side of the home opposite where they'd be sitting.

He'd be seen if he went for the door to the garage, so instead he decided he'd exit through the kitchen, go into the backyard, then quickly buttonhook to enter the garage through the man door at its rear. The keys were still in Eldon's vehicle; he'd pointedly left them there so the car would be usable even if one of them was dragged off by a demon or something. Obviously, opening the destroyed garage door wouldn't be a problem.

Once in the kitchen he paused, nose wrinkling at the putrid smell inside. His eyes found the door to the living room, then the demon corpse beside it. It still hadn't risen from the dead. Trying out his bravery, Callum crossed to the thing and poked it with his foot. Black goo — not congealed like blood; it'd started this thick — covered the toe of his shoe. So he kicked the demon, hard. It was like kicking a heavy sandbag. He struck it with the top of his foot like a soccer star but it barely yielded, flopping slightly and spraying the wall with flecks of the same black goo before settling back down. His foot took the brunt of the blow, hurting the dorsiflexion muscles below his shoelaces.

It'd felt good, though: kicking something. Venting anger. *Being bad.* Disobeying the man in the living room who claimed he knew everything, and had probably already turned his attention from solving problems to feeling up Nathan's nurse. And honestly: Was that really so unfair an assessment? For all Eldon's talk of stopping whatever was happening, he sure wasn't doing much about it. He was just as bunkered-in as Callum, albeit in much more comfortable fashion. Where were his attempts to reach better weapons, or anyone who might be able to help?

Callum considered the door. Considered opening it so he

could peek out and verify what he'd convinced himself was true: Eldon in there with Carrie on the couch, making out instead of making the world safer like he claimed. He decided against it. What mattered more — having an *I knew it!* moment to hold over Eldon, or reaching Nathan and Mary?

Nathan.

Immediately, Callum's newfound hard edge softened to putty. All of this, in the end, came down to Nathan. Mary was part of it, of course, but somehow he felt sure Mary would be safe. Her role in all of this was a supporting one. The main players were Callum and Nathan. As if everything that'd happened was a test.

Maybe it *was* a test. The more he thought about it, the more it felt true.

Nathan was the reason Callum was in pain — and, obviously, the reason Nathan himself was in pain. They were bonded by it. Mary had that same pain, but Mary hadn't grown angry at God for betraying her in the way Callum had. Callum, by contrast, had taken his pain to the place that made pain worse, then set it free like a spirit. That spirit had entered the black lake, taken form, and come back for him. Callum was shepherd to this town — to those inside it who chose his church, anyway. It was almost biblical, the way Callum's torment had externalized as a threat to everyone Callum had spent the last ten years of his life serving.

He used to bring them hope when he stood at the pulpit. Now, he'd brought those same people peril. It wasn't a big stretch to say that what God had done to Nathan had gone through Callum, mutated, and come out the other side as everything around them now. He'd had his chance, hadn't he? He was supposed to kneel and pray. To ask God for grace. Instead, he'd gone to Suicide Flats like a gambling addict breaks down and goes to Vegas. Had he chosen wrong? Had he failed the test? He'd been so angry recently, but now he wondered if all of that was part of the test, too.

Maybe he *was* bad. Maybe that's why instead of waiting for Callum to go to Hell for his sins, Hell had risen to find him.

Emotions warred inside. He had no idea, for a few disorienting minutes, how he actually felt. Was he furious or was he penitent? Was he filled with resolve, or filled with regret? Was he through being a doormat and finally finding his strength, or was he instead reconsidering the idea that meekness was might, and the meek would inherit the Earth?

Instead of leaving through the back door, Callum re-entered the back hall and took the stairs to the top floor.

Nathan's room was just as it always had been. They'd added a few medical devices, but they'd moved nothing and taken nothing away as Nathan grew sicker. All the relics of his boyhood were right where Nathan had left them before growing up too quickly: his electronics-building sets, his books, his tennis racket because despite Callum's hopes, the boy had never wanted to play baseball, never wanted to toss around with his old man. Callum's racket was beside Nathan's, because Nathan was the only reason Callum had bought it, the only reason he'd ever used it. Callum was a miserable tennis player. He'd tried to get better so Nathan wouldn't get bored and stop playing with him, but of course it hadn't mattered. Nathan had gotten *much* better and Callum had stayed terrible, but of course they still played. Because always and forever, Nathan had loved his father.

Callum sniffed. His eyes were watering. He swiped at them, feeling his resolution and confidence dissolve as anger became sadness. He didn't want this weakness. Not now. He'd need strength to do what he needed to do.

He moved to the bed. Touched the covers, which had been thrown back and not replaced. They'd never been a bed-making family. Then he sat on the bed, feeling it give too much beneath him. The mattress was getting worn out. It wasn't made for all the laying around that'd happened recently in this room. No kid Nathan's age was supposed to use it so much.

A swelling rose in Callum's chest. He felt suddenly disoriented, suddenly lost. The weight of grief, sadness, and most of all *guilt* was a thousand-pound caul atop him. He'd been so selfish. He'd sat with Nathan so much, spoken with him so much, but it hadn't been every minute, every second, every one of what was sure to be a limited number of remaining moments. Callum should have been here all the time. He should have slept here. He should have *worked* here. Why couldn't he? He didn't own a desktop computer. His real office was a laptop. So why hadn't he brought it into Nathan's room so he could be with his son while time still remained on life's big clock?

He cried. For a brief, miles-deep minute, he cried.

Then he sniffed, shook the feeling away, and stood with resolve.

Screw what was wise. Screw the warnings. Screw his own safety. And screw what Eldon Porter believed, if Eldon's way to deal with this was to sit around as do-nothing and cowardly as Callum had spent the last few months being.

Callum had work to do now that the apocalypse had come for his people ... or to die trying.

CHAPTER 20

TRIAGE

Eldon was planning, strategizing, trying to wrap his head around a plan of action that wouldn't get anyone killed and might actually make a difference. So far, he'd come up empty. He had one big idea, but it came with a fatal downside.

His first thought was to go to the lab. At the lab, he could at least investigate; he could at least learn something. It was better than his current strategy of sitting on someone else's couch and learning nothing. He could take a few samples from the dead fiend in the kitchen and study them — maybe figure out why, when Donnie shot the last one with the Paulson pistol, it'd grown stronger rather than weaker. He'd poked around its innards a bit earlier, but all he could do without proper equipment was gross anatomy with kitchen knives.

Going to the lab was a good idea, but it required crossing Fortune. From what he could see of Callum's neighborhood through the gaps between boards, things out there were getting worse, not better. If he tried to reach the lab, he'd never make it. Not unless he could reinforce the car somehow —

Mad Max style — which, to be fair, he was considering. Callum didn't have big metal plates lying around, but he had plywood. Maybe it'd be enough as long as he left Callum, who the fiends liked most, behind. No point in trying to sneak out if he planned to ring a bell as he went.

"I need to do something. I can't just keep waiting around," said Carrie, standing at what used to be a window.

She'd impressed Eldon — enough that if he decided to make a break for the lab, he might ask if she'd come with him. She was kind of a badass. She'd not only slaughtered a demon and kicked *his* ass; she'd also become coolly intelligent and surprisingly strategic as she'd calmed down, rather than going helpless like most people would. She was a doer, not someone who waited — surprising for a nursing student trained in caring and empathy, Eldon thought. The risk of putting her in danger, by taking her to the lab, might be outweighed by her value as an asset.

Did Callum own guns? Eldon should ask. It took longer to dispatch a fiend with guns unless you picked the right spot to shoot the first time, but guns could be used at a bit of a distance, unlike a Rollard. They only had one Rollard, but if Carrie came and one of them worked a firearm, that might be enough of a one-two punch to sneak through tight spots. Assuming, of course, that Fortune wasn't just one big tight spot.

"I keep thinking and thinking," Eldon said. "And I keep coming back to the same conclusion: I need to go to my lab. The chamber I've used to talk to the fiend hive mind is there, and it's not far from GEN."

"Who's Jen?" Carrie asked.

"*GEN.* G-E-N. They're the think-tank responsible for strategy and intervention plans regarding the other plane."

"What's that mean?"

"It means they plan for the worst. They make weapons. I'll bet they've got all sorts of goodies they haven't told anyone about. I even heard a rumor that they were researching ways to close rifts. They're supposedly ... developing something."

"What's it stand for? *GEN?*"

Eldon laughed. "You know, I have no idea."

"You can't close rifts right now?"

"No, but we haven't needed to. There seem to be rules about rifts that have made closing them feel by-the-way."

"Whose rules?"

"Science's rules." He laughed again. "Well, *their* science anyway. Science that we over here are still trying to figure out. Where I work, we don't know many of the 'whys' of the whole fiends-and-other-plane business, but we know a few of the 'whats.'"

"And what are those?"

"For one, rifts — which is what we call the 'doorways' between planes — only open inside the Gore Point. So we don't have to worry about one opening across the street, which is good. Another is that only one rift is ever open at a time. I have a small rift in my lab, but it's artificial and tiny so I don't think that one counts. It's complicated, but it doesn't look to any of us like the thermodynamics between the planes will support more than one at a time."

"Could you be wrong?"

"Sure. But I don't think we are."

"So *all* of the things outside are coming from *one rift?*"

Eldon nodded. "According to what we know."

"Are there other rules?"

"Theories. Things that *might* be rules, but we're still just guessing."

"Such as?"

"A lot of us think there might be a few well-defined, like-kind groups of fiends on the other side. We call them 'classes,' all of which are energetically unique. If that's true, classes would share the same energetic properties within the class, but be different from class to class."

"Different how?"

"For current purposes, it means there are different ways to kill them." He told her about the fiend at the mall: how Donnie had used the Paulson pistol that'd shown great promise in GEN's lab and only made it stronger.

"You have to kill *every one of them* differently?" Wariness had entered her voice. She looked to the boarded windows, beyond which hundreds of fiends were turning Fortune into meat and ruins.

"Every *class,*" Eldon said. "Whatever class is out there right now, it's not vulnerable to that kind of weapon."

"So what kills them?"

"Cast iron pans," Eldon said. "Rollards." He indicated the Rollard leaning by Callum's fireplace.

Carrie laughed a little, but it was an uneasy laugh. "But isn't there something bigger? Better?" *Something able to kill them faster and in greater numbers*; that's what she really meant. The impossible-sounding task of bludgeoning their way across town was the reason they'd so-far stayed put.

"I don't know, but based on how nervous my GEN rep seemed every time we talked about the possibility of a mass incursion, I'm not optimistic. The Paulson was new. Highly experimental. My guy at GEN said they acted like it could solve all our problems." Something growled outside, followed by the sound of enormous, booming footsteps. Eldon and Carrie went silent. After whatever-it-was was gone, Eldon finished his thought: "Obviously, they were wrong."

They sat in silence. What Eldon's words implied made the room oppressive and dark.

A shrill alarm sound rent the air. Carrie startled, but Eldon startled harder. She'd only *heard* the thing that made it, but Eldon had felt it vibrating in his pocket, forgotten from what felt like a thousand years ago.

He pulled Denny's device out and looked at it. For a while he saw only the face of a football video game. Slowly, he remembered what Denny had told him about reading it.

"What is it? What's going on?" Carrie asked.

"There's been an enormous energetic shift. I think ... *Jesus*. I think the rift I told you about — the one in my lab — just closed." He thought something even more surprising to go with it, but the detector was a crude thing. It gave him data, but the interpretation was up to Eldon ... and right now Eldon hoped the tiny bit of good news he was intuiting wasn't just a case of an experimenter seeing what he wanted to see.

"So? Didn't you say they close sometimes?"

"Yes, but that was before. They've always tried to stay hidden in the past, but there's been none of that since all of this started. We assumed closing rifts was their way of being discreet, so they could come and go without leaving evidence for us to find. Everything since has been no-holds barred." He didn't add the reason he thought that, because there was no point in scaring her: that according to all measurements and the hive mind itself, the mass expulsion over the past hours looked like chaos even from *their* side. It was less an invasion than mass hysteria — something even the hive mind couldn't control.

But was that a clue? It seemed to jibe with the good news he'd already been considering. If this was chaos, humans wouldn't be the only ones trying to stop it.

In fact, if this *was* chaos to humans and the fiend collective alike, the hive mind might be their ally. Hell's consciousness might be the reason his rift had closed. That's what Eldon thought he saw on Denny's little blinking machine: effluxing energy drawn back in the *opposite* direction of its usual entropy. Maybe the human authorities weren't the only ones trying to stop what was happening. Maybe the hive, by re-corralling all the Zen energy it could, was trying to stop it, too.

"Shit," he said.

Carrie crowded closer in panic, looking at the detector. *"What?"*

"No. It's a good thing. Look." He didn't want to mention the Hell's-ally theory yet; he'd have to get to the lab and try it out before even considering throwing any confetti. But he was already seeing something else — something that could help them in theory, but only if someone found another miracle.

"What am I looking at?"

Eldon shook his head. He could barely understand what he was seeing, so how would she? "A friend gave this to me so I could follow the fiend that went after Callum, back when there was only one of them. Now that there are so many, the signals are all over the place. I can't really tell where any of them are because they're absolutely everywhere."

"And that's *good?*"

"No. No. What I'm saying is, I can't see individuals with so many out there, so instead it's giving me an aggregate. I *think* it's giving me an aggregate."

"And?"

"The way I think this works—" And honestly he had no clue, but he knew the way Denny Brennan worked and therefore how he'd probably built the thing. "—is that the only way I'd see anything at all with so many of them would be if they were harmonizing — amplifying the signal instead of a bunch of conflicting waves of different frequencies cancelling each other out. I'd expect to just see noise if that was the case, but look." He pointed at part of the display, drawing her attention to a single large, coherent spike. "See how it's concentrated?"

"Harmonizing is good?" Her eyes said she didn't believe him. The spike didn't look reassuring. It looked like critical mass.

"I think ..." He almost didn't want to say it. Not only might it create false hope (or possibly "slightly less hopelessness" was more accurate), but it was also exactly the kind of definitive statement based on single-pointed evidence that led to bad science and ensuing bullshit conclusions. It was also all he had, though — the only possible straw at which to grasp. "I think it means there's only *one class* of fiends in Fortune!"

"That's good?"

"It's huge. It means that every single fiend in Fortune is vulnerable to the same weapon. They can all be killed the same way."

"What way? You don't mean Rollards and—"

"I mean an energy weapon."

Carrie's eyes lit. "Where is it? The weapon?"

Eldon's shoulders fell. *Oh, right.* They'd just had this discussion, hadn't they? GEN, being tied to the military and therefore exactly as paranoid as it turned out it needed to be, had thus far only developed the Paulson weapon as far as Eldon knew. Obviously using the Paulson again on this class wasn't a good idea.

He felt like a fool. Why had he shown his stupid, false excitement? He hadn't just gotten his own hopes up over the past handful of seconds; he'd also gotten Carrie's. He wasn't in a lab right now. Discovery for the sake of discovery wasn't as exciting today as it'd been yesterday. Who cared that he may have just proven the class theory ... which, in turn, implied that the one-rift/one-class idea held true?

It was a useless realization in practical terms. They still had no weapons beyond hand tools — no way to put the new information to use.

"It's—" Eldon started to say.

But he was immediately interrupted by a huge crash and the squealing of tires from the direction of the garage.

Eyes wide, Carrie looked his way. "Callum," she said.

But Eldon was thinking horrible, mercenary thoughts. He was done with theory. Done with too much caution, too much attempting to look after others. Delicate methods would not get them out of this. Now was the time for triage. For letting a few bad things happen if it meant good things might be able to happen too.

"It's exactly the distraction we need," he said.

CHAPTER 21

HUNDREDS. THOUSANDS

Eldon yanked the door to the garage open. Sunlight and chaos blasted from the right as he saw Callum, driving Eldon's car, jerk to a stop in the middle of the road and shift from Reverse to Drive. To his left, the man door to the backyard was open — presumably how Callum had entered. A sheared cable from the garage door was stuck in the car's grill, still with the derailed door attached to its other end. Callum had dragged it into the driveway like an anchor as he'd backed out.

Eldon stepped into the empty garage but stopped short of making himself visible to any demons still out there. He considered raising his arms and shouting for Callum to stop and come back, but he didn't. He'd meant what he'd said inside, heartless or not: *It's exactly the distraction we need.*

Callum stepped on the gas, squealing tires. The cable snapped as he sped off, causing the big garage door to scrape the concrete a final few inches. It rocked twice and was still.

The neighborhood looked nothing like the one Eldon and

Callum had driven into into hours earlier, before they'd boarded all the windows and stopped watching. There'd been two earth-shaking crashes since, and now Eldon could see their sources: There was a head-to-head collision at the corner, plus a single car that'd rammed an electrical pole down the street. The pole had broken at the base and was now leaning over the street at a 45-degree angle. The transformer was sparking, but the line hadn't snapped. If it had, they wouldn't have power.

Pieces of what used to be people were spread about like errant litter: a hand here, a head there, a torso with a bowling-ball-sized hole through it across the street — a wound Eldon couldn't help wondering at, curious whether it'd happened before or after the torso lost its limbs and head. Three nearby houses were on fire: smoldering more than flaming, with curls of black smoke making their way skyward like rising serpents. Other homes, on the hills in the distance, were actively on fire: five of them, Eldon counted. Some had enormous holes smashed into them as if by a giant fist, while others appeared broken-into and ransacked. Most of the houses nearby, though, were like Callum's: boarded and still, the block quiet amidst all its anarchy.

Carrie arrived at Eldon's shoulder. Eldon stepped back with her, spying a half-dozen demons entering his field of view: three human-sized grey things, one that looked like a huge cat without skin, and two large bipedal fiends visible only as moving shadows behind the houses across the street.

Seeing them, Carrie grabbed Eldon's arm to pull him back inside.

"No. Wait," Eldon said. "They don't want us. They're following Callum. See?"

They held still, hoping the demons wouldn't look in their direction. They didn't need to worry. The fiends only had eyes for the departing car — and once it was gone, they continued to plod after it.

"They'll kill him," Carrie said as they vanished.

"They might," Eldon said. "But there's nothing we can do about it now."

Freeing himself from Carrie, Eldon took a few more steps into the garage. He approached its street-facing edge, stepping over the ripped-through cables that'd once held the garage door in place. Their ends were strange flowers: individual metal threads unbraided, their ends pulled thin like taffy.

He peered around the door's frame, scoping the street. The only fiends he could see were the ones that were chasing Callum. As long as Callum kept driving, he'd outrun them. The real question was what might be coming from other directions, ready to meet him from the front instead of the rear.

"It's okay," Eldon said. "C'mere. Take a look."

Carrie did. They watched the fiends' departure, noticing others from farther afield now beginning to plot after Callum as well. It was like a migration. As if Callum was a modern-day pied piper, leading away the snakes.

Eldon pointed to a light-duty truck parked at the street. "Is that yours?" he asked Carrie.

"Yeah."

"I need your keys."

"You're leaving?"

"I need to get to the lab. I think the rift there closed because the other plane is pulling back its energy. We think they're mostly a hive mind: one intelligence for all of them. I have a way to speak to that mind in my lab. I need to try to contact it. To be sure."

"They're *mostly* a hive mind?"

"Single fiends sometimes individuate. Usually it only happens on their plane for hierarchy reasons: Their leaders need to have individual minds for the system to work; I don't have time to explain. But I think that kind of individuation might also be what happened here. The first fiend was a rogue, but it was connected enough to send its rogueness back to the hive. Sensing its thoughts is what caused others to become individuals and cross over, too. But the hive mind doesn't want too many individuals … *especially* in the lower castes. If that's right — and if *I'm* right about the hive mind closing the rift in my lab — it means the other plane doesn't want this situation any more than we do."

"You think they're trying to stop it?"

"I think they're trying to cut their losses," Eldon corrected. He didn't have time to explain that either: the reason individuated fiends were difficult to re-integrate into the hive, but more importantly how little the hive cared if they did. Single fiends were like skin flakes to the collective. They were toenail clippings, or hair on the floor after a haircut. Why bother going to all the trouble to clean up this little spill? They'd simply close the rift to keep more from leaving and let Fortune find its own way out … or burn to the ground trying. "What I'm saying is: I don't think we need to figure out how to close the rift in Cecret Lake. I think they'll close it for us."

"How many demons does your little gizmo say are already here?"

Eldon shrugged. "No way to be sure. Hundreds? Thousands?"

"Where's your lab?"

He pointed in its general direction.

"*Toward* the Gore Point?"

"On its other side," Eldon said. "But look." He showed her Denny's detector, aware she probably couldn't read it. "Almost all of them are going the other way — toward Callum, away from the lab."

Carrie took a moment. "Okay," she said. "Let's give the lab a shot." They seemed to be thinking the same thing: *One baby step at a time.* If the demons liked Callum so much, they should leave the neighborhood before others from nearer the Gore Point came past here on their way to Callum, replacing the ones that'd left.

Carrie returned to the house, grabbed the Rollard, and re-emerged. She handed it to Eldon. "What do you think I should take?" She moved to a pegboard on the back wall, hung with gardening tools. "Should I take a hoe? Or hedge clippers?"

"You should *stay here,* is what you should do."

"Mm-hmm. Mm-hmm." She nodded sarcastically. "Counter-proposal for you: Fuck your macho bullshit. We both go or you find another ride."

"It's not because you're a woman."

"Okay to go with Callum from the mall, though."

"That was different. I needed his house."

"Uh-huh. Cool story. I'm going."

"No, you're not."

"It's my truck. I've got the key." She patted her pocket.

Eldon looked at it. "I could take it from you," he said.

"You could try," she retorted.

"I'm not going to argue with you."

She snatched the Rollard from his hands. "Good," she said. "So we're agreed. But Eldon?"

He was still considering taking the key from her. But then he remembered the way she'd destroyed the fiend in the kitchen, and the way only Callum's intervention had saved him from her ass-beating.

"What?"

"Don't forget to grab yourself a hoe."

CHAPTER 22
EVERYTHING IS ENERGY

Callum saw the fiends turn to follow him as he sped out of the neighborhood. He'd expected it. For all his ego-protective shitting on Eldon's theories, he did believe what the man had said about Callum's point of attraction. He'd known it all along.

When he'd gotten to the entrance of Wasatch-Cache National Forest yesterday, his mind had grown cooler somehow, as if nothing really mattered. With it had come light-headed delirium: a lifting of his dour mood that, by comparison, had felt like ecstasy. Looking back, he supposed he'd halfway blacked-out after that. He remembered driving around the blockades now, even though he wasn't conscious of it at the time. He also remembered a feeling that something was covering his tracks: an obfuscating bubble of impunity that had caused the surveillance cameras to overload, showing nothing, to hide him.

Energy, Eldon had told him. *This all comes down to energy.*

It made Callum think of some of the things Mary had said as Nathan's diagnosis came, as he declined, as the worse-case-scenario had begun to seem more and more inevitable. It was sacrilege, almost, to say what Mary said to a man of God. But those had been desperate times with even more desperate times yet to come, and in that desperation Callum had wanted to believe *anything* other than what his so-called faith told him. After all, what good was faith if you had no faith in it?

Everything is energy, Mary had said, taking a page from her woo-woo friends. *We shouldn't focus on the darkness, but instead focus on the light. Cancer is energy, too. What if we can manifest something else, and send that energy somewhere that supports life instead of destroying it?*

To Callum, it sounded almost like praying. *Almost.* The rest, though, was hippie nonsense. But even so (even through his conflicted resistance, wanting to believe things he didn't believe at all because God had forsaken him and it couldn't hurt), there'd been sense in some of what Mary told him and in the brief respite that nonsense had given her: *Energy* was *energy, and in the end* everything *was energy.*

It wasn't just the church. It wasn't just the hippies. Even physicists agreed: In the end, everything was — or could become, or come from — energy.

Callum knew now that the demon that'd chased him from Cecret Lake had smelled him coming long before he'd crossed the border into the Gore Point. Callum's own intense pain had empowered it. He'd been like a battery the other side could draw energy from, growing stronger. He'd created his own carrier wave, with his anger and grief and guilt. The demons must have fed that power back into the human plane to make his visit to the lake possible: modulating the current flowing through the government's security perimeter, shifting Callum's brain waves to make him trancelike and mean, hiding him from their detectors so he'd be able to show up and feed them the emotional meal they'd smelled from afar ... and to give the demons reason enough to come over: initially just one, with others to follow.

His eyes flicked to the rearview. The demons from his street had been right behind him at first, but he'd lost them since. Turned out demons weren't as magical as legend said they'd be. They could die. You could shake them by driving away. In a way, it was disappointing. He'd spent his adult life defining things in terms of reaching for a Heaven he barely believed in anymore, and avoiding the eternal damnation of Hell. But if this was Hell, where was the beef? The dead people around him weren't still suffering, turning on torture spits over the Devil's fire forever. They'd simply been ripped to pieces.

If this was Hell, where was the unending pain the Bible spoke of? Where was the irony: sinners punished in ways that matched their sins, like an adulterer forced to fornicate himself into oblivion?

Locusts. That was the one Bible reference Callum found himself able to relate to what Hell had actually turned out to be. The fiends were winning because of their ferocity, toothsomeness, and surprise ... but more than anything there were simply too many of them to deal with — like locusts, or a roach infestation grown out of control.

This town didn't need a priest to save them. It needed an exterminator.

The thought gave him confidence. There was no holy reason to fear. Earlier today, Callum had felt possessed, but was it really *possession?* No, it was more like the unsettled feeling from a subsonic soundwave. Just more energy because everything was energy, in other words. No demon had crawled inside him, making him do things he didn't want to do. Their influence had simply triggered the darkest of what Callum *already* had inside him, then freed it from oversight. Instead of putting on a brave face, for once he'd refused to do so. Instead of burying his pain and being nice for the sake of other people, for once he'd let himself be an asshole.

In a way, all the fiends' influence had done was to cut through the socially-acceptable bullshit. They'd done no more than given Callum permission to act the way he truly felt. And that was good, because it meant he didn't need to fight a holy war. His job now was closer to evading a pack of wolves.

As he drove, some of the mania that'd invaded his mind earlier returned. It made him strong. He sat upright in his seat, refusing to be more afraid than he had to be. When single demons came toward the car, he steered into them instead of away. Every time his wheels crunched over one of their bodies, Callum found himself smiling. He could do this. They had no power over him.

They'll kill you in the end, though, he thought.

That might be true. But, counterpoint: *Who cared?* The nice thing about being as desperate as Callum had become was that he himself no longer mattered. He wondered why he'd spent his entire life trying not to lose his life. What was the big deal? The world was shit, life was shit, Fortune was shit, and at this point being ripped apart by black things from an eternally-burning plane sounded like a step up from what'd worried him yesterday. There were upsides to being killed, honestly. For one, he wouldn't have to be in pain anymore. He wouldn't have to act like he cared anymore. He wouldn't have to *resist* anymore.

The last one was a biggie. Trying to get on — to live day after painful day — was like holding onto a slipping rope in a game of Tug of War. Just hanging in there was taking everything he had. Now, though, he could drop that rope. He'd let go, surrendering entirely, if death was what it'd take to save his family. All that mattered now was Mary and Nathan. If Callum survived too, great. But if not? No big deal.

Nathan won't survive anyway, said that hectoring internal voice — not the demons, but Callum's own dark id.

Callum found himself undeterred. Maybe Nathan *would* die, but come Hell or high water (get it?), he wouldn't die today. Eldon's warnings meant nothing; Callum could see right through them. Eldon was a scientist, so Callum didn't blame him for connecting only the logical dots: for observing Exhibits A, B, and C and determining from them that X must be true. For the most part, that made sense. For the most part, *science* made sense. But the fiends had come first to a man who was at least nominally of God, and Callum was convinced *that* meant something, too.

Everything is energy.

Life consolidated energy. Death released energy. Cancer consumed energy. Prayer focused energy. Thoughts had energy; that's why MRIs were used in psychology research. And determination, Callum told himself — that had the most energy of all.

You tended to get what you expected to get, for better or worse.

Eldon believed that Callum's family was safe inside the Rampart? Well, maybe yes and maybe no. Eldon might have a magic box through which he communed with the other side, but Callum, by virtue of his time at the black lake, had experienced that same communion. He'd heard their thoughts and they'd heard his. And so although Eldon's beliefs told him one thing, Callum's intuition told him another.

If the Rampart repelled fiends, it would keep them inside Fortune. But did they *want* to stay inside Fortune? From what Callum saw as he drove — through massacred streets and over bodies, around and crashing through detritus-strewn obstacles — it looked like the demons were having the time of their dark lives. He knew an ecstatic frenzy when he saw it. The town Callum had known all his life was now one enormous demon rave: one big hotel room they'd trashed as they partied like Prince.

Two thousand zero zero, party over; oops — out of time.

So what the fuck? Callum figured that he, too, could party like it's 1999.

Oops — out of time.

Out of time for Fortune. Out of time for whatever dangerous game the government and GEN had been playing with the otherworldly creatures they'd known about for decades, but hidden from everyone else. Out of time for all those who'd never believed the chickens of Hell would eventually come home to roost. And out of time for Minister Callum MacReady, who'd stood by and taken all of life's crap without ever standing tall to fight.

What had he done, other than cower? What had he done, other than accept what came, claiming empathy but actually just acting like a doormat? What had he done since Nathan got sick other than cry and whine — other than think, in the end, only about himself and how he was affected? What had he done, through the pain, beyond smiling at his congregation and pretending he *had* no pain, that the world offered no pain to the righteous, that everything was fine and would always be fine?

Well, fuck that.

Fuck that *forever*.

Eldon believed the Rampart was safe, but Callum's no-longer-accepting-what-he-was-told,   no-longer-meek-and-mild gut told him that the Rampart was, in truth, Hell's biggest target. Humans had proven easy for the fiends to handle; they'd run, died, or hidden inside their homes. Only the Rampart threatened them. Only the Rampart, in truth, was in their way.

If they were going to party like it was 1999, they'd need a much bigger club to rave in. Fortune was quaint; the fiends actually wanted the world. That's what Callum believed, feeling their mind still out there, still inside him ... still just energy, into which any sentient mind could tune.

Mary and Nathan were safe inside the Rampart. For now.

But that would change when Hell outgrew its prison. Soon enough, the Rampart would be the *worst possible* place to be.

It might take millions of fiends to do whatever it took to breach the Rampart, strong as Eldon's people felt they'd made it against them. But they *had* millions. And they had *time*. What could anyone do about it? Maybe Washington was debating The Fortune Problem right now, and maybe soon they'd nuke it. But what if nukes felt more to the fiends like *heat* than *shockwave?* They *liked* heat; they'd lap it up if unknown factors let them survive the blast. Or what if they were fortified by nukes like the one in the mall had been forti-fied by the soldier's weapon? Washington surely knew it all, so were they wondering the same things now as Callum? Would they try to obliterate Fortune and hope it wouldn't make things worse, or would they stay their weapons instead, to wait and see?

Callum was sure of one thing: *Even if the fiends couldn't breach the Rampart, they'd eventually focus everything they had on trying.*

Maybe Callum was like a magnet to them, the way Eldon said. It was true the local fiends had chased him, and it was true that as he drove, they kept coming from all sides. Eventu-ally, Callum might be overwhelmed or run into a clot he couldn't drive over or through, but for now he had pedal to metal and enough reckless determination (an aspect his new, crude, non-doormat attitude called "far beyond giving the smallest of fucks") to get him through and keep him going. It didn't matter if fiends chased him. It didn't matter if, by the time Callum reached the Rampart, he had a parade of demons right behind him. They'd soon come to the Rampart anyway. If Callum's rush was doing anything at all, it was speeding up the inevitable, not causing things to happen.

He didn't need a lot of time. He only needed a little. He felt bulletproof now; not caring if he died had a way of doing that to a guy. He'd become fearless. He'd think nothing of pulling up, grabbing his family, and driving away. There'd be no escaping Fortune, but once he had Mary and Nathan, he could retreat again to his home. They'd all be near the city's center, obscured again by his root cellar, when the demons tired of destroying and killing and turned their attention outward toward the Rampart: the only thing remaining between them and freedom.

Why bother? said the familiar voice of Callum's morose, resigned-and-stepped-on pessimism. *Nathan will die soon no matter what you do. Even if you save Mary, your son will be just as dead from cancer as he was always going to be.*

Callum found he didn't care. He didn't want to listen to his own hectoring voice anymore. For his entire life, he'd believed others who were intent on telling him what was true. His parents told him to obey all the rules. The church told him to fear God. The people of Fortune, through their actions and their spinelessness, told him to eat his torment and act strong if it meant they could feel better. The law told him one thing. Society told him another. Since childhood, someone outside himself had told Callum MacReady who he was, what was true, and what he must believe.

But he was done with that. He was done believing anything that hadn't happened yet. The future was unwritten. There were no rules. And energy, in the end, was energy. So if he had to believe something, he'd damn well *choose* what he believed.

The Rampart's imposing wall loomed ahead. Callum drove on with demons to his right, demons to his left, and demons behind and flying above him.

Everyone dies. That's just how life works.

He stuffed down what remained of his fear and obedience, and instead focused everything he had on one unassailable, imperative idea: *Nobody he loved would die today. Nobody he loved would die for a very long time.*

The voice inside tried to tell Callum that he was deluding himself. But this time, unlike every other time, Callum turned toward the meek critic that lived inside him and defiantly fed its lies right back to it.

Maybe I'm deluding myself, but so what? he thought. *When aren't we deluded by* someone? *At least this time, the deluder is me.*

His hands tightened on the wheel. His eyes focused on the great wall ahead.

Hell came for him. For everyone.

But for the first time in his life, Callum refused to see it.

CHAPTER 23

COOL STORY, BRO

Eldon wanted to drive Carrie's car into the garage and reinforce it Road Warrior style for their trip to the lab, but Carrie argued that 1) they didn't have time, 2) they needed to see to drive, and 3) if there was any chance of survival, she'd rather not drill into her car's side panels with sheet metal screws if it could be avoided. Surely Fortune's apocalypse counted as *force majeure*. What, was her insurance company going to pay for bodywork just because there'd been a few demons? This was America: one nation under lawyers and the criminal insurance policies they create.

As soon as they were inside the truck's cab, Eldon noticed the object behind their heads.

"You have a shotgun?" Carrie was in nursing. He'd expected a Hello Kitty plushie hanging from the mirror, not a gun in a gun rack.

"I grew up on a farm."

"You didn't think to come outside and grab it?"

"Into the meat grinder?" She shook her head like he was an idiot. "No thanks. I was doing fine with a cast iron pan."

Eldon took the thing in his hands, feeling almost warm. "A shotgun is better than a hoe."

"Tell that to my garden."

Eldon tossed the hoe out the door and into Callum's driveway. His ability to fight demons had just leveled up. In addition to the shotgun itself, Carrie had an abundant stock of double-aught buckshot shells. He considered asking if she hunted, then decided the question was irrelevant. If she didn't, he didn't want to know why she had so much firepower in her truck.

They drove. They saw a few fiends, but nowhere near as many as Eldon had expected. He kept staring at Denny's thrown-together detector, wondering if he was reading it right. It wasn't a precision instrument; Denny had given it to him to track a single fiend, so monitoring a city full of fiends might be beyond it. But there was another possibility, too: that he *was* reading it correctly, and the truth was simply strange. It looked like most of the fiends inside Fortune were massing in a half-moon shape near — but not at — the south-end Rampart.

"This is so weird," Eldon said.

"What?"

"You know how I said the fiends might follow Callum?"

"Sure."

"Well, it looks like they're massing around him."

"That's what you said would happen," Carrie said.

"Yes, but ..." He tried to show her the screen, then remembered how hard it was for anyone else to read and took it back. "They seem to be *surrounding* him. They're coming toward him from all directions, but stopping short of actually engaging."

Carrie looked at the detector anyway. It showed a circle with a clear area in the middle; that much was obvious. The clear spot had to be Callum, with most of Fortune's fiends around him. Why had they chased him, if not to bring him down?

"Why would they do that?" Carrie asked.

Eldon frowned, slowly shaking his head. "They're letting him go where he wants. Or maybe they're *steering* him to where *they* want."

It was so strange. So very, very strange.

"Shit," Carrie said.

"I'll figure it out," Eldon told her, putting the detector away. "There's better equipment in the lab."

"No. I mean: *Shit.*"

Eldon looked up to see Carrie pointing through the windshield. A huge red thing with tree-trunk legs and downturned black horns was standing in the the road ahead with twenty or more smaller fiends around it like an entourage. The big one had to be thirty feet tall.

"Shit."

"That's what I said."

Eldon took a breath. He'd already racked the shotgun, a shell in the chamber. Now he rolled down the window and flicked the safety off.

"Take Elm Street," he said.

Carrie turned hard, speeding up.

"They're still coming. Maybe we should turn around."

"We need to get to the lab. Turn here."

Carrie again turned away from the fiends ahead, but they moved to block.

"We're heading in the wrong direction."

"You told me to turn!"

"I meant the other way," Eldon said.

"The other way is right toward them!"

"It's— *Look out!*"

Carrie saw the ambush just in time. Two black-and-red

striped things the size of fat Labrador retrievers leapt at their truck from beneath an overturned car, slapping the front quarterpanel and bouncing away as she yanked the wheel. One of their long-clawed limbs raked the hood, shredding it like wafer-thin tinfoil.

"Shit!"

In evading the Labrador things, she'd turned toward the big demon again. The smaller ones around it, as if they'd anticipated the truck's move, were rushing forward to close the distance. Now the truck was hemmed in on three sides — not checkmated yet, but moving in that direction.

Again Carrie yanked the wheel. Tires squealed; she barely avoided colliding with a downed electrical pole. It was topped with a smashed transformer, shooting fiery sparks. The truck rumbled over a curb, came briefly onto two wheels, then smashed sidelong into a blue corner mailbox. The box uprooted too easily and flew up to smash the windshield. The safety glass became a big, flexible spiderweb, impossible to see through.

"Watch out!" Eldon shouted.

"I'm watching out! You could fucking help, you know!"

Eldon considered the windshield, decided it was a loss, then laid back so he could kick it out. What the hell; at least he'd have a clear line of fire.

By the time the windshield was completely out of the way, the demons had more or less surrounded them. The big one was ahead and the smaller ones had fanned into two groups like big wings to the left and right. Carrie hit Reverse to counter, but the back lift gate rammed a row of cars parked along the street. She jockeyed around and found herself facing a dead end. Then she looked over her shoulder, planning to floor it backward, but saw that they were blocked in. All she could do was sit and idle.

She glared wide-eyed at Eldon. "Did they just do that on purpose? Did we just get ambushed?"

"They can't. They're mindless. Even the collective is mostly instinct. When I talk to it, it's not really talking. My mind interprets their intention, is all."

"Cool story. Explain it to *them.*"

Eldon's thoughts raced. Top-of-mind was deciding what to do next, but back-of-mind was still trying to understand. Everything GEN had told them and everything Eldon had experienced pointed to fiends being instinct-driven, not actually intelligent. What he'd just said was true: the raw energy coming through the communication cabinet in his lab was mass intent, not *thinking* in the way humans knew it. The fiends knew how to open and close rifts — and how to communicate with other species — in the way animals knew how to migrate, build shelters, and hunt. GEN had always considered them more like a dangerous colony of otherworldly ants than another sentient race ... no matter how cogent they seemed when they talked through the wetware of Eldon's brain.

"Maybe we can drive through one of these fences. Come out on the next street," Eldon said.

"Okay. What if we get stuck?"

"We're stuck right now."

Carrie's foot slipped off the brake. The truck lurched forward before she was able to step on it again. She was breathing heavy, near panic. Eldon knew how she felt.

"You said shotguns are good?" Carrie said, eyeing the one in Eldon's hands.

"If you hit them in the right place, which isn't always obvious. Rollards are better, if you know how to use them."

"Do you know how to use them?"

"Apparently. I did okay at the mall, but there was only one of them."

The demons came closer. Growling, drooling, mouths open and clawed limbs up.

"Go on," said Carrie. "Take it." She nudged the Rollard with one elbow.

"I'd have to get out."

"So get out."

"I'm not getting out."

"What? Big, strong man like you?"

Eldon was considering when the demons decided for them. Five of the smaller ones rushed toward the truck, leaping onto the hood and clawing toward the hole where the windshield had been. Out of instinct more than planning, Eldon raised his weapon and fired. The head of the closest one exploded, covering them with putrid brown-black sludge.

But it collapsed and slid away, dead. Emboldened, Eldon blew the head off of the next one, which also died and slid away. But when he tried with the third — this one more spider-shaped than man-shaped — it kept right on coming. Very quickly, it had one long arm inside the cab. Its flesh was hard, like an exoskeleton, and the limb was covered with stiff black hairs as big as pencils.

It was on top of Eldon seconds later. A mouth he hadn't even seen opened wide, exhaling putrid breath. It bit into his left arm above the elbow, bringing blood and pain. Eldon screamed, wincing, thinking all the usual horror movie cliches: *Will I become one of them now? Is this mummy rules or zombie rules?*

Then the bulb with the mouth on it fell from view. Eldon looked down and flinched hard, seeing that Carrie had managed to cut its apparently-a-head off with the Rollard despite their close quarters. The head was now in his lap.

"DRIVE!" he shouted.

He juggled the bleeding demon head as Carrie stepped on the gas, wanting nothing less than to touch it. He finally managed to toss it onto the hood, where it struck the thing's body. Both head and body fell to the ground.

Carrie knocked the Rollard toward the backseat to drive, nearly severing Eldon's arm. He pushed its sharp parts the rest of the way back and gripped his bleeding arm, unable to see the demon bite fully and too distracted and freaked-out to feel it yet. The car lurched forward and stopped, lurched forward again and this time kept right on going. They jolted upward hard enough that Eldon hit his head on the cab's ceiling, bringing stars. He heard a roar and knew she'd run over one of the fiends. In the side mirror, its mangled body got up and dragged after them.

But they'd escaped the worst part of the pincher, now outside the ambush circle. The remaining fiends came hard.

Eldon racked the shotgun and pumped rounds into them: seven eventual rounds with a reload, and yet only one demon was wounded enough to fall. He wondered, as a scientist, at the physiology of it: something for his mind to do because the alternative was panic. Was he destroying their brains? Was that what this was, and they simply kept those brains in different places from fiend to fiend? Or did they not *have* brains, and killing them required something else?

Once the truck was mostly free, demons stopped being what scared Eldon most. Suddenly, the top spot belonged to Carrie's driving. She literally had the pedal to the floor, being none too picky about how straight she drove ... or if she drove on the actual road, or what was in her way. Despite reservations about getting stuck, she'd apparently decided after what'd just happened that driving over hill and dale to get away was worth the risk.

She flattened a fence, barely avoided driving into a back-yard swimming pool, smashed what looked like an empty home's screened-in porch and then its gazebo, and finally came through into the K-Mart parking lot. Eldon found himself thinking of *The Blues Brothers* and how Carrie, like Jake and Elwood Blues, would be right at home driving through the causeway of a mall. *What* obstacles? In a hot enough panic, this truck could plow through anything.

"Is it following?" Carrie yelled. *"Is it following us?"*

Using the singular, she had to mean the big one. Eldon twisted to look over his shoulder (the rearview and side mirrors were gone now, taken down by the spider-thing and the Jones Family's decimated backyard fountain, respectively) and was relieved to see the huge demon growing smaller. It'd apparently made its move, and that move had failed. Demons couldn't think, plan, ambush, or strategize. He told himself again that those things were true, even though he had good reason, now, to believe otherwise.

We're okay. We're alive. A tiny, panicked Eldon somewhere deep inside kept repeating the words, willing them to be truer than they felt.

"IS IT FOLLOWING US?"

He turned back. "No. And neither are any of the others with it." The truck bounced over another curb. Eldon put a hand on one of Carrie's hands, white-knuckled on the knurled steering wheel. He said, "Easy. Slow down."

She stared white-hot at him, furious that he was telling her what to do. But then the fear began to drain away and she nodded briskly, understanding.

She shook herself out, finding a bit of composure. "Where's the lab?" she asked.

Eldon squeezed his bitten arm, winced, and decided it was just a surface wound. He'd live — and horror movies be damned, the worst he'd suffer from it was an otherworldly infection ... which, now that he thought on it, didn't exactly sound like a picnic. What kind of microbes thrived at 300C? They'd be tougher than Earth pathogens, surely.

But they were okay. They were alive.

"Sixth and Bayview," he said, pointing. "You can't miss it."

CHAPTER 24

I'LL PRAY FOR YOU

Mary MacReady was listening to the sounds beyond the Rampart's walls like a woman waiting out a tornado. The GEN people who worked here had told her, Nathan, and her co-worker Mallory Malloy something she didn't know Eldon Porter had already told her husband: that the Rampart was more than a physical barrier, and if there was a safe place in all of this, "inside the Rampart" was it.

So far, that had proven true. The Rampart's inside reminded Mary of the time she'd visited Hoover Dam: all concrete, pipes, and sharp echoes. There were precious few windows, and the few that existed were more like portholes. Even so, she could see that although hundreds of monsters had passed by, none had approached and until recently none had stayed. Their hosts wouldn't reveal what made the monsters keep their distance, but they had conveyed two unsettling things to go with it: Yes, Hell had more or less risen on Earth as long as you weren't too picky about the terminology — and yes, Mary and the others were stuck inside the Rampart until ...

Until ...? Mary had prompted when the man who'd been

speaking stalled out. She prompted again, but it seemed nobody wanted to complete that particular answer. Maybe because there *was* no answer. How long would they be in the Rampart? There was no way to know.

Over the past few hours, Mary had learned something else as well: That some very intriguing inventory had been hidden from her during yesterday's audit. She'd expected the usual industrial supplies, kept in what originally seemed to be a storage room. What she *hadn't* expected was that the utility door at the back of the storage room opened into a massive, high-tech interior — or that inside that interior, there were row after row of what looked like brushed-steel, double-sided battle axes.

The people here worked for GEN, but they were clearly junior. They'd tried to call their HQ for information and orders when everything began, but none of the lines were working. That left them to their own decisions and devices. So they'd grabbed the axe things, which they called "Rollards," and waited to use them. But they hadn't needed to. What they'd been told about the Rampart was apparently true. The monsters (called "fiends," as if the GEN folks knew they existed and were only a little surprised to see them — far less than Mary, anyway) hadn't come close enough for Rollards to be necessary.

So they'd shut themselves in and waited. And waited. Mary had mostly busied herself by worrying about Nathan, but he'd thwarted her by remaining high on his good day — the health-iest-seeming day he'd had in weeks. There was nothing to worry about beyond the obvious.

Nathan, sensing his mother's distress, had flipped and begun comforting her instead of the other way around. *It's okay. Dad will come.* Mary didn't have the heart to tell him that as good a man as Callum was, he wasn't exactly a warrior.

They were supposedly safe, and that meant Callum — not Mary and Nathan — was the one in danger. And where had Callum been when everything went down? Turned out he'd been at the mall. She'd gotten that much from hearing the GEN people talk as they watched their many instruments, calculating something Mary couldn't fathom: This began at the mall, they'd said, and a local minister was being referred to as the fiends' "prime acquisition target."

Mary had asked about that. They told her she'd misunderstood. They hadn't been talking about the mall at all. Then, they'd gone back to talking about the mall — about how something called a "Paulson" was *definitely* not the solution to whatever this was. And they'd kept talking about that prime target — not their target, but the monsters' somehow.

"Ma'am?"

Mary stood. She'd been half asleep with Nathan fully asleep on her lap. He'd gone deep, though, and she found she could set him aside without waking him.

"Where's Mallory?" Mary asked. She looked around, having lost her co-worker.

"Top level, ma'am. We've decided it's necessary to force-evacuate."

"You mean leave the Rampart?"

"Yes ma'am."

"But those things are still out there."

"We'll be evacuating through the *other* side, ma'am: crossing to the far wall, then exiting outside of Fortune."

Mary didn't understand. She'd asked about that long ago. If Fortune was the problem and they'd ended up inside an unapproachable wall *around* Fortune, why couldn't they just escape through it into the outside world? They'd had one enormous reason why not, and once explained, Mary had agreed it was far safer to stay put.

"You said you couldn't turn off the power running through the Rampart's center," Mary told the GEN man. "You said we'd be fried if we tried to cross to the far side."

"There's a magnetically-shielded pod used by the maintenance crew," he told her. "We think it might get us through."

"'*Think,*'" Mary repeated. "'*Might.*'"

"The Rampart's current is never completely off, but it can be decreased for maintenance. That's when the pod is used. It's always been safe for the techs who use it."

"So you've lowered the current?"

"No, ma'am. I'm afraid that can't be done locally, and we can't reach the control facility."

"So you're saying you want to shuttle us across a billion-volt forcefield in a tin can and hope for the best?"

"That's a bit of an exaggeration, ma'am." He swallowed. "The situation has changed. We have reason to believe the Rampart may not be entirely safe anymore."

"What? Why not?"

The GEN man swallowed again.

"Are you actually worried about your security clearance?" Mary said. "If you want me to risk my son's life to get out of here, I'm going to need more than you're giving me."

"I can't say, ma'am. I'm sorry."

"Do you have kids?" Mary asked.

"Y-yes, ma'am. I do."

"What would *you* do, with your kids, if you were me and someone wasn't telling you the truth?"

He said nothing. Mary stood firm, content to wait him out no matter how long it took — or to stay here and die in a way that was at least inevitable rather than choosing to leap into the fryer.

The man surrendered. He looked around, saw that none of

his colleagues were nearby, and spoke the next thing very low. "We think they're dismantling our power lines."

"Who?" Then she realized. "Wait. *Them?* The ... the 'fiends'?"

"We don't think there's a lot of time. I'll be straight with you: They don't like that we're keeping them inside. They want out, and I'm not confident anymore that we can stop them. If anyone is here when the power fails, all of this just becomes one big wall. It won't hold them for long."

Mary looked up, to the stairs Mallory had presumably climbed with the others.

"You're speaking straight?" Mary asked.

He sighed. "What's the point of not, I guess."

"Do you really think the 'pod' you're talking about will be able to cross that much electricity?"

"Theoretically."

"Only theoretically?"

"Let's just say I'd rather take my chances," he said.

"What if I wouldn't?"

"Well ... *Mary?*"

"Mary," she confirmed.

"Well, Mary, I'll keep being straight with you since we've come this far. I knew a little about what the Rampart was built for, but the reality of it is a hell of a lot worse than knowledge from any book. What I see out there scares the life out of me. I'm not staying. If you don't want to go, I won't force you ... but I'm not going to stick around with you, either. If you stay, you'll be on your own."

Mary lowered her voice. She was suddenly very scared — more scared, now that this moment had come, than she'd let herself be so far.

"My son has cancer," she said low, so Nathan wouldn't wake up. "A few months ago it did something to his heart.

They put in a pacemaker. It's supposed to be a really good one. Shielded and all that. But ..." She didn't want to say the rest.

Now the GEN man looked at Nathan before returning to Mary. He said slowly, "The pod should shield it."

"'*Should*.'"

Another GEN worker — the tall black woman whose cheekbones made Mary jealous — appeared at the top of the stairs. "Glen?" she called down. "We need to go."

The man — Glen — met Mary's eyes. She'd never seen someone before look so ... *human*.

"There's only one pod," he said. "We can't send it back. If you don't go now, you don't go."

Mary stood. Thought. Breathed, waiting for the next moment to come.

"Please," Glen said.

"I can't risk it."

"*GLEN?*" the woman called.

"I can't risk it either," Glen told Mary.

"I know. Thank you."

Then he did a strange thing. He took a small silver cross from around his neck, put it in Mary's hands, closed them, and closed his own hands around hers. He didn't know Mary was a minister's wife, wearing a cross of her own. She didn't tell him. The moment was too tender.

"I'll pray for you," he said.

"And I for you," Mary said.

He took the stairs two at a time, rushing now, finally letting buried fear bleed through his facade. At the top he looked back and paused, but after that he was gone ... and Mary and her sleeping son were alone.

. . .

THAT WAS A HALF HOUR AGO. Nathan had woken not long after the others left, and when he did, he seemed much worse for wear. Rather than invigorating Nathan, the nap looked like it'd taken years off his life. That was the way his ups and downs had been all along: Hope became false hope; false hope became despair. Every good day was nothing but a tease — a brief respite between worse times.

"Where's Mal?" he asked. He was clammy now. Sweaty. Mary had made the right decision not to chance his pacemaker. The way he looked now, with this one-eighty flip from solid to feeble, she was convinced that even without a feeble heart the electricity itself would have killed him. Everything was energy, and Nathan's energy was fragile. Just look at the boy now: He could hardly lift his head.

"She had to go. They all had to go, Nate. It's just you and me now."

Mary expected questions after that, but Nathan just settled back down. "Oh," he said.

Something boomed from beyond the walls, on Fortune's side of the Rampart. She didn't know what it was and didn't want to know. A person shouldn't be asked to recalibrate everything they'd ever believed about everything in the course of one afternoon: *Heaven, Hell, other dimensions, the fragility of life and death.* Society was a thin veneer over chaos; all it'd taken to upend everything was an attack by something unexpected. Although: *Was* it unexpected? GEN had clearly known something. So where were the weapons and plans to face them? What contingencies had the government put in place: paranoia on the public's side for a change?

She thought of the man, Glen, and the nugget he'd let dangle: *We think they're dismantling our power lines.*

Monsters were supposed to be monsters. They weren't supposed to be electricians. Maybe he'd meant that their rampage was *disrupting* the lines — meaning accidentally — but that's not how it'd sounded to Mary.

They don't like that we're keeping them inside. They want out, and I'm not confident anymore that we can stop them.

So that boom outside? It could've been anything. Mary couldn't get to the portholes easily, but she wasn't sure she wanted to look out anyway. The fiends could be building a catapult out there for all she knew, to storm this literal rampart.

A small hand took Mary's. She looked down, broken-hearted for so many reasons.

"It's okay, Mom. Dad will save us."

She could only press her lips into a bloodless line, then attempt to bend it into a smile. If she'd needed proof that God killed innocents too, that was it. Callum wasn't Arnold Schwarzenegger in *Commando*, come to save his daughter with grease paint and muscles. He was the man after whom the phrase "mild mannered" had been coined. He was a quiet preacher with a predictable haircut who couldn't successfully do a pushup.

Something boomed again. This time, Mary would swear the walls shook. She pulled Nathan to her, his cheek to her chest, smoothing his hair.

She wanted to say something simple and positive: *"I know"* would do. But instead she said nothing, quietly beginning to cry.

Thirty seconds later, she heard a car engine growing louder and louder.

Squealing tires.

And then a crash.

CHAPTER 25

STANDOFF

Callum steeled himself for battle. It was easier now that his goals were crystal-clear and he no longer cared about surviving. If the fiends wanted him, he'd just have to let them have him. He was here to deliver a car in which his family could escape; that was all. Callum going with them would be a nice bonus, but it wasn't at all required.

All that mattered was getting them into the car. Using himself as bait should draw the fiends away from the Rampart's door, away from the car. They'd have time to get to it and escape. As long as Callum could reach the Rampart (easier than he'd expected; the fiends were more *following* him than *attacking)*, as long as Mary and Nathan were actually inside (which he wasn't sure about in the least), and as long as he could get their attention and draw them out while he created a distraction, this would work.

He sped on. If he kept his gaze straight ahead, he'd never know there were demons inside the city. They refused to surround him. Refused to fall upon the car and use their claws and talons to rip it to pieces. *Why?*

You know why. You know what they want.

That was a lie, though. Callum was sure it was a lie. It was *so much* a lie, it was only mostly true. Callum definitely had no idea what the voice in his head was talking about. This morning's pseudo-possession had *definitely not* — and we're talking *zero chance* — unlocked something that'd always buried deep within him. Callum was *not* a changed man now, with a dark side no longer afraid of the light and relegated to his inner shadows. So no, it *wasn't* true. Callum *didn't* know why they wouldn't attack him. Others, yes, but not Callum. He *definitely* had no clue what they wanted from him. He was one hundred percent (give or take a hundred percent) sure of it.

The dark voice inside him chuckled at that. The laugh seemed to say: *It's just me and me in here, Callum. I am you, you are me, you are I, I am we. And WE? WE can believe whatever we want.*

The Rampart grew larger in his windshield. No threats approached from any direction; they simply kept their distance and observed, waiting for the next twist like any good audience. Through the mental scar left by the demon mind, he could almost hear their thoughts. Almost, but not quite. He knew that whatever this moment was, it wasn't the one the fiends wanted from him — yet. They trusted him, though, or trusted some unseen future. *Do what you want right now,* they seemed to tell him, *because what comes next is so inevitable.*

Callum shook it away, driving faster. He didn't want permission. He didn't want consensus. He'd finally grown bold; he wanted opposition enough to prove it. It wasn't bold to do what you were *allowed* to do. So he drove, eyes locked, wanting to fight, pretending for all he was worth that he wasn't — somehow — doing exactly what Hell's mind wanted him to do.

How could it? Why would it? No. This is right.

The fingers of his left hand gripped the wheel hard enough that he imagined he might pinch it to taffy. Eyes forward, he used his right hand to reach into the backseat. *Why?* He realized his idiocy right away. Weapons were always in the rear during car chases in the movies, but that was because the prop department put them there. Callum had grabbed nothing before rushing from his house. Nothing at all. Not a machete, not a shovel — not so much as a pocketknife. How exactly was he going to fight them?

Never mind. You don't have to fight. You just have to cause a distraction.

Callum could do that. The only problem was that if he looked right and left, he saw at least thirty fiends watching him in both directions with another thirty to the rear. If he ran, they'd take him. *In seconds.* How much time would he have bought Mary and Nathan if he gave his life that easily? How far would they get if Callum couldn't resist enough to even slow them down?

He felt something change inside: a pushing-aside of thoughts as if they were physical things. The sensation was beyond unnerving. He felt as if his mind itself was being rearranged by some intrusive hand: a psychological force he found himself unequal to — one that seemed to exist only to remind him that all his feelings of control were illusions ... and something deeper, whenever it chose to, could seize control of him at any time.

His vision blinked out, and suddenly he saw nothing.

The Rampart was gone.

Fortune was gone.

Callum saw himself standing on some sort of a raised dais,

surrounded *not* by his own decimated city but instead by an audience of thousands — maybe millions — of grey-skinned fiends. Every one of them was the same: slight, angular, sexless, and with half their heads missing. The creatures seemed to have been slashed through head and skull on a horizontal bias, revealing a wet brain: working, throbbing as if it wasn't a brain at all, but instead a beating heart. They had mouths, though: dark, hateful, tooth-filled holes below the brain, open and downturned in a perpetual hiss.

Ahead, like a king on a throne, as a massive red beast with huge horns. The largest fiends he'd seen paled in comparison to its size.

The enormous thing looked at him: right at Callum. Then, very clearly — in Callum's own voice, as if his brain had been hijacked and used to translate their thoughts into his language — he imagined its words.

The balance has changed. The infection will spread. You will not be safe. We will do what we must. And you *will do what* you *must.*

Callum wanted to open his mouth to ask what that meant, but he had no voice. None of what he saw was real. The huge fiend had said what it needed to say, having delivered the one-way message it'd reached from the other plane into Callum's mind to deliver. The question was: Why had it spoken to *Callum?* Why him, out of everyone?

You know why. You know what they want.

His own voice this time. His own shadow side.

The vision began to fade. Callum became aware of time again, aware only subsequently that he'd lost awareness of time to begin with. The vision had dream logic. It'd taken less than a second, but it felt like he'd been in that foreign place for hours.

Reality came rushing back. He was still behind the wheel of Eldon's car, still driving very fast because he was scared to death and because he needed to believe that *speed*, not *permission*, was the reason he would successfully reach the Rampart unmolested.

He was still approaching it. With extreme, out-of-control speed.

He startled. Hard. He'd been focused on driving before the vision interrupted him, but now, thrown so suddenly back from his mindspace into his corporeal body, Callum found himself panicked. He couldn't re-enter this quickly. His focus was overcome by a driver's version of the bends: too much demon-thought in the blood, soon to pop him like a champagne cork.

Callum found his senses. He slammed the brake with both feet, convinced that pedal force was all it'd take to stop two thousand pounds of steel. The Rampart had grown too close in the time he'd spent away. Now, he'd meet it with extreme prejudice.

Seeing he'd never brake in time, Callum spun the wheel hard left at the same time. The turn dug both side wheels into the wall's concrete apron, grasping for desperate purchase. Several cars were parked nearby; Callum clipped one delicately enough to remove a lens from a Jeep's headlamp without so much as scratching the rest.

Come on, baby. Slow your roll ...

He'd turned too hard. Now, he thought, he'd simply roll into the Rampart and explode. The tires held, though, and after a few feet of drift, most of his momentum returned to the intended direction of travel. He careened, half-sideways but no longer at deadly speed, at the Rampart twenty or so feet from the door he'd been aiming for.

Still too sharp. Gonna bust the engine. But then how would Mary and Nathan use the car to get away?

Certain he was destroying the car's drive train, Callum

wrenched the wheel again. The car nosed away, the wheels slid in a cloud of acrid smoke, and the Rampart screamed at the passenger-side door.

Callum had time to think: *Well, this is it. This is what death looks like.*

There was an enormous crash. With it came a bone-jarring jolt. Callum was thrown sideways, not forward, the seat belt clawing at the side of his neck instead of stopping him from the front. The safety glass in both side windows exploded like a bomb, peppering him with hard glass confetti.

The lights went out. And after that, sleep.

DISORIENTATION.

Lights, sound, and a memory he couldn't reach but that he somehow knew was life-and-death important.

He fought through confusion, imagining his will as the biggest bouncer in his headspace, shoving lesser thoughts aside with elbows and fists. It took only seconds to remember where he was, what had happened, and most importantly why he'd come. He remembered the vision that'd caused his crash, too, though he didn't have time to sort the details.

Mary. Nathan. You have to get their attention, and then you have to run.

The car was still on. Still idling. Engine still running. He put it in Park without killing the engine, knowing Mary would have a hard time driving it away if Callum forgot to give her the keys.

The rest of his reorientation took milliseconds. His lap was full of glass, but it was all cubes, not the deadly shards of plate glass. His neck hurt but was unbroken, and he seemed not to have been crushed or impaled. The car itself was intact; he remembered the speed at which he'd struck the Rampart and judged it, with his cobwebbed mind, to be insufficient to have done more than require bodywork. He was sitting level; hopefully that meant none of the wheels had broken off at the axle. He'd also had the good sense to smash the passenger side of the car instead of its driver side, which meant Mary would be able to get in and drive without a problem.

Callum wiped his forehead, saw a lot of blood, and force-decided it was because scalp wounds bled copiously instead of considering how dead he might already be. With fumbling urgency, he opened the door and fell out of the car more than exited it. He rolled, scrambled, and stood. The car looked okay. They'd be okay, even if Callum wouldn't.

Callum prepared to run. How much time had passed? How long had he been blacked out? He didn't think it was long; smoke from the tires still hadn't entirely dissipated. They'd be on him now. On him in seconds.

That's when Callum noticed the calm. Very slowly, like tiptoeing to avoid waking a sleeping baby, he turned his head. When his neck stabbed pain, he began to turn his shoulders as well, then his torso and feet.

The world had gone quiet other than the running engine. Not far off, he could hear the snap and crack of house fire. Beyond that Fortune had gone cathedral-still.

The fiends were watching him. Waiting.

There had to be two hundred demons around him. They'd formed a semicircle bisected by the Rampart's tall stone facade with the area around Callum and the car, for maybe thirty yards in every direction, completely clear. It reminded him of the perfect circle that forms if soap is added to dishwater skimmed with grease: a retreating of oil from soap. Every one of their dark, evil eyes — for those that had eyes — were on him.

It was quiet enough that he could hear them breathing.

Did demons have lungs? Did they breathe oxygen, if their world was so hot? If they didn't, how could they survive here? He, Eldon, and Carrie had discussed some of it before they'd John-and-Yoko'd up and sent Callum into the root cellar like some sort of third wheel. *I think they may become what we expect,* Eldon had said. *I think their bodies, as we see and experience them, are too coincidental for things to be otherwise.*

What did that mean? And did it matter? Why would it matter, here and now?

"Callum?"

Callum nearly collapsed in relief, short-term though it was. Mary was standing at the open Rampart door, seeing Callum before she saw the demons. Then she saw it all and took a step back, but then stopped.

"Nathan?" Callum said.

"He's here." Then the boy's face appeared at his mother's side, looking unsteady on his feet. Why had they come here? Carrie implied he'd been more well than he'd been in ages, but to Callum, Nathan looked like death warmed over. He should have stayed in bed. Maybe then he'd've been safe.

They're safe now, Callum. Hurry.

"C'mon," he said low, as if the only reason the demons hadn't attacked was because they hadn't heard them. He waved small, then big. "Come on. We have to go."

Mary looked out. At all the creatures. At how alone and weaponless the three of them were. But she wasn't waving Callum in her direction like he'd half-expected, either, and that meant she'd never considered the Rampart to be particularly safe — or maybe its status as a safe haven had changed.

Mary came forward, her arms protectively wrapped around Nathan. Her head was on a swivel, eyes jittering from place to place like mice in a cage.

Callum waited for the demons to approach, but they stayed where they were.

Breathing.

Salivating from toothsome maws.

"Why aren't they coming at us?" Mary asked, voice low and wary.

"Doesn't matter. Get in the car."

She went to the rear door.

"No. Driver's seat."

"I'm not up to driving. You got here somehow. You made it through this."

"You *have* to drive. I'm not going with you."

"*What?*" She looked like he'd spoken in another language.

"They're interested in me. I don't have time to explain. You go. I'll keep them here."

"Callum, you don't even have a weapon."

That wasn't true, though, was it? He'd gotten enough bits and pieces over the past hours to believe something absurd: That maybe he *was* a weapon — a weapon against his own species instead of theirs. Or maybe *pathogen* was a better word. What had the big red thing said in his vision? *The balance has changed. The infection will spread.*

And what did you do with an infection you couldn't cure? They'd known the answer as far back as the Civil War, with its abundance of gangrene and bone saws.

What did you do with an infection? You cut it out.

"Drive," he told Mary, backing away.

Mary didn't move.

Callum snapped. He had nothing left. Nothing at all.

"DRIVE! Do you want Nathan to live or die?"

Her face worked. He saw it now: how terrified she was, how at-the-end-of-her-rope she was. They all were — every soul in the city of Fortune.

"Please," he said. "Let me do this. Let me do the right thing, for once."

"Callum, you—"

"*Please.*"

Mary stared for another second, then briefly closed her eyes before reopening them. She got into the car and turned her attention to the wheel and pedals. She drove a little then: just along and then away from the Rampart, eliciting a horrid symphony of scratching metal. She was still close to Callum, and her windows were down.

She turned the nose of the car toward the horde. Callum nodded and moved in the opposite direction.

"Come on," he said to the fiends.

Nothing.

"Come on, you bastards! You want me? Come get me!"

He took more steps away from the car. The semicircle didn't budge. They watched him. Waiting for something.

He waved his arms. He plucked a rock from the ground and threw it into the mass, where it bounced off two unmoving fiends.

"*COME GET ME!*"

From the corner of his eye, he saw Mary close her eyes. She looked down, a few tears falling, trying to press emotion back inside.

"*You hear me? It's me you want! Come over here and get me!*"

Nathan was crying. Protesting. As little as Mary wanted to leave Callum, Nathan wanted it a thousand times less. As sick as he was, he kept trying to climb over Mary and out the window. She had to hold him down, and restraining him only made her cry harder.

Callum ran at the demons, leaping at the front row to take them on with his fists. They rebuffed him easily, apathetically, seeming to watch with pity for this poor fool embarrassing himself at their feet.

Mary began trying to drive off, into the circle of fiends, but they weren't budging there, either. She'd never get through, if they didn't swarm for Callum.

Something pushed Callum's back. He looked behind to see a thing that looked an upright half-bull, half-elk with its hoofed limbs out.

"No," he said, understanding. "I'm not going with them. You want *me*. Take *me*."

The beast snorted. It took a step toward Callum, then shoved him again at the car.

"No."

Now several of the fiends roared. They were becoming an agitated mob, their patience growing thin. At the same time, the circle began to constrict around Mary and Nathan in the car. Some pawed the hood. Others crowded the broken side windows, while Mary and Nathan cowered inside. She seemed to be considering flooring it and trying to plow through them, but that was ludicrous. They were five or six deep. She wouldn't make it three feet.

Callum considered the bull-elk thing as it came forward again, preparing once more to shove. The message couldn't be clearer: *Go where we say or they die. Not you. Them.*

"Why?" Callum asked.

Demons growled. Hissed. Snorted. Now that the car and Callum had come away from the Rampart, the demons were moving to complete the circle between the humans and it. They still wouldn't touch the Rampart or go closer to it than six feet; apparently whatever made them fear it was still going strong. But as much as they could, they were pinching Callum and his family away from the wall. Soon they'd be completely surrounded with nowhere to go.

"Just let them go. Just let them be," Callum said to the bull-elk, knowing there was no way any of them would understand. But did he really need an answer? No. He'd known on some level where this would end from the moment it began ... and it wasn't here. It wasn't *here* at all.

You know why they're pushing you toward the car. You know what they want.

It was true. Entirely true. He didn't need the demon voice inside him anymore to know it, and he didn't need more visions. He'd known, in some oblique, no-details version, what the big red thing in his vision had meant.

We will do what we must. You will do what you must.

Callum, though he preferred not to, understood perfectly.

Wordlessly, he went to the car. He thought he'd summoned enough bravery, but he still had the largest hurdle left to go.

Mary waited, with questions in her eyes, as Callum opened the driver's door. He looked down; she slid into the passenger seat; he sat and put his foot on the brake. He shifted into Drive, numb and cold.

"Callum? What is it?"

"You'll be safe," he said.

Not a guess. This was something he knew.

"Why? What's going on?"

He said nothing, and began to drive.

CHAPTER 26
END OF DAYS

Eldon wasn't new to this. He'd had practice, just today, of getting quickly into places with the hounds of Hell at his heels. Carrie hadn't, though. He had to encourage her. Aggressively so. Most people weren't used to ramming their way into buildings.

"Come on, cowgirl," he said. "You've got a truck with a gun rack. Prove you're not a poseur."

Carrie didn't smile. There'd been a time when people used to smile, but Eldon could barely remember it. She looked scared. Like he was scared. The game was not about being composed in any sort of permanent or lasting way. It was more about holding your fear back as much as you could, hoping the force of it didn't explode into panic and get you killed.

"Aim for the big doors," he said, pointing. "All you need to do is drive fast and not hit the brake until you're in."

At first, Eldon had wondered why GEN assigned him a lab inside a disused fire station, but he'd quickly come to understand. The citizens of Fortune didn't realize how involved the government was in their city. From where Eldon sat now, however — with his military liaisons and the spy-vs-spy signs and countersigns he had to give every time he picked up his scrambler phone — Fortune felt more like a covert military occupation than a town. That's why Wasatch-Cache and the entire Gore Point area were only *nominally* closed, not *officially* closed. It's why the security cameras were hidden and the barricades looked like polite suggestions rather than ironclad decrees enforceable with bullets. And it was why, when GEN had needed a civilian laboratory to do its dirty work, it'd built one inside a building the city government already owned: an old fire station, complete with big red doors and a slide pole.

Eldon scanned the area, finding it free of fiends for the time being. He wished Carrie would hurry. Now was the time to crash their way in if they wanted to survive. This — here and now — was their window of opportunity.

It was strange, though, how calm things had gotten. After outrunning the last group of fiends, Eldon and Carrie had seen very few of them and been attacked by none. Based on energetic predictions, the Cecret Lake rift had probably pumped out five hundred or a thousand individuated demons by now, meaning Fortune should be sick with them. And yet, there'd only been those few remaining in Callum's neighborhood. There'd only been the one small-but-mighty gang of fiends — the gang that'd almost taken them down. There'd been very few others. Denny Brennan's detector suggested that a big group was about a mile north of here, but the rest — the vast majority — had massed on the other side of the city near the southern checkpoint of the Rampart. That, of course, was where Callum had gone.

"Come on, Carrie," said Eldon, growing anxious. *"Andele."*

Instead of driving forward, though, Carrie reached for her door handle. "I've got another idea."

She put the truck in Park and got out. She walked to the

building, squatted in front of one of the doors, then pulled it up like opening a garage. Counterweights took the door the rest of the way once it was in motion. After it was up and open, Carrie got back in the truck and looked at Eldon like he was an idiot.

"Men," she said. "Always wanting to break things."

She drove inside. They exited the truck, Eldon still staring at her as if she'd done something wrong.

"It's okay, big guy," Carrie teased. "I'll let you close it."

Eldon pressed a button on the wall to lower the door. Nothing happened. "Power's out," he said.

They'd anticipated that. As they'd driven, they'd twice seen entire blocks of interior lights die before their eyes. The whole city's power was failing, sector by sector. The last to go would be the Rampart, because it's power was excessively redundant. Every grid in the city fed it. As long as one lit-up lightbulb remained in Fortune, the Rampart would have power. Thank God for that, but it meant the clock was ticking. How long *would* it be before the last of the electricity — and then the Rampart — failed?

Carrie returned to the big door and lowered it using the guide ropes. She managed to refrain from mocking Eldon about doing all the work. Afterward, the garage, empty of fire engines since long ago, was eerily quiet.

"This way," Eldon said, heading for an archway.

They moved through a door, then down a long hallway. Nothing inside seemed to have been decimated. That was a good sign; it meant the communication chamber would still be where he'd left it this morning. If any of his co-workers were inside, they'd probably be alive. It was no problem that the electricity was out. The power Eldon needed didn't come from transmission lines, and the lab had big skylights that would provide enough light to work.

"This is it," Eldon said, arriving at the lab door.

Carrie was holding the shotgun. She gave a curt nod and stood ready. But there was no need for readiness. Unlike in Fortune at large, all was well inside the lab.

When they entered, Brianna practically tackled Eldon in a relieved hug. As they embraced, he thought at first that she'd crapped her pants in fear (no judgement there, by the way), but then he realized the smell was more organic than fecal — like rot, not shit.

It wasn't coming from Brianna, either. It came from someone else inside the lab: Denny Brennan, his clothes and hair matted with goo.

"Don't ask," Denny said, noticing their stares. But of course he told them anyway.

THEY CAUGHT EACH OTHER UP. Denny told them how he'd discovered a weapon that worked on the class of demons currently in Fortune in the grossest possible way. Brianna told them that the rift in Eldon's lab had closed but they didn't know why. Eldon then explained about Callum and how his emotional distress had started this — how Callum's visit to Cecret Lake yesterday had given the fiends a taste of mental energy they'd never felt before and how they'd been driven to frenzy by it. He also gave them his theory on why the rift had closed — a theory he confirmed after mind-melding with the other plane using the communication chamber, seeing as the hive mind would only speak to him.

They discussed. And discussed.

Nobody knew what plans the fiends in Fortune had for Callum. Their minds were mostly separated from the hive, so even the hive couldn't help. The humans confirmed one thing, though: The invasion had indeed grown beyond the collective mind's control. There was no way to call the individuated minds home, so the collective had chosen to cut them off. It'd pull its energy back and close the rift, leaving Earth to deal with the fiends that were already here.

"There's something else," Eldon told Denny, Brianna, and Carrie. "Until the Cecret rift closes, which will probably take a while for the hive to do, there's still a psionic tendril between the individuated fiends and the hive mind. There's so many of them in Fortune experiencing the same thing that the experience is feeding back to the hive in the other plane. What the Fortune fiends are seeing, the collective mind is seeing too, by proxy. Because of it, the fiends still in the Hell plane are going a little bit crazy like the ones here are going crazy. At this point, I don't think that 'experience' can be taken back. It's part of their collective mind now, for better or for worse."

"What are the fiends on our side experiencing that's infecting the hive?" Brianna asked.

"*Lust* is the best word I have for it. They've always been interested in us, but now it's turned into an obsession — a mindless, species-deep mass obsession. It's as if they were bugs, and what's happened over the past two days taught them to move toward light. You know how bugs always move toward light? Well, pretend that's learned behavior instead of instinct and you'll pretty much get what I mean. What the fiends didn't used to do, they'll now do like it was second nature. Like instinct. They won't want to stay in their plane anymore. Now, they'll always want to move toward us like bugs move toward light. It's the new normal."

"What's that mean?" Carrie asked.

"It means it will keep happening," Denny said. "The most-poisoned individuals among them have already come over, so if the hive mind closes the rift now and lays low, we might get a honeymoon that'll last a while. But the 'lust for us' that Eldon mentioned will build. Sooner or later they won't be able to control themselves, and they'll start opening rifts again. Different classes of rifts, with different classes of fiends coming out of them. We'll need unique weapons to deal with every class and every rift. If Fortune survives, we'll need to prepare. We have to find ways to deal with new incursions as soon as new rifts open so that *this*—" He raised his arms to indicate the city's destruction. "—doesn't happen again."

Eldon had been thinking the same thing, but because he'd been inside the chamber and experienced the collective mind directly, his thoughts were more gut feeling than scientific conclusion. They'd need a standing force in Fortune: a militia specifically trained to fight demons. If the hive mind was as infected with thought-lust as he believed, they wouldn't be able to count on that same infected hive to close rifts from their side the next time one formed. That meant humans would have to learn to close them. GEN would need to gather its ashes, find what it could in the rubble of its destroyed building, and re-formulate the rift-glue it'd been playing with. Denny called it "stitching resin." He compared the theorized procedure for rift-closing to be like sewing a rip in spacetime itself.

"Okay," Carrie said, exhaling, taking everything in. "But what about the situation we're in right now? Forget tomorrow — how do we get through today?"

"We're on our own, for one," Brianna said, though they'd mostly covered that already. "The hive doesn't like that it's lost control of so many individuals, but their solution is to cut their losses and move on rather than clean it up. They'll close the rift. That'll at least stop more fiends from coming. But after it's closed, we'll still have a few hundred fiends left on our side to deal with."

"A few hundred *at least*," Eldon said. "I'd say it's closer to a thousand."

"What about the army?" Carrie asked. "Can't the army or the government help?" She looked from one scientist to another, but clearly they already knew the answer to that, and the answer wasn't good.

"The government won't intervene unless the Rampart falls," Denny Brennan said with bitterness in his voice.

"Why not?"

"Oh, the usual reasons. *Power. Greed.* Zen Element is extremely valuable, both in terms of money and as an unexploited technology. Especially *weapons* technology. Element acts as if it defies entropy. Instead of moving from order to disorder without an infusion of energy like everything else in the universe, Zen's natural movement is from disorder to order. Instead of falling *apart*, it falls *together*. There's been a cottage industry around raw Zen Element since it was first discovered, but what homemade wrinkle creams and scar treatments can do is *nothing* compared to what's possible with refined Element. A few grams of refined Zen could power a city for weeks. It could regrow hair on bald men. It could reverse all kinds of diseases."

"What's Zen Element got to do with this?" Carrie asked.

"Everything," said Brianna. "Element comes from their blood and bodies. And I mean ... look around you. Just *look* at how much fiend biomass has entered Fortune in the past 24 hours. The government doesn't want to stop this. Why would they want to *stop* a gusher of the most powerful substance in existence? This is Christmas to them. They'll wait it out for as long as it takes, licking their chops."

The group sat with that. Then the overhead lights, which had been off, flickered on and off again. There was a sizzle and a flash of sparks from outside. When Eldon ran to investigate, he saw that the transformer across the street had fried. He saw something else, too: In the distance, where the land rose slowly, a grid of several still-lit-up blocks suddenly went dark.

A few seconds later, another block of lights went out.

Then another.

Denny was beside him, watching the homes go dark one by one.

"Eldon, let me ask you a question," he said. "What would you do, if you were a group of beings that fed on angst and fear, and you found yourself trapped somewhere with fewer and fewer people inside to feed on ... but a whole bunch more just outside?"

Eldon felt cold. It was happening. The last of Fortune's electricity was dying, but it wasn't a side effect or happenstance like he'd imagined. What they saw through the window was clearly deliberate. Systematic. This wasn't power *failing*. It was power *cut*.

When Eldon didn't answer, Denny went on. "I know what *I'd* do. I'd break out. Whatever it took, I'd break out of my prison."

Everyone said that other than the hive mind after it was filtered through a human mind, the fiends were like locusts more than humans. They were a swarm, nothing more. They weren't intelligent. They were horrors driven by instinct and the need to feed ... and yet here they were proving those suppositions wrong.

Here they were, taking Fortune's infrastructure apart piece by piece.

"We have to stop them. Somehow," said Eldon.

Denny held up a big bottle of graphite. "I think I know a way to do just that," he said, "but it requires some travel."

. . .

CARRIE HAD ALWAYS LIKED apocalyptic fiction. It was more fun in books, though, than it'd turned out to be in practice.

They left the lab without a single fiend to stop them — all four crammed into Carrie's pickup truck with Denny and Brianna knees-to-chin in the tight backseat. They'd driven as far as they could toward the power plant where the fiends were doing their sabotage, but were stopped before they could reach it.

About a mile from the plant, they encountered an impassable roadblock. It looked at first like a pileup collision, but on closer inspection Carrie couldn't imagine how such a collision could have happened. The angles were all wrong. The incorrect parts of the vehicles were crushed: Two cars sitting nose to nose showed damage at the rear, not up front where they'd have needed to hit each other to make sense. Some cars were upside-down or on their sides, but they showed no body damage consistent with rolling — if the places they'd supposedly rolled from and to even made sense, which they didn't.

"This didn't happen on its own," said Eldon. "This blockade was *built*."

Everyone had figured that out. None of them wanted to think about what it meant. Across the hoods, trunks, and roofs of the piled-up vehicles choking the road to Fortune's power plant were huge scratches spaced several feet apart. Carrie could only imagine the size of the hands that must have picked them up and stacked them here like Legos.

They climbed out of the truck and continued toward the power plant on foot. Between them they had one Rollard, one shotgun with a handful of buckshot shells remaining, and an axe from the old fire station's equipment locker.

Denny, without an obvious weapon, was carrying an improvised bomb of his own making: something he called a "Rattler," and which he'd freely admitted might not work at all. He'd found a globe in the brigade room above the lab, filled it with carbon dust harvested from the lab's filters and graphite from the stock cabinet, then sealed it with epoxy. He'd left an open slit on the globe's top, into which he stuffed a wad of plastic wrap smeared with a cocktail of lab-grade potassium, anhydrous sodium, and blood from the fiend Brianna had killed. Denny called the wrap a "fuse," but it wasn't really a fuse. Carrie had tried to understand for a while but given up quickly. She was just trying to hang on; she didn't care about the details.

"Like I told Brie," Denny'd said when it was finished, "it's not really not a bomb. At least, I hope it's not. When I exploded my way out of that fiend, a real bomb's shockwave would have killed me, but it didn't; it only blew the fiend to bits rather than both of us. That tells me it's more than just an exothermic reaction. It's more than just a burst of energy. My best guess is that it's resonance. A kind of chain reaction — like in a fission reactor, but without physical contact between the molecules."

"But it's just a guess," Brie had said.

"It's a *good* guess," Denny had replied. "You know who you're talking to, don't you?"

Carrie had no idea "who Denny was," but Eldon and Brianna hadn't asked questions after that. Apparently he was the Larry Bird of scientists. Kind of looked like a fat Larry Bird, too.

Watching Denny and his non-bomb bomb now, as they walked side by side in the same way she'd imagined Boulder's contingent entering Las Vegas when she'd read *The Stand*, Carrie hoped the poofy-haired GEN man knew what he was doing. It was Greek to Carrie, but that was okay because what else could she do?

If she understood things correctly, most of the fiends in Fortune were chasing Callum somewhere (*"leading* him somewhere" were the words Eldon had used, though Carrie didn't understand why) and most of the rest had massed a mile ahead of them, at Fortune's power plant, to cut the city's power. If they succeeded, the Rampart would no longer hold the fiends. They'd spill into the world and kill out there the same as they'd killed inside Fortune. Worse, all three scientists seemed to think that breaching the Rampart would infuse the fiends with so much new emotion-lust, it'd energize the collective and send *even more* fiends through the Cecret Lake rift, which the detector said wasn't closed yet. Things would spiral from there: their so-called "hive mind" no longer able to seize control enough to *ever* close it. If that happened (if a critical mass was reached and the hive mind became the minority to the individuated ones), there might be no stopping this. It wouldn't just be goodbye Fortune; it might be goodbye *Earth.* Goodbye *humanity.* The military would be useless if things went that far — and of course, no other countries' armies would be able to help because they'd be ignorant, seeing as the US hadn't shared what it knew about the other plane and its occupants.

Carrie wasn't being noble when she thought about how she'd rather die than let that happen. It was simply a longer-term breed of self-preservation. She'd read enough apocalyptic books to know she had no interest in living through the apocalypse. Dying quickly at the hands of an angry fiend sounded a hell of a lot better than living for weeks, months, or years in what Earth might soon become.

She didn't know or care how (or if) Denny's bomb (which apparently wasn't a bomb) would work. He'd described it as a chain reaction at a distance. He'd compared it to using sound waves to shatter crystal, too, thinking Carrie might know the cliche of opera singers breaking wineglasses with their voices.

They have Zen in their blood and we don't, he'd told Carrie before they'd left, wanting her to understand because Denny, in addition to being the Larry Bird of scientists, was a teacher at heart. *If the Zen Element and absorptive graphite in this Rattler starts a reaction — technically an* anti-*reaction; that's anti-entropy for you—"* And then he'd laughed, though Carrie hadn't seen what was funny. *"—that reaction might telegraph to them even if we're a hundred yards away. If they can hear the chunks of graphite hitting the globe's interior, that's probably close enough to rattle their insides.*

There was, however, a catch. Denny seemed to think his Rattler would only work once: the "priming" Zen smeared on plastic wrap inside the fuse would be used up after one shot and that would be it. That meant that even if they were able to stop the fiends ahead from cutting the Rampart's power, they wouldn't be able to do much about the hundreds or thousands of other fiends in the city. But Carrie was training to be a nurse. She should be pleased to be even a small part of their planned world-saving. No need to save the world *entirely* on her first try. That was just crazy.

With the fiends almost entirely massed at the power plant or steering Callum somewhere unknown for reasons unknown, very few were roaming free anymore. Once out of the truck at the blockade, they were able to walk in the open. They walked four abroad, the way she imagined all apocalyptic warriors walking. In her mind, she even heard theme music: a score for this movielike moment, heralding their forthcoming victory.

Eldon suddenly stopped walking, staring ahead. They could see the plant now, and a group of fiends over the next hill.

"Shit," he said.

Carrie was about to ask what he meant. They had the Rattler, and she'd convinced herself it'd work ... or if it didn't, they'd at least die quickly. The decision was easy, even if its outcome was uncertain. So what fly had Eldon seen in the ointment? What could possibly be *shit*-worthy — *there's-a-problem-here*-worthy — that they hadn't expected?

Then she saw it. She saw the problem, and it was a big one.

They'd arrived at the top of a low hill: just enough to raise them above the shallow dish of land in which the power station was situated. From here, they could see everything.

Still far ahead — out of Rattler range, surely — was a group of fiends surrounding transformers and capacitors and towers and cables. Those were the ones they needed to get to, if they wanted to stop this.

But much closer to where they stood was a secondary line of fiends: an outer perimeter they'd never get through with one Rollard, one axe, and one shotgun. If they used Denny's Rattler to break through it, that'd use up the Rattler and make it useless against the inner circle. They'd have cleared the way to a situation they could no longer stop once they reached it.

Eldon stepped back, squatting low. The others did the same. Once they were out of sight, yet to be seen by the fiends, a horrid pall fell over all of them. Eldon put his face in his hands, and Denny set the Rattler aside without a word.

They'd never get through the outer line of fiends to reach the ones in the center. Not soon, and maybe not ever.

In the hills, a grid of lights went dark, then another.

Time was almost up. The end was less than a five-minute walk away ... but in the time they had, there was no way for four people with four weapons to reach it.

CHAPTER 27
CUNNING

Callum had all sorts of ideas for ways to escape. Unfortunately, the demons had them first.

At first, he'd wanted to distance himself from Mary and Nathan — not a way for *himself* to escape, but at least a way to ensure his family's safety now that the Rampart was about to fall. When the fiends wouldn't let them separate (maybe for leverage, or maybe because it increased his emotional turmoil, which they found delicious), he'd thought maybe he could outrun them in the car. But they'd surrounded the car the whole way, as if they knew he planned to make a break for it.

No way out. How can anyone think they're not intelligent? They've certainly stayed ten steps ahead of you, Callum old boy.

He could see cunning in them. He could feel it in his heart, which still held tendrils of the dark force that'd taken him over at the mall this morning. And then he thought: *Was that only this morning?* He couldn't believe it.

It was all coming back. All happening again. Soon enough

here he was, at the park gate just like the fiends wanted him to be.

Driving around the gate, just like he had before.

Heedless of the security cameras because even if they could see him this time, nobody was watching the monitors. Why would they? This situation had spiraled far beyond anyone's control.

Time was running short for the fiends; Callum could tell that from what remained of his bond to their minds. That's why they'd wanted him to drive instead of walk: so he could reach the Gore Point before time ran out. There was a rift under the lake; it'd opened after Callum left the first time and had subsequently birthed everything now inside the Rampart. That rift wouldn't last much longer, though. He sensed a tug-of-war over it: one force rushing to close it while the fiends around him rushed Callum toward it, knowing their only hope to keep it open was for Callum to get there first.

Oh yes. He knew what they wanted him to do. He didn't want to do it, but his fate had been sealed the moment Mary and Nathan came to him — probably the reason the fiends had allowed Callum to pick them up in the first place. After that, the demons had their leverage. After that, it'd simply been a matter of following the only choices that wouldn't get them killed.

Yes, Callum had had many ideas about escape, but the demons had had them first. He knew a car could outrun them, but they'd formed a gauntlet to guide him: twin walls of bodies between which Callum was supposed to drive. He'd thought maybe he could plow through them — just yank the wheel sideways, run down one of the gauntlet walls, and drive anywhere but Suicide Flats — but they'd anticipated that; every fiend in the gauntlet had its claws out, held low enough to spear his tires. If he tried to leave the line, they'd cripple the car and drag his family out of it.

The gauntlet was long and straight. From the Rampart to Wasatch-Cache was four or five miles, and yet the entire distance had been lined with fiends. It reminded Callum of Hands Across America. How many of them were there? Were they somehow recycling: fiends at the back of the line coming forward to cover the car again after it'd passed? How could they, though, if they couldn't move faster than he could drive? The alternative — that every fiend he passed was unique, and he never passed the same ones twice — meant there must be thousands of fiends in Fortune. He tried to do the math (fiends were X feet wide, divided into five miles), but it was just whistling in the dark. Just a way to distract his mind so it wouldn't focus on where he was, what stakes they'd set, and what he'd soon have to do.

Mary asked questions. Callum pretended he didn't know the answers. He tried, awkwardly, to hold a discussion they could have had yesterday — one that ignored all the demons around them. Mary thought he was doing it for Nathan and tried to play along, but Nathan was in and out, not well, trying to keep a brave face for his parents' sake. All of them were trying to put on airs for the other two.

Time passed, somehow, as the living nightmare played out.

It was early dusk by the time they arrived at the park gate. Callum tried to bargain with the fiends outside, arguing absurdly in English for them to let his family go. *I'll do whatever you want if they can get out of the car and leave safely,* he said. They were demons, though, and they didn't understand. Or didn't want to. Or had thoughts of their own, maybe, like: *You'll do whatever we want no matter what. Even if we shred their non-vital parts to ribbons. Even if we torture them. You'll do whatever because you have no choice, if you want them to live.*

Callum had cast his die. He shouldn't have gone to the Rampart. Mary and Nathan might have escaped without him. *With* him, though, they'd become bargaining chips. Now, maybe they'd survive but maybe they wouldn't. Those who thought they knew so much had turned out wrong: demons were *plenty* intelligent. Intelligent enough to make a deal. The only question left, then (and the answer didn't matter; it's not like Callum had options) was whether they were intelligent enough to keep the deals they'd made.

Were demons honorable in their agreements? Were they fair? The answers to those questions seemed obvious, but what was Callum to do? Should he take a risk now and find out the hard way, or do what they commanded and at least have a chance?

He parked where he had before, amused after turning off the engine to realize how obedient-to-the-core he was. He'd actually pulled into a parking spot. Not the handicapped spot, either, which was closer to where he was about to go. He'd parked perfectly between the lines, so he wouldn't find a ticket when he returned to the car later on.

But he wouldn't *be* returning to the car. Not today. Not ever.

Callum was down to his final minutes. The end was close.

Even from here he could see the undulating, shimmering light of the rift's aurora in the darkening sky as he stood from the car, with his demon escorts around him.

CHAPTER 28

NOTHING

"Okay," said Eldon, sitting up straight on the opposite side of the hill from the two groups of fiends. "We're just going to have to run for it."

"That's idiotic," said Carrie.

Eldon looked over. Hadn't she been a nursing student this morning? Hadn't she basically been Callum's son's babysitter?

"You saw what I saw, right?" Carrie went on. "They're not in one big group. They're in two: the ones in the middle, taking apart the power station to kill the electricity, plus the circle farther out. Do you think they picked that arrangement randomly? Do you think they'd set up like that just to be fooled by runners?"

"What — you're saying they *know* we have a weapon with limited range?"

"That's exactly what I'm saying," Carrie said. "They've perfectly defended against it. Unless we can get past the outer line, we'll be too far away to hurt the group in the middle. If we use the Rattler on the outer group, it'll be used up and, again, we can't touch the group in the middle. You think that's a coincidence? Weird defensive choice for any old weapon, don't you think?"

"Maybe you should leave this to the people who know a thing or two," Eldon said.

"Men?"

"Scientists."

"She's right," said Brie.

Eldon stared at her, feeling betrayed. It was one thing for the only female scientist to disagree with him, but another to do it at the exact moment he'd been accused of misogyny.

"She is, huh?"

"She is," Denny agreed. "GEN's spent a lot of time trying to understand the interplay of their hive mind with the phenomenon of individuation. We think, like *you* think, that they have a leadership caste — maybe even a king of some kind. If that's true, those in charge would have to be individuals. At least *partial* individuals. So this isn't new. Their evolution would already have had to solve it. They're either able to communicate without telepathy or able to use their telepathy selectively and partially rather than completely. I already used a Rattler, remember? I blew myself out of a serpent. Other fiends saw that happen. My guess is that even the individuals here have at least a rudimentary mental collective. They're set up perfectly to defend against a Rattler because they know a Rattler works. Because they know that by now, we'd've made another one."

Eldon wanted to protest out of pride. He slouched instead, knowing that Denny — and Brie, and even Carrie — were right. He'd liked it better when everyone thought the fiends were nothing more than swarm animals. Even if they weren't the usual definition of "intelligent," which they might well be, they were at least *instinctually* intelligent. They knew how to identify a threat, then guard against it. If Eldon, Carrie, Denny, and Brie simply tried to storm the outer line, they'd be dismantled like machines made of meat. They'd only peeped the fiends over the hill briefly before ducking down to stay unseen, but even that glimpse was enough to dissuade someone with a brain. The fiends weren't just lolling around over there. They were attentive, readier than ready.

"What if you broke the Rattler in two?" Eldon asked. "Make two small Rattlers instead of one big one."

Denny shook his head, shifting the firehouse laundry bag in which he'd placed the globe-bomb. "I don't have a second shell, or a way to glue the first shell back together if I did. I'd have to make a second fuse, and I don't have that either. But more importantly, it wouldn't work because a smaller Rattler wouldn't be big enough to take out the center group. Even if we were able to use half of it on the first line, we wouldn't have enough left to stop the ones taking apart the power lines."

"And we don't have a way to get more lab-grade graphite or carbon," Brie added. "Not quickly enough, we don't."

As if to emphasize Brianne's point, something briefly illuminated the darkening sky over the hill: a pop, fizzle, and shower of sparks as the fiends cut another line, and another grid of homes went dark. They were racing a ticking clock. As soon as the last of the power died, there'd be no point in storming the circle at all. How much longer could they have before the fiends' job here was done, and the Rampart became nothing more than a pile of stones?

"Maybe we could throw it," said Eldon. "Throw the Rattler over the first group and hope it gets close enough to the second group to do some damage."

"It's not actually a bomb," said Denny. "You know that, right? It's not 'throw and blow up.' I have to *operate* it."

"Besides," said Brianna, "is your arm that strong? It's not a football; it's a globe. We'd need a catapult to get it that far, and that's assuming it wouldn't break on impact."

"We can't just do nothing," said Eldon.

Nobody replied. *Nothing* was unacceptable, but it was also their only option.

Eldon was furious. They'd come this close, and now they were just going to let the world end? They'd come *this close* … and now not only was the Rampart going to fall, but Hell's mainline was also going to yawn wide to feed the rampage? He'd been checking the detector every few minutes, frustrated by how much trouble the hive mind seemed to be having in closing the rift. He knew what was making it difficult, and he almost had to admire the fiends for it. The demons in Fortune hadn't captured or killed Callum at the Rampart. Instead, the detector seemed to suggest they'd driven him back to the Gore Point. Because he was their prime emotional source, Callum's presence at the Gore Point seemed to be powering-up the rift in the same way he'd caused it to open in the first place.

Clever demons. They'd found a way to use Callum like a battery: a way to increase the rift's energy enough that the hive mind couldn't close it. As he moved closer to the rift, sealing it would become harder and harder. And if he *entered* the rift? Why, it might just rip all the way open. It might even expand, making the entire Gore Point one big rift from end to end.

"We *won't* do nothing," said Carrie.

Eldon practically gaped at her. Wasn't that exactly what they *were* doing? Hadn't she just knocked down the only possible course of action they had? Anything was better than nothing. He'd be damned if they planned to just sit here and wait for it all to be over.

Eldon wanted to know Carrie's plan — what "not doing nothing" looked like.

But she would only watch him with an inscrutable Mona Lisa smile, surer of their non-plan than she should be as the wan light of the distant rift grew brighter on the horizon, as Fortune's time on Earth grew shorter and shorter.

CHAPTER 29

THE MALLEABILITY OF BELIEF

Fiends surrounded them. Callum could smell their death. He could feel their heat. The clear area around Callum, Nathan, and Mary wasn't big enough to extend his arms all the way. They were lined up four or five deep around the family, taking no chances.

One of the demons shoved him, grunting.

"Don't rush me."

It roared. Demon spittle dusted Callum's cheek. Mary cringed back. Nathan, barely able to stand, wrapped his arms around his mother's middle.

"I have to leave," Callum told Mary. "I have to go on alone. It's the only way to keep you safe."

She began to scream, cry, and gibber without meaning. She clung to him, refusing to let go.

"No. *No*, Callum. Don't you dare leave us!"

"It's the only way. It's the only way they'll let you go."

"You don't know that."

"I know they'll never let you go if I don't."

She sobbed into his chest. He wrapped his arms around her. Nathan joined them, holding close.

"Shh," he said. It was easier to be strong for them than to face his own future. "You'll be okay."

"I want *you* to be okay too!"

"Shh," was all he could say.

It went on for a few minutes. One of the fiends growled, then put a clawed hand on Mary's shoulder to pull her away. Callum snapped instantly, no longer remotely afraid. He shoved the hand away, then charged the fiend without thinking. He managed to knock it back, clawing at it, swinging ineffective fists. The thing startled away from him, then leaned in and roared again.

Quiet returned, but he really had to leave now; the writing was on the wall. The rift was still out of sight, but its aurora kept growing brighter and brighter as the sky darkened. It looked like weightless fire, its lazy, hypnotic motions diffusing in all directions.

He pulled himself away from his family, then turned to the fiend he'd shoved. It retreated a half-step. Callum, who'd spent his life meek, found it incredibly satisfying. "If I do this, you will leave them alone," he said.

Its jaws opened. A line of hot drool descended to the ground slowly, like a spelunker.

"If you touch them," Callum said, "I'll cross your side of Hell to end each and every one of you."

When it didn't respond again, Mary said, "Callum, it doesn't understand you." She'd politely omitted the obvious: that there was no way for Callum to possibly deliver on his promise.

Without breaking contact with the demon's red-yellow eyes, Callum said cooly, "It doesn't matter. *I* understand me."

He stared it down for another few seconds, then turned to

his wife and son. He embraced each of them in turn. After, he lowered himself to face Nathan the way his father, when Callum was young, used to face him. *Man to man,* Dad used to say.

"Listen to me, Nathan. I want you to really listen to me."

Nathan nodded.

"I want you to be okay. Do you understand me? Whatever it takes, however it happens, in whatever way it's possible — I want you to be okay without me. Can you do that?"

"Callum ..." said Mary. She was thinking of the doctors, the disease, the way Nathan looked right now. The kid had a heart condition atop his terminal cancer. He could easily have a heart attack from all of this, and die right now.

Callum looked up sharply to silence her. To silence her doubts. She wasn't allowed to have doubts right now. Callum had lost most of his faith over the past few months, but right now he needed to believe what he was saying. He needed to have *faith in faith,* and doing so would take all of them.

Over the past hours, he'd had a lot of time to think. A lot of time to watch, and wait, and see what happened. And in that watching, waiting, and seeing, he'd started to believe something he'd never considered before: that all belief was arbitrary — every bit of it. That was good news. It meant he didn't need to wait for faith to find him. It meant that faith was a choice he could make: to believe what he wished to believe because *every* belief — good or bad, fact-based or blue-sky supposition — was only a guess. No single belief was a lie because until the future came, everything about it was a lie.

I can believe what the world is showing me, he thought, *or I can believe that somehow, some way, it will all be all right.*

Fool, said that internal voice — the detractor that'd hectored him his entire life.

But *was* he a fool to believe what he chose instead of what others insisted was real? The demons wanted him to enter the rift — to give himself to its power and give his power to it — and because they held all the cards, that's exactly what Callum was going do. In that way, it made no difference what he believed. But in another way, it made all the difference in the world. He could go to his death beaten, or he could go to it standing tall. What else mattered in the end?

"Can you promise you'll be okay?" he asked Nathan again. "Can you do that ... for me?"

"I can do that, Dad," Nathan said.

Callum hugged him, stood, and hugged Mary again.

Then he turned away and the demons followed. They left Mary and Nathan standing alone, almost as if they'd heard Callum's threat and believed it.

Callum did not look back. He couldn't. The bridge had been passed, and he had a new fate now.

Ahead the aurora throbbed brighter and brighter as he walked through Suicide Flats with Hell's minions around him. But Callum didn't need the aurora to see, even in the darkening sky. Because he'd decided:

No matter what, he'd carry his own light with him.

CHAPTER 30

OUT OF TIME

"Jesus," said Denny.

He'd taken the detector back from Eldon. He was operating it in ways Eldon hadn't, clearly exploiting options Denny had never bothered to explain.

When the others looked over, Denny's face was lit from below by the detector's display. The sky, save the occasional gush of sparks from over the hill as the fiends worked, was nearly dark.

"The rift is getting bigger. It's growing by terawatts."

"Because of Callum?" Brianna asked. In the absence of options, they'd spent the last bit sharing the rest of their thoughts, knowings, and theories, such as the fate and purpose of Minister MacReady.

"Basically," Denny replied. It meant the answer was more complicated but he didn't want to explain because it all boiled down to the same practical thing. "That big group of fiends — the one that stretched out in a line from the Rampart — is mostly at the Gore Point now. They're moving through Suicide Flats. I *think*. The energetics are pretty far beyond what I built this to measure. Right now, it's kind of like trying to keep track of someone shining a flashlight as they walk into the sun."

"Can the hive mind still close the rift?" asked Carrie. She understood the least, but insisted on being part of the discussion. She was so pushy. No wonder Eldon had come to like her.

"It either can or it can't," said Denny. "There's nothing we can do about it at this point. In my humble opinion, Fortune can't get much more fucked than it is right now, so I don't care too much about the rift itself in the short term. A thousand fiends inside Fortune, a hundred thousand … doesn't make a lot of difference, really. The Rampart is what matters. *Keeping them in* is what matters." He looked up, watched a new fountain of sparks fly into the sky, and after it they watched another section of city go dark around them. "I hate to say it, but I'm starting to agree with Eldon. *Something* might be better than *nothing*. We're almost out of time."

In the absence of ideas, they'd thus far chosen to discuss what they knew and hope new ideas came. Maybe time would change the situation, giving them options. Maybe the outer ring of demons would decide to join the others in the middle. Maybe they *weren't* defending against Rattlers and it was all just a coincidence, in which case they could take them by surprise. Maybe they'd break up, or get bored. Who knew? Carrie had been obnoxious about it. She kept saying that everything was for a reason and the right things always happened in the end, so if they just hung back, a solution would eventually present itself. To Eldon, it sounded like hippie bullshit. *Hoping* would get them nowhere. *Trying* at least gave them a shot.

"Look," said Denny. "I'm guessing at the Rattler's range. I don't know how far away it'll work. Maybe we should just get as close as we can and take a shot. It also might rattle for longer than I think it will. It might kill the outer line, but keep rattling as we run for the center. Like I said, I've only been guessing."

"Your guesses aren't usually *guesses*, Denny," said Brianne.

Denny shrugged. It was true.

"We should keep waiting," said Carrie.

"No," said Eldon. "I'm through waiting."

"There will be a way. There's always a way."

Eldon snapped. "Says what? Your inner eye? Your guru? For fuck's sake, there can't be more than one or two grids left before the Rampart falls! *We are out of time.*"

"How's your smash and grab worked so far, Eldon? Punch first, think second ... right?"

"Listen, goddammit," said Eldon, moving closer to Carrie. "We're *under attack.* We're talking about things that can be touched and felt and counted here, not some fucking will o' the wisp. So here's what we're going to do. We're going to get out of the lotus position and off our meditation pillows, and we're going to go in swinging. I'm okay with the Rollard. You've got your shotgun, and Brie can back us up with the axe. All we need is to punch a hole in the defensive line so Denny can get through with the Rattler. In fact — sorry, Denny, but maybe someone in better shape should do the running. You take the gun. Now, that's as good a plan as any. If we take them by surprise, we might get lucky."

"And we might not!" Carrie was whisper-yelling, but still Eldon wanted to shush her. Or maybe he wanted to encourage her — make her louder, not quieter. If the fiends heard them and came running, they'd at least be forced into action. In fact, maybe that was even better: cause a distraction first, so the line would break up and come to them. If they did that, then maybe, just *maybe* ...

A flash of from the Gore Point interrupted him. All four heads whipped toward the light of the rift's distant aurora, where a power source called Callum MacReady had just started to rip Hell wide open.

Without thinking, Eldon stood to his full height. He was visible now; all the fiends over the rise would need to do would be to turn what passed for their heads. But none were looking toward (or sensing, with various sensory apparatus) the humans. All their unholy eyes were on the rift's aurora. It had grown bright red and yellow, as bright as a second sunrise.

The line of fiends were impervious. The light wasn't surprising them. They'd known the rift would expand, and now their most crucial moment was nigh.

But then, just as Eldon was about to run at the line whether his compatriots followed him or not, something in the aurora changed.

And the change, finally, *did* surprise them.

CHAPTER 31

BEAUTIFUL

Cecret Lake was a dark mouth yawning in the parched ground of Suicide Flats. Its water had completely drained or boiled away, leaving a sludgy black residue on its emptied sides. From where Callum stood, he could see water, presumably from an aquifer, seeping through the soil and trying to refill it. Instead, the water trickled down the slopes into the maw of Hell. It made it to the lip of the fire-filled rift at the lake's bottom, then flashed instantly to steam.

The rift was a sun burning inside Cecret's shallow bowl: a captive, enormous flare rising from the world's blackest fire pit. To Callum, its plasma-hot breath, full of ionized particles, looked like a geyser made of flame. It was a building-sized blowtorch ... and they expected him to walk right into it.

It's okay, he tried to tell himself, though he'd lost a lot of the resolve he'd had minutes ago. *I choose to have faith. I choose to believe this is all for the best.*

It was a hollow hope. A stupid prayer. *All for the best?* He was about to walk into an eye of fire.

He tried to think of Nathan.

At first, he could only see Nathan as he'd been: in bed, barely able to sit up, looking up at his parents from what Callum worried each day would become his deathbed. The image evoked despair, fear, and pity. And guilt. Because as soon as he thought of Nathan, he was there all over again. He was at the door of Nathan's room, not wanting to enter. He'd been a coward so often. He'd thought of himself so often. Had he really had Nathan's best interests in mind, or had he instead been praying secretly for it to end?

Nathan was on the way out; there was no longer much doubt about that. He could rally for short times — even sometimes battle back the cancer's advance a little — but it always returned to the same thing. It'd been months and months of fighting. Months and months of struggle for no sustainable reward. So a person had to ask: Who was winning, as the situation dragged out? Not Nathan; he was always in pain. Not Mary. Certainly not Callum, who had to stand in front of a church each week and pretend he believed God would save him — maybe not on Earth, but certainly Nathan's soul in Heaven.

It'd been shallow comfort. He hadn't really wanted to have faith. Faith required suspension of the moment: a sort of spiritual holding of breath, making *now* last longer while a hopefully-brighter future took shape. Faith was exhausting. As time went on, it became crippling. The more time passed with Nathan worsening, the more painful faith became. It'd been easy to believe at the beginning: faith for beginners. But as the days darkened, faith became a million-pound weight. It was lifting all of the sensible universe, trying to believe that some nugget of difference had been hiding beneath it.

No. That's not what you believe.

A new voice. Or rather, a very old one. Callum hadn't heard

that particular mental voice since he'd been in seminary —
back when he'd been nothing but sunshine and good intentions. Back then, he'd held firm to his faith — not just in God,
but in people, in nature, in the perfect order of things. Back
then, he'd really believed that all happenings could be good
happenings. There was order to the universe, even if humans
refused to understand it.

*Don't let the doubts in, Callum. Don't you dare let guilt and
hatred define you.*

His eyes went to the rift. It was fiery red: the color of his
anger. The color of his rage. The color of all the terrible things
he'd thought and felt as life turned its thumbscrews. The
longer he watched, standing on the lip of the empty lake with
demons behind him — not pushing, but waiting for this
voluntary sacrifice — the more he began to see the rift as a
physical embodiment of his own worst pieces. And was that
really so absurd? He knew he'd brought the thin spot at the
lake's bottom the fuel it needed to open in the first place. He'd
chosen to be angry and desperate instead of hopeful. He'd
chosen to mourn what he was losing instead of appreciating
what he still had. He'd still had Nathan. He'd still had him even
now. He'd had Mary, and he'd had his friends, and he'd had all
the small blessings life had given him. He'd had his life so far,
and his home, and the bounty of nature. He'd had clean air and
a life free of physical danger. But had he brought optimism to
Suicide Flats that day? Or had he brought a glass that was
already half empty?

You'd had every right, said the dark voice. *God had left you.
You were losing your son.*

True. That's what he'd felt. But wasn't belief a choice? Hadn't
he just decided that? He'd told Nathan to do something Callum
himself had never been able to do: to simply *decide to be okay.* What
if he'd done that yesterday? What if instead of coming to the lake

with blackness inside, he'd come with light? Would that have fed them? Would the first fiend have hungered at optimism and gratefulness? Could all of this have been avoided, if Callum had chosen the hard path instead of accepting the feelings that came easy?

The rift was him. He was the rift. The rift was fury, like he'd been fury. The rift was all that was wrong. All the pain. All the illness and sadness and horror and pain.

So choose, said the voice of a younger, better Callum. *In this last moment, where you have no more choices, you can still choose what you believe.*

In front of him, the red rift flickered. Some of its effluxing jets of fire sparked blue, purple, green — the way a fireplace does if you toss a penny among the logs.

You're going to die today, Callum MacReady, said the voice of light. *But* how *will you die? Will you choose to walk into Hell, or will you go with chosen joy, and make your own Heaven?*

Movement caught his eye. He looked up and, beyond the circle of demons around the rift, waiting like druids around a sacrificial altar, he saw a human head. A human shoulders.

The complete form of a human boy.

It was Nathan, standing alone in the trees. He wasn't coming forward; he'd stopped where he was. Callum's first thought was that Nathan shouldn't see this; a boy shouldn't have to watch his father die. But then a strange thought occurred: *Is that really what he's watching, Callum? Is he witnessing surrender, or a triumph?*

He could see Nathan's face. He did not look afraid and he did not look mournful. As Callum watched, he raised a hand: almost a wave, but not quite. The gesture suddenly told Callum all he needed to know.

Nathan *would* be okay. If not on Earth, than at least until he left it.

The flame sparked blue. Yellow. Green.

Nathan might live. He might die. But he was not afraid, because he was watching his father face his own ending and Callum, too, was not afraid.

An explosion of purple. A rush and a jet of orange, crimson, emerald green. The effluent became less violent. Less like a blowtorch and more like a wave. Or a dance.

The fiends around the edges of the lake began to stir. Their lines broke, undulated, shifted and separated.

It was true, he realized: *He was not afraid.*

Mary came up behind Nathan, rushed as if he'd gotten away and she'd just caught him. *She* saw now, and she too stood and waited. Her face was more complex than Nathan's, awash with more adult emotions. But she met his eyes. And he met hers.

And he felt not hate, not pain, not regret, not guilt … but love.

And he could feel those emotions — love, and gratefulness, and acceptance, and joy — feeding into the rift instead of the terrible emotions he'd fed it thus far. It wasn't what the fiends wanted. He refused to give them what he'd given before. He refused — because he could still make choices, could still decide to believe — to deliver the horrid, intolerable pain that Hell expected and wanted of him.

The rift began to cough. To churn. Its colors shifted like a prism, its entire energy changing. Instead of pure, deadly red, the aurora was now wavering curtains of color: not the look of hate, but of a rainbow.

Callum sank into it. He let himself become it. The aurora billowed out to him, enfolding him, making him part of it. It no longer wanted to destroy. Callum refused to let it, if he was its source of fuel. He would not be the power cell that destroyed the world. If he was to give it power, it would be power he'd chosen.

The demons began to chatter. To growl. He could feel them behind and around him, shaking him, clawing at him, opening his flesh in an attempt to shift his spectrum back to darkness. But Callum had made his choice. He watched his wife and son, and he was grateful for what he'd had.

"It's beautiful," he said.

A huge dark hand pushed Callum from behind. He tripped, then tumbled down the empty lake's shore. When he stopped, he was still shy of the rift. But now it was beckoning him rather than threatening him. It was not Hell's door he stood at, but God's welcoming arms.

We are what we choose to be, he thought. *We go where we choose to go.*

He sent his mind out to Mary. To Nathan. To the people of Fortune. To the people of the Earth. And he remembered — he remembered that old quote about being the change you wanted to see in the world. He almost laughed, even though he suspected he was fatally bleeding. He laughed because he'd never seen this coming. He'd never known things would work out as beautifully, as perfectly as they had.

He *was* the change. He could be all the change the world needed right now, if he chose to be.

Callum crawled forward, knowing all was well. And as he entered the rift, finally leaving his body, he realized he was smiling.

CHAPTER 32

RED ROVER

Two miles away, all eyes watched the aurora transform. It no longer looked like a rift. It was more like a self-contained rainbow.

Eldon stared, gape-mouthed. Even Denny, with all his knowledge and equipment, was speechless. The fiends still hadn't noticed them. How could they? They could only see the rift. They could only feel the strange new energy that came from it — an energy that even the humans could feel: no longer menacing, but something else entirely. Standing in its electromagnetic wind, Eldon felt almost buoyant. The world had become a child's birthday cake, and on the wind was nothing but happy wishes.

"Go," Carrie said. *"This is our chance!"*

Without waiting, she ran right past him. Half of Eldon wanted to protest, if only because he didn't want her thinking she'd been right all along. But she had been, hadn't she? Maybe everything didn't happen for a reason, and maybe things didn't always turn out if you were patient enough to wait. But they had this time. This time, there was no question they had.

The demons were entirely scattered. Entirely distracted, confused, upended. They looked to Eldon like they were losing their minds. He ran forward, stood next to Carrie as she watched, unhurried, and waited for the situation to mature into what it was trying to become. The sky wasn't dark anymore. Daytime had returned to Fortune by the rift's illumination, and all that was missing from the multicolored light show was unicorns.

"You said *now*," Eldon told her.

But Carrie was laughing. *Laughing.* Something was coming right at them from the Gore Point, and it made them feel drunk. Eldon, who'd lived a serious life, found himself almost giddy. Twenty-nine years old and he felt like a little kid again.

Carrie took his hand and held it very tight.

"*Red rover, red rover,*" she shouted at the fiends, literally giggling. "*Send Satan over!*"

Then she ran. And, half-dragged, Eldon ran beside her. As his feet caught up with him, as he gave in to whatever strange force was causing this shift and this emotion, he wanted to tell Carrie that she had it wrong. The people with linked hands weren't supposed to run in a game of Red Rover. They were supposed to hold tight while the runner from the other side tried to break through. It was a game of sprained muscles and torn rotator cuffs. It was a game of pure childlike foolishness that would probably die in the 1990s. But then the thought went away, and he ran with her. As if they'd known each other forever. As if this was the best day of his life, and there were nothing but blue skies ahead.

When they hit the first fiend, it didn't see them coming. Their conjoined arms slapped it forward at the neck, driving it into the ground. But still they ran on, Eldon remembering with fantastic absurdity that he was still holding the Rollard in his left hand while Carrie still held the shotgun in her right. They clotheslined another two confused demons that way, then broke apart as they hit their fourth. Carrie laughed as she fluidly moved both hands to her shotgun, blowing a grapefruit-sized hole in the chest of a big horned thing that made the mistake of running at her.

Eldon swung the Rollard. It became a game. He axed, forked, stabbed. Axed, forked, stabbed. Blood flew. Bile spattered. It was the best time he'd ever had. Demons roared. Bellowed. *Screamed.* But they were outmatched now; all they'd been expecting and braced for had upended in two quick seconds.

Callum, you beautiful man, Eldon thought. He didn't know what had happened ... but he knew, somehow, that Callum had done it.

Shotgun blasts. A flash of motion as Brianna used her axe. They were practically unopposed; the fiends' disorientation was that great. Anyone could rack up kills here. Even ...

Where was Denny?

And then Eldon saw him: that fat little dork with his popcorn hair, running so fast down the far side of the hill between them and the power station that it looked like he'd overbalance and fall on his face. He carried the absurd globe in front of him like a nerd late for geography class.

It took long seconds before Eldon remembered their mission. The demons around them seemed to remember it at the same time, spotting Denny's rush for the power station at the same time Eldon did. Most had already spied him and were rushing toward him — enough that Denny quickly disappeared into the crowd. Even the fiends that Eldon and Carrie had been fighting soon turned and tried to run at Denny ... so Eldon and Carrie, with their respective weapons, killed them from behind.

The clot behind Denny thickened as he approached the fiends dismantling Fortune's power grid.

There was a tremendous roar, but it was too late. Whatever Denny did to activate the Rattler — a shake, it seemed — sent a concussionless shockwave out from the center. Eldon felt it pass, but there was no force to it. Instead of annihilating him, it cleared his head. In the bleat between the wave and the next thing, he found himself clearheaded enough to look at Carrie and smile.

Then it was like the center exploded, soundless, and all the fiends within the blast radius began to rupture like balloons, keeling over dead.

Eldon fell to the grass. Carrie fell beside him. Amongst all the dead, they laid on their backs and watched the shimmering aurora like teenage lovers watching the stars.

Eventually the light in the sky began to dim, slowly, as the distant rift closed. It took long and beautiful minutes to fade, like sunset.

Eldon, again with Carrie's hand in his, never wanted it to end.

CHAPTER 33
LEGIONS AND STITCHERS

SIX MONTHS LATER

"Well," Carrie said, flopping onto the couch hard enough to push it backward an inch, "I'm fired."

She was smiling at Eldon. Aggressively so. It felt like a middle finger, that smile.

He waited for more. He'd grown careful about being drawn in by Carrie's baiting. As soon as she'd realized how serious he was all the time, she'd started being excessively chipper on purpose. It wasn't really an attempt to draw him out or improve his outlook on life. It was mostly just to fuck with him.

"You seem pretty broken up about it," he said.

"Mary. Mary fired me. That bitch."

She was still smiling. Eldon sat up, understanding. Now he really did feel a bit less serious. "You're kidding," he said.

"No. Not kidding at all. I'm totally out of a job."

"Remission?"

Carrie shook her head. *"Cure.* Do you know how reluctant doctors are to use that word? I asked her if I could look through Nathan's scans myself, just to satisfy my curiosity. Not only were they completely clean; his oncologist actually wrote 'cure' in the discharge report."

"My God."

"Will you thank Denny for her, for getting Nathan into the trial? For both of us?"

"Of course."

"Give him a big kiss. From Mary."

"I'll get him a bottle of that bourbon he likes."

Eldon felt dazed. He'd known Zen Element could undo cell damage. He'd seen that much in his own work, but he'd secretly thought it wouldn't go much beyond eye cream for rich women. He should have known. He should have believed Denny. Denny had said all along that comparing raw Zen Element to refined Zen Element was like comparing a cap gun to a bazooka, but ... *a cure for cancer?* How did that even work? Cancer was cells proliferating *too* well: life being *too* abundant. Did treatment with an anti-entropic kill tumors, or make them into something more productive? He'd have to look into it. Right now, most of the uses for Zen Element that'd exploded in the past months felt about as scientifically grounded to Eldon as magic.

"So Mary's happy? To say the least?"

"She is." Carrie moved to sit beside Eldon, wanting to be close. The second bit of furniture in their living room was called a love seat for a reason. She put her head on Eldon's chest and said, "But it's bittersweet. It makes her miss Callum. She says he should have been around to see it. That he never really had much hope for Nathan's condition ... but what a difference a few months make."

"He had hope," Eldon said.

Carrie was quiet. Then she said, "Yeah, I guess he did."

They stayed that way for a while. The wall clock ticked. A loud, big-machine engine started across the street: the Jacobys' contractors, firing up earth-movers to put in their swimming pool. The Jacobys were new. Nice folks. They'd moved to Fortune at the same absurd time as so many others came to replace the dead. That was the power of government spin, Eldon supposed. Yes, the whole world knew now that other planes and fiends existed ... and yes, most people thought of them as *Hell* and *demons* despite the propaganda. But last year's invasion had been officially declared a "statistically unique event" certain to never happen again, and that white-washing (plus a lot of evidence-hiding and unheard-of govern-ment-incentive homebuyer programs and tax credits) had let Fortune boom again. Never underestimate the power of greed and telling people what they wanted to hear, Eldon supposed.

"You know, I was thinking," Carrie said. "It's strange. Denny said that Zen Element refining was still in its infancy, right? There are some things they've figured out, but suppos-edly the big leaps are still years — maybe decades — away?"

"They are. But that's because we didn't know a lot of our processes are backward for use with Zen. It makes sense now, but we're used to things like NMR and spectrography obeying the usual laws of physics. You can't scan something with an electron microscope if it re-orders electrons, though. Some-times the electrons don't even seem to go anywhere. They just kind of vanish."

"Yeah, right," said Carrie, not caring about this part. "But I mean, how exactly did scientists figure out to try what they're doing now? What changed to make refining Zen Element easier now than it was before? When did it start to happen?"

"When a new kind of pre-rift popped up and got GEN thinking in ways it hadn't before. It showed them that Zen Element exhibits a Heisenberg response at macro levels under certain conditions." Again Eldon thought: *Magic, not science.* But it *was* science — just backwards.

"Yeah yeah. But *when?*"

"When the energetics started to change."

"And when was that?"

"After the rift."

"After *Callum.*"

Eldon considered that. It was fair. "Okay, sure. After Callum."

"You remember what Mary and Nathan said. They saw him go in. Whatever we felt at the power plant, they felt up close. At the epicenter, y'know?"

Eldon knew what she was getting at, and it — like the backwards science — wasn't very surprising in retrospect. Eldon was still the only human that the slightly-changed hive mind would talk to through the communication chamber, but even as the hive mind grew less talkative and more aggressive, it still responded to Eldon's thoughts. He'd never once opened his mouth to communicate with the other plane, so how else could they be speaking if it wasn't psychic? If it wasn't, in some way, thought-reading?

In the same way, based on everything Mary had told them about that day, even GEN believed it was Callum's own energy — his own psychically-linked mind — that'd changed the rift. It certainly wasn't the rift itself or the demons around it. They, like the demons at the power station, hadn't *wanted* different energy. They'd been so disrupted by it, in fact, that it'd spoiled their plans and allowed the rift to close right in front of them.

It wasn't the hive mind that'd changed the energy that day, either. Eldon knew because as well as he could, he'd asked. And so, after all the other possible influences were eliminated, the only factor remaining was Callum. And it made sense: If Callum's dark emotions had called the first fiend across the boundary, his better emotions would affect them, too.

Mary said Callum had gone into the rift smiling. *Smiling.* Given that and the rest, it was more negligent to ignore the *Callum-as-change-agent* theory than to embrace it.

"Well don't you get it?" Carrie said. "Callum's the reason the refiners figured it out. *Callum's* the reason Zen Element took such a big leap. You see? Mary wishes Callum could be around to see Nathan live his life ... but Callum is the *reason* Nathan is *able* to live his life. If not for him, there'd be no cure!"

"That's a bit of a stretch, don't you think?"

"It's not a stretch at all."

"Scientifically speaking," Eldon said.

Carrie, returning her head to his chest, punched him lightly in the stomach.

It was true, though, if he set aside his evidence-based needs for a minute. He didn't need test tubes and chromatography to measure what'd happened that day with Callum. He'd *felt* it, and so had Carrie. So had Nathan, and Mary, and Denny, and Brianna. So had the people of Fortune, in fact; all those good vibes were probably the reason so many of them emerged from their hiding places that night to kill hundreds of fiends with chainsaws and machetes ... which in turn was probably all that kept them from attacking the power plant a second time. If Eldon ignored his need to dot all the I's and cross all the T's, the facts were plain: Mary said Callum had made Nathan swear he'd be okay ... and six months later, *Nathan was okay.*

But he couldn't tell Carrie that. He couldn't tell her how

perfectly it'd all worked out. Truth was, if Callum hadn't started the demon invasion by accident, he wouldn't have had a chance to finish it on purpose the next day, thereby causing the epiphany that made Zen refining take its big leap. He couldn't tell Carrie that if none of it had happened, Nathan MacReady would almost certainly be dead by now. Eldon had a million reasons why her logic was shit (a lot of other people died, so was "the grand plan" honestly to sacrifice most of a city to save one boy?), but he knew that if he said any of that to Carrie, she'd deflect him effortlessly. *You just haven't seen the full picture yet,* she'd say. *Have some faith, will you?*

"I have news too," Eldon told her.

"You *also* got fired?"

"The opposite, actually. The Legions voted today on who they want to head the formation of three more Brigades."

Carrie sat up, genuinely pleased. "And you won?"

"Unanimously."

"That's amazing! They still need more Brigades for cleanup?"

Eldon shook his head. "We've pretty much found and killed all the leftover fiends from the original rift. Last week some guy found one of those little round ones — the Pac-Man-looking things they call 'chomp-daddies' — in his shed, but that's what we're down to now. Hard to believe how many fiends came out of that rift. I checked the master tally about a month ago and it was almost a thousand. Even *after* the first night when citizens killed ... what? Like six or seven hundred of them? Even after that, almost *a thousand* were still marooned when Callum's distraction allowed the hive mind to shut the door."

"So what are the new Brigades for?"

"Protection from *new* rifts."

Carrie sat up.

"I think it'll be okay," Eldon said. "Like Denny predicted, we got a nice, long quiet period before enough pressure built up in the other plane. Now GEN says the pressure's back and it's only a matter of time, but we used our time well. We did our homework. *GEN* did its homework. Denny thinks they've got a pretty good idea of the classes of fiends that exist over there now, and they have a pretty good idea how to kill each of them. They've made new Legion weapons for us — one for each class of fiend. We have enough weapons, we've been training with them, and we're more or less ready. They won't catch us unprepared this time. This time, we'll be ready."

"You're just going to walk up to new rifts and kill what comes out, huh?" Carrie said, sounding doubtful.

Eldon pulled her closer and kissed the top of her head. "We'll be okay."

"If the hive mind is infected now, how will you get the rifts closed?"

"GEN has the stitching resin ready, too. That's also part of my new job — hiring and training more people."

"More Legions?"

"Different function. We're calling them 'Stitchers.'"

They were quiet again. This time the silence felt heavy, as if Carrie was troubled. She had good reason. The briefing Eldon had been given — only some of whose content he was allowed to share with his fiancée — had bothered him plenty. The nature of the other plane and the Gore Point had changed. The two worlds used to merely inspect each other, but now things felt closer to a cold war. Eldon was less scientist than ever lately. He was — and would increasingly need to become — more of a warrior. He'd headed the lab in peacetime ... but as what GEN called "riftfare" ramped up in the coming years, it'd be Eldon who led the Legions in their new normal of wartime.

"We should go for a walk," Carrie said. "Get out of the house. Distract me a little."

"We could go to Wasatch-Cache," Eldon said. "Did you hear? They've gotten so cocky since Cecret Lake refilled with blue water, they've reopened everything but the spot around the old rift."

"No thanks," said Carrie.

"Oh, come on. There are a whole bunch of new freak settlements in the Flats. They're sacrificing goats and everything."

"They're not really sacrificing goats, are they?" Carrie asked.

"No. *Shh.*"

"Did you just shush me?"

"I *'shh'd'* you," Eldon said. "There's a difference."

"You know, we met with me kicking you in the balls."

"I apologize," he said. "Please treat my balls kindly."

The were quiet again. The banter was less fun than it should be.

"How about we just walk around the neighborhood?" she finally said. "You know ... pretend it's not Hell on Earth?"

Eldon smiled at her. "It's a date."

AUTHOR'S NOTE

I started writing professionally in 2012. And before you start cracking wiseass jokes about how "professional" it is to write about people being kicked in the nuts, I'll clarify that I meant "authoring books for a living," not "being mature." I've done the first for over a dozen years as I write this. I'll let you know if I ever accomplish the second.

In that time, I wrote about 150 books. So it's notable that, in the two years immediately prior to writing *Suicide Flats*, I wrote exactly zero. I'm still trying to find the answer to why. Part of the answer, I know: I'd separated from my previous publisher and taken most of my rights with me, necessitating a shit-ton of administrative work to get my pre-existing books back on sale. That work — including all the stuff readers don't know about that's required behind the scenes — was a literal year's worth. So in some ways, I wasn't writing because my mind was on other things, and because I simply didn't have the time.

But there was another reason — one I had to write this book to find out. See, I began my professional writing career (there's that word again) as what we call a "pantser": an author who wrote by the seat of his pants with very little idea what was coming next at any given time. It wasn't an ideal approach. I tended to get lost in the weeds. Things got much easier when I started writing books with Sean Platt, with whom I've written most of my stuff. Sean would come up with a big-picture idea and an outline, and we'd discuss (and then modify) that outline before I started writing. As time went on, we found a rhythm wherein I'd end up ignoring most of the outline, but Sean was always there reading new words right behind me. We'd meet, discuss, make a new next-chapters plan, and then I'd return to the races. Then, when I'd finished the entire rough draft, Sean would edit it and make it shine.

We called our approach "plotsing," because it was somewhere between the two accepted types of writers: the "pantser" I'd been and what authors would call a "plotter," who follows a strict outline. We worked the middleground, and for a long time, it worked.

Problem was, we were also teaching writing to other authors at the time, and teaching made me think about elements of story structure I'd never even *considered* in my own writing because it came intuitively to me: three acts, an inciting incident, rising action, climax, resolution, stakes, character arcs, and a whole lot more. Once those things were in my head, I started applying them to my own writing. After all, it wouldn't hurt to have some awareness of what I'd been doing naturally, would it? We'd always ended up with layered, complex books with a million intricate loops and callbacks, so I started trying to find newer and cooler ways — this time using what I'd reinforced in myself by teaching it — to write layered, complex books with a million intricate loops and callbacks.

But as things turned out, being aware of what I'd always done by gut *did* hurt. Thinking about story analytically was a bad idea: the whole "trying" thing. See, my previous books *became* layered and complex ... but they never *started* that way. The best ones began with dead-simple ideas: a gunslinger rides a unicorn instead of a horse *(Unicorn Western),* an overweight guy becomes a vampire only to find he's not good enough for the world's pretty vampires *(Fat Vampire),* a murderous shapeshifter is on the run from the law *(Cursed),* or what we thought of as "*Downton Abbey* with robots" *(Robot Proletariat).* Those ideas were straightforward with no layers at the beginning. The layers were an effect, not the cause, and naturally showed up as I wrote.

At the time, I hadn't understood something I fully accept now: that I don't actually *invent* my stories. In truth, I've always *discovered* them. Stephen King has a metaphor for his own process that he gives in his book *On Writing* that I couldn't agree with more: that stories are like buried fossils. The writer discovers something interesting just barely peeking out of the ground (the seed of an idea), then pokes around with the tools of their trade to see what it is. The shape of what's buried, though, only reveals itself as the writer excavates. Until then, the writer is just as clueless as the reader. Using that metaphor, I've always unearthed very elaborate stories ... but when I first discovered them, they were nothing more than tiny pieces sticking up from featureless ground.

Failing to realize this was (in addition to life getting in the way and all that administrative work) the main reason I didn't write for two years: I was sabotaging myself by overthinking things. Instead of immersing myself in flow, I'd begun taking my old, gut-level writing process and inspecting it with a microscope. I'd started insisting on knowing the shape of the fossil was before I dug it up, in other words. Or, worse: No matter what the fossil might *actually* be, I wanted to shape it myself, and turn it into something else.

In the beginning, I'd written on instinct: too much self-assured swagger to think about what I was doing. But now, instead of just bulldozing ahead like I used to, I'd started to think about it. I wanted to see how my mind worked, so I broke down my process to see if I could figure out what made it tick. I started saying to that natural, ephemeral process, "I command you to make *this specific thing* for me." But it didn't work that way. I couldn't tell the earth which fossils I wanted it to give me. Doing so only ensured I'd find no fossils at all.

And so slowly, I shut down. I managed to write a few books in those years by muscling my way through them, but the resulting novels were left-brained, analytical endeavors that weren't fun for me at all. The books came out well (my mind-bender *Pattern Black* is one of them, and it's a reader favorite), but I didn't enjoy creating them. They were slow and artificial to write instead of the care-free abandon of my early years. By the end, I hated those books and just wanted them to end. (Although yes, I did learn to love them in time.)

To make matters worse, my constant collaborator Sean wasn't able to write with me during those problematic years ... and still won't be able for the immediate future as I write this. That meant that if I was going to write, I'd have to do it alone. I've always had trouble writing alone. I can do it (after all, I wrote all of our collaborative first drafts alone in addition to my twelve solo books), but Sean was my security blanket. I knew he was there even if I never asked for help. Just knowing support existed was somehow enough.

So there I was in the middle of 2024, completing my administrative work and running out of ways to convince myself that it was okay to not be writing. I knew I was kidding myself. I knew it was time to write again, but I'd failed a few times in the interim: started a few books I found myself unable to finish. I was burned by it all. I wanted to write, but I didn't have the heart to fail again.

Starting *Suicide Flats* turned out to be the answer.

Suicide Flats was like re-learning with training wheels. It gave me a cheat. I knew it'd take place in the world of our *Gore Point* series, and that gave me a "seed crystal" to build from that a fresh story world wouldn't have. Although my new story — which, again, I had to write entirely on my own — didn't yet have a plot, it at least had lore. I knew there were *rifts* and I knew there were *demons*. In the core series, I'd established a lot about the two planes and how they interacted with one another. I even had a timeline. What's more, *Suicide Flats* was supposed to be a short story at first. I'd forgotten how to write a *novel* ... but I could write a *short*, couldn't I?

Turned out, those things were only Dumbo's feather. But hey ... as long as Dumbo believed the feather was what made him fly, he could fly.

I started *Suicide Flats* with a simple premise: a demon comes out of Cecret Lake, others follow, and a rampage ensues. That was about it. I figured it'd be a romp and little more. But I still needed characters, so I came up with Callum MacReady. I don't know where I came up with the name "Callum," but "MacReady" was from John Carpenter's *The Thing*, which I'd just re-watched. (It's Kurt Russell's character: Mac the pilot.) I like to choose a protagonist who'll resonate well with the story's contents, so I figured a minister would be ideal for my new story about Hell. I even had a model in mind: Mel Gibson's character from *Signs*. Just like Callum, Mel's minister had lost his faith. I figured I could rip the idea off: my minister would need to re-find his faith in the same way.

At first, the going was rough. But as I wrote more and more of *Suicide Flats*, I started to find my rhythm. I remembered all the little tricks and nuances I used to take for granted: ways that used to make writing come alive for me, but that I'd never noticed before because they were so automatic. Now that I was seeing writing from the perspective of someone who couldn't do it automatically anymore, I saw all those little tidbits and how delightful they were ... and it was magical.

For one, I always used to try to get my book covers in advance so I could look at them for inspiration while I wrote. The book covers, too, were part of the fossil I was uncovering, so I knew there was truth in them. Why was there smoke on this new cover, for instance? I found out when Callum is in the mall, possessed, and he notices how the connection between fiends and the people they possess looks like black smoke. And why was the book called "Suicide Flats"? I'd picked that name as a placeholder because the cover had to have *some* name on it, but I'd always intended to change it. Then, as I wrote, the story revealed itself ... and I understood why I'd plucked that name out of all possible names from my subconscious.

For me, writing's never been about invention. It's been about looking around, seeing what's there, trusting that it's there for a reason, and finding out how it fits. Like the smoke. Like the fact that I suddenly discovered that I needed the perspective of someone "in the know," so why not invoke Eldon Porter? In *Gore Point*, Eldon never actually appears. He's a background character who exists only as an influence on his two sons, Adrian and Ray. But now here we were back in 1989 and I thought, "Wait, I understand now: my in-the-know character must be Eldon."

I'd written Carrie, Nathan's nurse, only because Nathan couldn't be left alone. That was her only purpose at first: to be a way Callum could leave after Mary left. I figured Carrie would be a mention, nothing else ... but then Callum and Eldon ended up needing to go back home, and that meant revisiting Carrie, who'd stayed there. She ended up being a huge part of the story. She even, in the very end, turned out to be Ray and Adrian's mother. Her future motherhood isn't spelled out, but the clues are there. Her middle name is "Adrian," for one — and her thing is saying that the universe has order and that everything happens for a reason, which is the heretofore-unnamed mother's thematic purpose in *Gore Point*.

Watching all those pieces fall perfectly into place right before my eyes was invigorating. My old joy came back. I remembered *how to do all of this writing stuff.* Silly that I'd thought I'd forgotten.

Suddenly it was all returning, like it'd never left.

In my younger, headier days, I used to write to music — loud music with lyrics. I liked to write to Eminem in particular, and nobody understood how I could find flow with his rapid-fire words in my ears. Those other people's doubts eventually got to me, and over time I lost the ability to write to music. I eventually gave up. During my left-brained, no-fun writing years, I wrote only to white noise.

But as *Suicide Flats* revealed itself to me (and as it became a full-length novel: a much larger fossil than I'd bargained for), I decided to try writing to music again. I needed a soundtrack that matched the book's mood, to help me immerse while I excavated the buried story. Between the dark cover art and the dour first chapters, I knew I wanted something bleak. I chose Morphine's *Cure for Pain* album, which is slow and low. (That's an Easter egg, by the way: I named a chapter "Cure for Pain.")

As the story's action began to ramp up, though, Morphine's soundscape began to feel too sedate. I was entering more of a Rage Against the Machine feel, so I started listening to that instead.

Then, toward the end when shit gets real and emotion gets deep, I switched back to Morphine: always suiting mood to mood, art as the inspiration for art.

Words flowed. The narrative assembled itself with my support, not because I commanded it. When the story grew complicated and its themes loomed large, I decided to trust it to know what it was doing. I didn't *need* to know how to untangle the story and resolve the loose ends. As long as I had faith, I knew the fossil already was what it was.

This wasn't just the first book I completed in two years. It was also the first book in *six or seven* years that finally felt like old times, and returned the joy I'd missed so badly.

I'm proud of *Suicide Flats*. Even though I wrote it, the ending made me cry. I think that can only happen when a writer accepts that although they pressed the keys on the keyboard, they weren't actually the author. I merely took dictation. I merely excavated what was already there. Like all my favorite books, *Suicide Flats* came from somewhere else. The story was already written. I was just lucky enough to find it first.

I hope you enjoyed this book. It's the first of a whole new renaissance.

Johnny B. Truant
Austin, Texas
November 8, 2024

WANT MORE DEMONS?

First things first: If by some chance you got to this book without reading the core Gore Point series, you need to go read that right now FO SHO:

GORE POINT: A trilogy about demons who claw through from Hell to our world, and the brigades who fight them.

Adrian and Ray Porter have spent their lives battling demons that claw into our world through a thin spot: a hellish and dead place with a black lake at its center, nicknamed "The Gore Point." But as the rifts begin to change and grow for the first time in decades, can they keep the planet from becoming Hell itself?

You can get *Gore Point* from the usual bookstores, or you can get it cheaper at JohnnyBTruantBooks.com

READ ALL OF THE GORE POINT BOOKS?

Then how about something new? All of my books and suggested reading order is at JohnnyBTruantBooks.com, but personally I'd suggest:

DEAD CITY: a biological thriller about a zombie plague, the drug that stopped it and created a fragile mixed human/zombie society, and how it all fell apart … maybe on purpose.

You can get *Dead City* from the usual bookstores, or you can get it cheaper at JohnnyBTruantBooks.com

ENTER THE TRUANTVERSE

When it comes to stories and the worlds they live in, books are only the beginning.

Visit JohnnyBTruant.com/join to get my best books sooner and cheaper than the other stores.

My list doesn't suck like so many author email lists. Seriously. It has unicorns.

ALSO BY JOHNNY B. TRUANT

Winter Break

Pattern Black

Pretty Killer

Cursed

The Bialy Pimps

Namaste

The Target

La Fleur de Blanc

Axis of Aaron

Devil May Care

Screenplay

The Island

Burnout

Sick and Wired

UNICORN WESTERN:

Unicorn Western

The Wanderers

A Fistful of Magic

Shimmer to Yuma

The Man Who Shot Alan Whitney

The Spectacular Seven

Open Meadows

Save the City

Save the Girl

Save the World

Longshot

THE INEVITABLE:

Robot Proletariat

The Infinite Loop

The Hard Reset

Cascade Failure

Reboot

En3my

DEAD CITY:

Dead City

Dead Nation

Dead Planet

Dead Zero

Empty Nest

THE DREAM ENGINE:

The Dream Engine

The Nightmare Factory

The Ruby Room

The Pandora Core

The Engine Convergence

The Tinkerer's Mainspring

GORE POINT:

Gore Point

City of Fire

THE BEAM:

The Beam: Season One

The Beam: Season Two

The Beam: Season Three

The Beam Season Four

The Beam Season Five

Future Proof

Plugged

The Future of Sex

THE TOMORROW GENE:

The Tomorrow Gene

The Eden Experiment

The Tomorrow Clone

Null Identity

COMEDIES: